GOING ORGANIC CAN KILL YOU

I left the cart outside the door, grabbed a fresh stack of towels and stepped inside, pausing on the threshold. No response from the feet on the bed. I took a few steps forward, noting a book called *The History of Yoga* sitting on the coffee table, along with a laptop and small printer. Now that I was inside the room, I could see it was a man. Another two steps and I spotted the price tag sticking out of Maxwell's yoga pants.

I studied his inert form, both hands bent at the elbows and tucked under his body. Odd way to sleep, but at least I hadn't disturbed him yet. I stepped with a little more confidence now and quickly entered the bedroom. As I picked the bath towel off the floor, I heard a phone ring. My hand flew to my pocket, but I'd left my phone in my purse back at the house. The ringing was coming from the bed.

Shoot, what was Maxwell going to say when he woke up and saw me in his bathroom?

"I'm here to replace your towels," I called over my shoulder, throwing a clean towel on the rod and turning around.

The phone rang again. Maxwell hadn't moved. Either he was a sound sleeper or something was wrong.

I stepped over to the bed and looked at Maxwell's face.

His eyes were wide open but unfocused.

Holy crap.

Maxwell was dead!

Going Organic Can Kill You

Staci McLaughlin

KENSINGTON PUBLISHING CORP.

http://www.kensingtonbooks.com

KENSINGTON BOOKS are published by

Kensington Publishing Corp.
119 West 40th Street
New York, NY 10018

Copyright © 2012 by Staci McLaughlin

All rights reserved. No part of this book may be reproduced in any form or by any means without the prior written consent of the Publisher, excepting brief quotes used in reviews.

All Kensington Titles, Imprints, and Distributed Lines are available at special quantity discounts for bulk purchases for sales promotions, premiums, fund-raising, and educational or institutional use.

Special book excerpts or customized printings can also be created to fit specific needs. For details, write or phone the office of the Kensington special sales manager: Kensington Publishing Corp., 119 West 40th Street, New York, NY 10018. attn: Special Sales Department, Phone: 1-800-221-2647.

Kensington and the K logo Reg. U.S. Pat. & TM Off.

ISBN-13: 978-0-7582-7500-4
ISBN-10: 0-7582-7500-5

First Mass Market Printing: July 2012

10 9 8 7 6 5 4 3 2 1

Printed in the United States of America

Going Organic
Can Kill You

1

"That pig got out again."

I glanced up from my brochure notes as Gordon Stewart, manager of the O'Connell Organic Farm and Spa, strode into the kitchen, tie flapping over his shoulder, face mottled. His slicked-back hair glinted in the overhead lights. Not for the first time, I wondered if its black color was his or came from a Grecian Formula bottle.

"Clients don't want filthy animals running amok while they're relaxing," he said to Esther. "You're lucky that news van left." He turned his attention on me. "Dana, I saw you near the pigsty. Did you leave the gate open?"

How did I get sucked into this? "Not a chance." I focused back on my list of spa promotion ideas, but kept one ear tuned to the conversation to find out what happened with the pig.

Esther stuck the needle in her cross-stitch and laid her WELCOME TO THE FARM sampler on the table. "Good heavens, I don't know how little Wilbur keeps escaping."

As owner, Esther O'Connell had hired me a month ago to promote her new farm and spa. Considering how much farmland she'd razed to create the ten cabins and pool area complete with an adjoining Jacuzzi and two patios, the spa portion now overshadowed the farm side, but all herbs, fruits, and vegetables served at meals were grown organically in the nearby vegetable patch.

I'd been back in Blossom Valley for six weeks, following a nine-month stint of unemployment in San Jose. When Mom had mentioned my job status, or lack of status, to Esther, she'd hired me after her original marketing guy quit to become a blackjack dealer in Vegas.

Esther stood, her ample belly under her light blue cotton blouse jiggling against the table edge. "I'll round him up, but I hope he doesn't get the best of me again. I never thought I'd get the smell of manure out of my hair after the last time."

An image of Esther floundering in muck while wrestling with Wilbur filled my head. Not good, especially now that guests were roaming the property. I flipped my notebook closed. "I'll help." Sure, I only wrote the marketing materials for the farm, but how hard could catching a loose pig be?

"Then get to it," Gordon said. "We don't need a squeamish client throwing a fit during opening weekend. Everything has to be perfect."

"Wilbur running around will remind people they're at a farm, too, not just a spa," I said, wondering why Gordon didn't catch the pig himself if he was so worried. After all, the manager's number one priority at any place was to make sure the customers were happy. If he felt the spa guests wouldn't like loose animals, Gordon needed to lasso that little piggy. But then he might get his dress shirt and shiny shoes dirty.

I followed Esther out the back door and down the path that led through the herb garden, my Keds crunching on the pea gravel. The striped rosemary saluted us in the warm morning sunshine, while the bright green cilantro swayed in the light breeze, the herbal scent filling the air.

As we rounded the clump of oak trees, I heard snorting and grunting mingled with the fainter clucking of hens. We stopped at the pigsty and I leaned over the top rail, watching the pink pigs root in the mud, snuffling over mystery bits. Sure enough, only four pigs. Wilbur had escaped again.

"Oh, no. Where could he be?" Esther touched my arm. "If this weekend isn't a success, I'll be ruined."

"Don't worry, the clients already love this place." I pushed off the rail and turned to face her. "We have all the amenities these people expect, right down to the thread count in the sheets. No one can complain. Well, except for that Maxwell guy, but complaining seems to be his hobby."

"That's what I'm worried about. You know how fickle these celebrity types can be. 'The swimming pool is too cold.' 'My mattress is too firm.' And like Gordon said . . ."

I waved a hand dismissively. "Forget Gordon. He's wound up because the press is here."

Esther had been excited when a production company had wanted to scout nearby locations for an upcoming horror movie and made reservations at the farm, even if she'd had to cut her rate by thirty percent. The extra attention from the Bay Area and Hollywood newspapers and TV stations that the film crew generated seemed like a good trade-off for the lost revenue. With enough press, the stars would soon see Esther's spa as the go-to place for relaxation and rejuvenation.

I'd noticed the press myself in the form of one very hunky reporter for the *Herald*, Blossom Valley's weekly paper. When I wanted to know what was happening in the world, I read the *San Jose Mercury News* or the *Press Democrat*. When I wanted to know what time the Fourth of July parade started in town, I scanned the *Herald*. The cute guy with the dimples in his cheeks hadn't interviewed me yet about my marketing position at the spa, but I was keeping my fingers crossed.

"Gordon knows these media folks are important," Esther said.

"But he thinks one bad review will shut the whole place down," I said.

Esther clasped the front of her blouse, clearly worried.

"Not that anyone will write a bad review," I added before she panicked more. "When people get wind of the Hollywood types staying here this week, they'll be pounding down our door."

"I hope so. But I've heard people at the feed store talking and they're not crazy about an organic farm. Think the place is too highfalutin, especially with the yoga classes and spa food."

A pig stuck his snout through the fence and bumped my leg. I patted his head, the coarse bristle on his skin scratching my palm. "You'll always find naysayers. Most people are thrilled that you're bringing out-of-towners into Blossom Valley. The downtown needs a boost before more businesses go under." Already, the vacancy rate on Main Street was hitting an all-time high.

"I don't know if my little farm and spa can help the town much, but I'll give it my best shot. Thank God I have you and the others helping me. I couldn't possibly do this alone, now that my dear Arnold is gone."

Her eyes filled with tears. I reached out and squeezed her hand, her words reminding me how she and Mom had bonded at a widows' support group. Her wrinkled flesh was clammy to the touch and my heart ached at the sight of the grief etched on her face, reminding me of my own pain when my father passed away last year. I instinctively reached up and fingered the St. Christopher medal he'd given me years ago and that I always wore now.

"Let's track down Wilbur," I said, shaking off my melancholy. "Before he freaks out a guest."

I left the pigsty, looped behind the chicken coop, and

started down the paved walking path that led past the cabins, studying the dense bushes that lined the walkway for any sign of hoof prints. The soil at the base of the foliage was soft and crumbly from that morning's sprinkler session, but offered no clues as to the location of the errant pig.

Esther trotted behind me, alternating between calling Wilbur's name and whistling as if Wilbur was a dog instead of a pig. I was pretty sure Wilbur wouldn't respond to her pleas, but at least this distraction kept Esther's thoughts away from her husband and his death from cancer a few months ago.

As we approached the pool and the large patio on the other side, Esther stopped whistling. Maroon crepe-paper streamers cascaded down the backs of the deck chairs. Silver and gold balloons hung from the posts of the redwood pergola that partially covered the expansive patio. The banner that we had strung between two posts, proudly proclaiming O'CONNELL ORGANIC FARM AND SPA, had loosened on one side and now drooped toward the brick below.

The dozen or so guests had arrived Thursday night, serenaded by The Kicking Boots, Blossom Valley's country-western band. The drummer couldn't keep a beat and the lead singer was tone deaf, but Esther couldn't argue with the rock-bottom price. Between the questions from reporters and the chatter of the locals who'd been lured to the opening by the promise of free food, no one noticed the off-key performance.

The party had wound down around one, when the guests dispersed to their rooms. Once the staff stopped replenishing the food trays, the locals had disappeared faster than a lizard when you flipped over a rock. Yesterday had been subdued in comparison, as guests lounged by the pool, soaked in the Jacuzzi, or hiked on the nearby farm trails in the warm May weather.

Now, across the pool's clear blue water, Christian Harper led four guests in a series of yoga postures on the smaller patio. At the moment, everyone was concentrating on the Proud Warrior pose, while Christian studied their forms, bending a knee here, straightening an arm there. Though I'd been working here a month, I barely knew Christian; but then, I'd been creating brochures and fliers in the office to advertise the big opening, and he had only joined the staff a few days ago.

In his mid-forties, Christian was lean and tall and sported a long brown ponytail. His tank top and electric blue biker shorts emphasized his well-defined biceps and quads. According to Zennia Patrakio, the farm's forty-two-year-old cook, he was once an accountant but had gone on a spiritual retreat to India a few years ago and found his true calling. Esther had hired him to teach yoga and Pilates. When he wasn't directing a class, he provided massages for the guests.

Right now, Christian was eyeing the young blonde in the boy shorts and sports bra who stood closest to the pool, as if he'd only recently discovered the difference between girls and boys. I'd met a few of the guests opening night and remembered she was an actress named Tiffany Starling. In her early twenties, she'd booked her stay to celebrate landing her latest role, something to do with a giant octopus and man-eating crabs. She'd told me about a handful of other movies she'd had roles in, and while I'd seen a couple, I couldn't remember her face at all. Since they were all slasher films, she'd probably played Victim Number Two or Dismembered Body in the credits.

I'd met the woman now posing next to her, Sheila Davenport, this morning, when she'd come looking for aspirin. Her smooth skin and rich auburn hair made her appear to be in her early forties, but the creases in her neck and lines on her cleavage suggested she was a good decade older.

She took one look at my bare earlobes and ringless fingers as I handed her the pills and gave me a card for her jewelry design business just over the hill in Mendocino.

I watched as she brought her legs back together and squatted into a chair pose, her short hair gently swaying with the movement. Yoga was clearly nothing new for her.

Next to her was a plain-looking woman I hadn't met yet, and on the end stood Maxwell Mendelsohn, his thighs quivering as he tried to maintain his posture while also looking around the other woman to watch Sheila. A little romance in the air?

Esther had approached me yesterday afternoon to get my opinion on why Maxwell was here. He'd refused to eat the wild rice and tuna salad for lunch, calling it "rabbit food." Not that I'd ever seen rabbits eat tuna. He'd complained that the curtains were too thin to keep the morning light out and whined incessantly to Gordon about the spotty Wi-Fi reception. Even now, his Bluetooth was lodged firmly in his ear, matching his close-cropped business hairdo. Judging by his wobbly tree stance and the price tag peeking out of the waistband of his yoga pants, yoga was not a form of exercise he normally practiced.

As I watched, Maxwell's right leg, the one supporting all his weight, swayed from side to side. His arms pinwheeled as he crashed into the woman next to him. She somehow managed to put her other leg down and stop Maxwell's momentum before he toppled them both.

"This damn malarkey," Maxwell said, his voice carrying over the water. He glared at Christian. "You don't even know what the hell you're doing." He snatched up his terry cloth towel from the nearby redwood bench and stalked off toward the cabins.

Christian watched him go, and then turned back to the other students. "Release your pent-up breath. Let the negative energy flow from your body." He bent forward. "Now try Downward-Facing Dog."

Esther tugged on my sleeve and I snapped back to attention.

"Sorry, we've got a pig to catch," I said. We started down the path again.

"He's probably rooting around the vegetables," Esther said with a quiver in her voice. "Eating tomorrow's lunch."

"I bet we get him before he can do any real damage."

We rounded the bend to find Wilbur, a pink and brown piglet, knee-deep in arugula, snorting happily as he ripped another set of dark green leaves off the plant. The scent of pepper filled the air.

"Wilbur, no!" Esther shrieked.

Wilbur's head shot up. Esther lowered her voice to a more soothing timbre. "You need to go back to the pen. The other pigs miss you."

I dug a black-and-white elastic headband from the back pocket of my jeans and pulled my dishwater blond hair into a rudimentary ponytail, getting ready in case Wilbur made a run for it. Esther inched toward the pig and he watched her approach. I looked past them at the nearby low hills, the lush green from the spring rains already fading after the temperature had noticeably risen in the last two weeks.

Standing among the vegetables, I tried not to think about the fantastic job offer that had come in from a major computer company days before I was set to depart for Blossom Valley. Although any twenty-eight-year-old would be thrilled at the offer, I'd had my reasons for refusing the job, but helping Esther catch a loose pig only added doubts to my decision.

I watched as Esther got within arms' distance of Wilbur. As she reached out, he gave a snort, pawed at the ground, and ran between her legs. He headed straight toward me, a wild gleam in his eye, bits of arugula hanging from his lip. Did pigs even have lips?

Not knowing what else to do, I launched myself at the pig, landing with an *oomph* as Wilbur easily sidestepped me and thundered past. I craned my head around in time to see him pound across the patio and disappear through the back door of the kitchen. Well, crap, now he was in the house.

"Dear, are you all right?" Esther asked as she helped me to my feet.

I dusted off my jeans and GOT MILK T-shirt and tucked an escaped lock of hair behind my ear. "Just peachy." No need to mention the giant bruise to my ego. That little injury would remain a secret. "But we'd better catch that pig before he tears the place apart."

As if Wilbur heard my comment, a loud shriek emanated from the house, followed by the dreaded words, "A pig! A pig!"

I looked at Esther, her eyes wide, her face gone pale.

"Oh, no," she said. "The guests!"

2

I broke into a run as I streaked toward the house, glancing over my shoulder once to see Esther huffing and puffing her way down the trail. Rescuing the guests from the pig was up to me, not that I had any idea what to do. I darted in the side door to the dining room and came to a sliding halt on the tile.

One of the guests, a woman whose name I didn't know, stood to one side. She pointed toward the hall, her mouth hanging open. "A pig ran by."

"Don't worry, I'll catch him." I just hoped she didn't ask me how. I was still working on that part.

As I tried to think up a pig-catching plan, I detected a humming sound. What the heck? I made my way down the hall to the lobby where Zennia sat on the floor, humming loudly, her long black braid hanging over her shoulder. If I didn't know any better, I'd swear she was humming the *Green Acres* theme song. Wilbur lay on his back before her, Zennia slowly scratching his belly. When she caught sight of me, she put a finger to her unadorned lips.

"I've hypnotized him," Zennia whispered.

"How do you hypnotize a pig?" I whispered back.

Zennia ran a hand along Wilbur's side. "You must look

at the pig to find his inner soul, what makes him tick. Then you can communicate with the pig."

When I looked at a pig, all I saw was bacon, but I kept that to myself.

A puff of breath sounded behind me and Esther came in from the hall. "Oh, goodness gracious, Zennia, you've done it again," she whispered. "You are a genius with the animals."

With a slight groan, Zennia rose to her feet, her long crinkled skirt swishing around her legs as she moved. "He should be a doll now. If you'll get something to carry him in, Esther, I'll help load him. He's young, but too big for you to handle on your own."

"Be right back." Esther darted toward the other side of the lobby.

Zennia headed toward the kitchen and I gestured at the pig, which now appeared to be napping. "Is he okay to leave like that?"

"He's in a trance. Once he's back with the other pigs, he'll snap back to normal, but for now, we can leave him in the lobby."

I glanced around for any sign of Gordon, crossing my fingers that he wouldn't get wind of the pig on the floor before Esther could return. Somehow I doubted he'd be okay with the arrangement.

"Wilbur seems happy here on the farm," I commented as we emerged into the kitchen.

Zennia rinsed her hands under the faucet. "Nonsense. Animals need to roam free, not be penned for the amusement of the guests."

"Wilbur wouldn't stand a chance in the wild. A coyote would eat him the first day." I had no idea if coyotes ate pigs, but it sounded like a good argument.

Zennia harrumphed and dumped a pile of green beans on a plate.

Esther came into the kitchen, pushing an empty bellhop cart. Zennia looked at her pile of beans, sighed, and followed Esther as she went to pick up Wilbur. I trailed along, curious to see how they'd get the pig on the cart.

Back in the lobby, Esther tilted the cart on its side next to Wilbur, leaning the top bar against the wall. She seized his front legs while Zennia took hold of his hind legs. With a mighty heave, they lifted part of Wilbur off the floor and shifted him toward the cart. His midsection seemed to catch on the lip, so I leaned down and gave him a shove, flinching at the squishiness of his belly under the rough skin. With Zennia holding the frame on one side, Esther grabbed the other and tilted the cart upright, Wilbur sliding into the middle without a single grunt. I wondered if Zennia had slipped Wilbur one of her herbal concoctions, rather than merely hypnotized him. That was one zonked-out pig.

Esther released the cart to wipe a hand across her brow. "Whew. Glad that's done." She placed both hands on the metal frame and pushed the cart out the front door. I watched as she made her way past the side windows toward the back of the house.

I briefly wondered if I should have escorted her. Surely she'd be fine now. I went into the kitchen, washed my hands, and poked around in the fridge, sliding the packages of tofu and edamame to the side in hopes of finding something fattening and unhealthy. But only more tofu and a variety of vegetables stared back at me. I shut the fridge door.

Zennia tossed mystery ingredients in a bowl, prepping for lunch. Time for me to work on those brochures in the office. I'd gone three feet when I heard my name.

Esther stood at the open back door, her pants and shoes splattered with mud, her hands completely encased in brown goo.

"Esther, what happened?" I asked.

"Wilbur was madder than a wet hen once I got him back to the pen. He put up quite the fight." She glanced down at her clothes, her hands held out as if in surrender. "I'm afraid I lost the battle."

Oops. Guess I should have gone with her after all.

Zennia set down her bowl and handed Esther the towel hanging off the oven handle.

"Best get cleaned up. Lunch is served in five minutes and I barely have time to finish the quinoa and mango dish as it is." Tiny round bits, what I could only assume was the quinoa, covered her apron. Zennia swiped at the black strands of hair that had come loose from her braid and turned back to the bowl on the counter.

Esther gasped. "Five minutes? What am I going to do?" She turned pleading eyes on me. "Dana? I hate to be a bother again, but any chance you could serve lunch? I can't get washed up that fast and we can't keep the guests waiting."

"Of course Dana will help," Gordon said, walking into the kitchen from the hall and making me jump. The guy needed to wear a bell.

I had been on the verge of agreeing to help Esther but now I paused. Gordon would automatically assume I was helping because he'd given the orders. Couldn't allow that.

"Gee, Esther, I have an awful lot of my own work to finish up. Gordon, you could serve lunch." Judging by the glower on Gordon's face, he wouldn't be helping.

"Not possible," he said, raising his clipboard and waving it at me as if that explained everything. "My work for this opening weekend is too important for me to waste time waiting tables."

And my work wasn't? Esther watched our little exchange, her hands still held far away from her sides, like a brown pelican in flight. I glanced out the window and saw a few guests drifting toward the dining area. With only fourteen guests, serving wouldn't take long. And I couldn't abandon Esther just to spite Gordon.

"What goes out first?" I asked Esther.

She let out the breath she'd been holding and looked at Zennia.

"We'll start with the potato and green bean salad," Zennia said, gesturing to the small plates at the end of the counter. "Then we'll serve the vegan fish sticks with the quinoa."

I looked at a plate of potatoes and green beans tossed with diced celery and green onion. Zennia had been using Esther and me as guinea pigs all week while she tried out recipes to serve the guests. This plate was the most normal thing she'd made to date.

"At least it has mayonnaise in it," I mumbled under my breath.

"Of course," Zennia said. Guess she didn't need her hearing checked. "It's my own recipe with silken tofu and mustard. Much less saturated fat than those store-bought jars."

I made a face at the plate, then chided myself for being such a food snob. Maybe the tofu mayo was delicious. If nothing else, I'd drop a few pounds while I was working at the farm.

I lifted the first two plates, balancing one on my forearm and picking up a third, and headed back down the main hall. I hung a left into the dining room. Eight round tables covered in cream tablecloths filled the space, a narrow vase of daisies sitting in the middle of each. Framed photographs of the farm and Blossom Valley from fifty years ago hung on walls recently painted sky blue. Esther had told me she wanted the guests to feel like they were still outside as they sat down to dine. At the back of the room, French doors led to the picnic tables on the larger of the two patios.

After several trips back and forth, I paused to assess.

Three people were actually eating the vegan fish sticks, while everyone else poked at their food with a fork or shoved the slimy-looking quinoa around on the plate to cover the sticks. Based on the fishy smell rising up from the food, I didn't blame them. Zennia had explained this morning how she used kelp granules in the breading to give the fake fish sticks their taste. I'd have to dig around in the pantry for something edible when I took my lunch break, since I already knew the fridge was a loss.

While I was trying to recall if Zennia at least kept crackers in the kitchen, Sheila burst into the room.

"Did I miss lunch? I lost track of time." She sank into a chair at the nearest empty table. She'd changed out of her yoga attire and into a floor-length sundress with a chunky necklace and matching bracelet.

"I'll get your salad," I said, walking out the door.

By the time I returned, Sheila had placed her napkin in her lap and was holding a fork. She must have worked up quite an appetite at yoga.

I set a plate of potato and green bean salad in front of her, then looked around the room. All the guests were accounted for except Maxwell. Was his absence due to his dissatisfaction with the food or embarrassment over his little yoga spill?

I wandered over to his assistant, Logan Manchester. In his late twenties with brown hair styled like Justin Bieber, he texted on his BlackBerry. His fish sticks and quinoa lay untouched.

"Any idea if your boss is having lunch today?"

Logan kept his eyes on the PDA screen. "I report to him. He doesn't report to me."

Yikes. Perhaps I should call Logan's mother and tell her she'd raised a rude little boy.

"We can hold an extra plate if he'll be eating here," I said.

Logan sighed and looked up. Dark circles underscored his brown eyes, all the more pronounced against his pale complexion.

"If you wouldn't mind. God knows I don't want to be the one to tell Maxwell that he missed lunch." He reached into his man bag and extracted a sterling silver fork and knife. He set these at the place across from him, then pulled out a bottle of Evian water. He caught sight of my raised eyebrows. "Maxwell is very particular."

"I'll be sure to place his fish sticks in a tidy row." I straightened a daisy that had fallen over in the vase and propped it against the others. "How long have you worked for him?"

"Six months." He raised his head a little higher. "I got hired as his assistant's assistant and Maxwell promoted me when that guy left. I've lasted longer than anyone."

At six months? I wondered if Maxwell fired all the others, or they fled screaming from his particularities.

"Congratulations." I noticed some diners were leaving already, no doubt frightened off by the food. "Do you think he'll be along soon? I need to clear the other tables."

Logan shrugged. "He may have gotten a call. He's an important producer in Hollywood, you know."

Over half the guests were related to the film somehow, but everyone's exact identity and affiliation to the movie was a bit hazy in my mind. "Famous producers still need to eat."

I moved to the neighboring table and picked up a plate. Whoever had been eating here had made it through half the sticks before giving up. I tried not to breathe as I lifted the plate, lest I catch a whiff of kelp granules. "I'll keep an eye out for him while I clean up."

Logan was already back to reading his e-mail. "Thanks. He told me to be here at noon, sharp, so I'm sure he'll show up eventually."

I finished clearing the rest of the plates, then left Logan alone in the dining room, Maxwell a no-show. Zennia was not in the kitchen when I dropped off the plates, so I searched the pantry and snagged a box of wheat crackers, a step up from those fish sticks. I retreated across the hall to the office, nibbling a cracker, and booted up the computer.

I'd finished the bulk of the work for my marketing contract but had two more brochures to complete. I blocked my mind from thinking about what I'd do when the job wrapped up. It'd taken me almost a year to get this contract after the start-up I'd been working for in San Jose shut down due to lack of venture capital funds. I didn't relish the idea of starting over. Again. Especially in a town like Blossom Valley, where jobs were few and far between. But I'd made the decision to return home after my father's death from a heart attack, and I had to make it work. For my mom's sake as well as my own.

After the computer finished warming up, I checked my e-mail, felt a pang of loneliness when I saw my empty inbox, then opened InDesign. I brought up the brochure file as the maid, Heather Koubek, walked in, slightly out of breath. Her brown hair was swept up in an untidy bun, exposing a long scar on the side of her neck. Without her usual wedge shoes, she was under five feet, her thin body dressed in cut-off jeans and a white T-shirt, a hole along the bottom hem.

"Dana, Esther mentioned how you served lunch for Zennia." Her tongue ring flashed in the light as she spoke. "I was hoping you'd help me with the rooms."

What was that phrase Mom was always spouting off? No good deed goes unpunished?

"I don't know the first thing about housekeeping. I can barely keep my own room straightened."

Heather touched her jeans pocket; the outline of the

object inside reminded me of a cigarette lighter. "You wouldn't need to clean anything. I did all the rooms this morning, but I was having trouble with the dryer and couldn't finish the towels in time. You'd only need to pick up the dirty towels and drop off the clean ones."

Didn't sound too hard. "And what will you be doing?"

Heather's face went blank. "Sorry?"

"You said you were too busy, and I was wondering what you'll be doing while I replace the towels."

Heather fingered the hole in her shirt. "Well, I, um, have so much, lots of different, um, things."

Well that was nice and specific. I looked at the computer screen and half-finished document.

"You could change the towels when you get back," I said.

"I wouldn't want to risk having a guest get mad about dirty towels. I'll make it up to you, I promise." She tossed the passkey at me and I automatically caught it.

Before I could protest, she'd backed out the door and disappeared.

I stared at the empty doorway, wondering what she was hiding. A secret rendezvous with a boyfriend? A sudden aversion to dryer fluff?

I heaved myself out of the desk chair and headed for the laundry room. I studied the old washer and dryer, relics from the seventies. If Esther was going to make this farm a success, she'd have to upgrade her laundry unit. The dryer alone was a huge energy hog. But I knew she'd sunk her entire savings into building the cabins and renovating the public portion of the house. After a few booked weekends and the revenue that would come with them, she could focus on the behind-the-scenes maintenance.

The clean white towels were stacked neatly on a shelf, a maid's cart with a rolling hamper parked nearby. I placed the towels on the cart and pushed the cart out the door. When the wheels hit the sash, the cart wobbled and threat-

ened to topple. The bright white towels cascaded to the
floor. I muttered under my breath, refolded and restacked
the towels, then placed one hand on top to avoid a repeat
performance.

I wheeled the cart out the door and down the path
toward the cabins. I passed the pool area where Tiffany
lounged in a deck chair in the world's tiniest red bikini, a
butterfly tattoo appearing to flutter on her right thigh as she
rocked her leg back and forth. Christian was now leading
two guests in Pilates, but he glanced at Tiffany every few
seconds. Esther had mentioned a "No Fraternizing with
Guests" policy, but the sight of Tiffany's tattoo had apparently erased that discussion from Christian's memory.

Oh, well, not my problem.

Past the pool, the cabins waited. The walls of each cabin
touched its neighbor, giving the appearance of one long
building, the rough-hewn wood giving the place a rustic
air. Each cabin had a square window that faced the pool,
the water reflected in the panes.

I slowed the cart and stopped at the first cabin. What exactly was the procedure here? While I'd received plenty
of clean towels in my time, I'd never delivered them.
Should I knock? Listen at the door for any sounds?

I knocked, waited thirty seconds, then yelled, "Hello? I
have towels." No response. I let myself in with the passkey.

The room was devoid of personal items, making me
wonder for a moment if the cabin was vacant. I was sure
Esther had sold out for the big weekend. I spotted a
zipped-up suitcase in the corner and decided this client
must be one of those people who didn't unpack when they
went on vacation.

I looked at the towels in my hand, then at the lonely
room. I couldn't leave it so empty. Spreading out a bath
towel on the bed, I rolled up both sides, then curved one
end to create a neck, recalling the trick I'd learned when

my parents dragged me to a towel origami class on our one and only cruise a few summers ago. I quickly made a matching shape and set them on the bed, two swans facing one another, their necks and heads forming a heart. Let's hope the occupant wasn't on a solo retreat to recover from a failed relationship. That could be awkward.

I headed for the next room. Again, no one was home, but this time it was evident someone was staying here. Stockings and shoes were strewn across the floor. A Hollywood rag I didn't recognize was spread over the coffee table, Brangelina staring back at me from the page. The bathroom counter was covered in make-up jars and tubes. I wasn't even sure what some of the products were for. Based on the shiny gold minidress laid out on the bed, I guessed this was Tiffany's room. If she wore the dress to dinner, it would at least distract everyone from whatever invention Zennia was whipping up. I changed the towels and left.

Next door, costume jewelry was scattered across the coffee table, large colored beads and plastic crystals lying loose among other pieces. A catalog lay at the end. On the nightstand, a jewelry case sat alone, its velvet exterior proclaiming its value. I glanced over my shoulder, though I knew I was alone in the room, and cracked the case open.

I gasped.

A ruby and diamond necklace was nestled on a satiny pillow. I snapped the box closed and let go of it like the fire in the diamonds was burning my hands. Who would leave such a valuable-looking piece lying around in their room? That necklace belonged in a safe. I swapped out the towels and hurried out, feeling guilty, and all I'd stolen was a peek.

The next room held a case of Evian water, a bag of silverware, three new packages of boxer briefs, and a laptop computer. The open closet door revealed starched white dress shirts and khaki slacks. Logan, Maxwell's assistant, must be staying here.

Three rooms down, seven to go.

I wheeled the cart down to the next room and stopped. After my usual knock and thirty-second wait, I tried the knob. The door was closed but not latched. Had someone not latched the door on their way in or out? I knocked again, this time a little softer, listening for any sound. Nothing.

I pushed the door open and stuck my head in. Down the short hall, a pair of feet hung off the edge of the bed. I promptly withdrew.

Shoot, someone was napping. Finish the rest of the rooms first and come back in hopes they'd be awake? But with so few rooms, I'd be finished in another ten or fifteen minutes. I'd better sneak in and try not to wake whoever was asleep.

I left the cart outside the door, grabbed a fresh stack of towels, and stepped inside, pausing on the threshold. No response from the feet on the bed. I took a few steps forward, noting a book called *The History of Yoga* sitting on the coffee table, along with a laptop and small printer. Now that I was inside the room, I could see it was a man. Another two steps and I spotted the price tag sticking out of Maxwell's yoga pants.

Didn't that tag itch?

I studied his inert form, both hands bent at the elbows and tucked under his body. Odd way to sleep, but at least I hadn't disturbed him yet. I stepped with a little more confidence now and quickly entered the bathroom. As I picked the bath towel off the floor, I heard a phone ring. My hand flew to my pocket, but I'd left my phone in my purse back at the house. The ringing was coming from the bed.

Shoot, what was Maxwell going to say when he woke up and saw me in his bathroom?

"I'm here to replace your towels," I called over my shoulder, throwing a clean towel on the rod and turning around.

The phone rang again. Maxwell hadn't moved. Either he was a sound sleeper or something was wrong.

I stepped over to the bed and looked at Maxwell's face. His eyes were wide open but unfocused.

And what was that funny smell?

Holy crap. Maxwell was dead.

3

I stumbled back, gripping the bathroom doorway behind me to keep from falling. Holding the wood frame, I waited for my breathing to steady, the crackers in my stomach threatening to rise up. After several inhalations, the nausea passed. Throwing up next to a dead guy would not be good.

I looked once more at Maxwell, my stomach doing another flip-flop, then released the doorframe. I didn't fall over. So far so good. I took a tentative step forward and stopped.

Maxwell's wide-open eyes seemed to call to me from the bed and I glanced over. Was he truly dead? What if he had a pulse?

I inched to the edge of the bed and held my index and middle fingers near his neck. God, I was about to touch a dead guy. Why, oh why? But if the tiniest of chances existed that he might be alive, I had to know. I squeezed my eyes shut and thrust my fingers forward until they made contact, shuddering at the cool flesh. I held my breath and counted to fifteen, not detecting the slightest flutter. Maxwell was definitely dead. I jerked my hand back.

How had he died? He'd looked healthy at yoga class.

But people dropped dead of heart attacks all the time, even those in their mid-fifties, as Maxwell appeared to be. I needed to call the police. And tell Esther.

Poor Esther. A death on opening weekend would completely unravel her. After all the time and effort she'd put into the farm and spa, only to have somebody die. And a Hollywood somebody at that. The press would gobble it up.

A piece of white paper sat on the nightstand, a stark contrast to the brown of the oak. It was the only item on the wood surface. Had Maxwell killed himself? Was this his suicide note?

I glanced at the door, then back at the note. I needed to call the police and I'd left my cell back at the house.

But Esther would want to know how Maxwell died, and the note might tell me. I stepped up to the nightstand and leaned over, careful not to touch anything. Police on those cop shows were always lecturing people about not touching evidence. I wasn't sure the note was evidence, but I wasn't taking any chances.

A feminine scrawl, full of loops and curls, stated, "You know you want me. Meet me behind the chicken coop at eleven tonight." The letter was unsigned.

Definitely not a suicide note.

But who had given it to him? Sheila, the woman he was watching at yoga?

I'd have to think about it later. Right now, I needed to get back to the main house, alert the cops, and prepare Esther for the onslaught of reporters. If Maxwell was the hotshot producer that Logan claimed he was, the paparazzi would be camped out as soon as the news hit the Web.

I hurried from the cabin, making sure to lock the door behind me on my way out. No sense having a guest accidentally stumble onto a dead body while I was away.

Although I felt like I'd been in the cabin for hours, it must have been only minutes. The sun was still high in the sky, the warmth bouncing up from the cement path. The faint sound of splashing in the pool reached my ears, along with laughter and the occasional shout. The guests wouldn't be laughing for long. Maxwell's death was sure to cast a pall over the coming week.

Brushing these thoughts aside, I hastened down the path, past the crowded pool, and into the coolness of the house. The kitchen was empty, Zennia on her afternoon break before dinner preparations. The homey rooster clock and the gingham curtains were at odds with the tragedy I had to report. I hurried through the room to the nearby office, where I picked up the telephone receiver with a trembling hand and punched the nine, followed by two ones.

An operator came on the line at once, asking my emergency.

"I'm at the O'Connell Organic Farm and Spa. One of the guests has died."

"What is your name?" The voice was smooth and unhurried.

"Dana Lewis. I work here at the spa."

"Do you know the identity of the deceased?"

Barely. We'd hardly met. Yet . . . I suddenly felt close to him. "He's Maxwell Mendelsohn, a guest at the spa." My thoughts were jumbled together, piling on top of each other.

"And you're sure he's dead?"

I remembered the glassy stare, the odd smell, the lack of pulse. "I'm sure."

"Are there any signs of injury or trauma?"

"No, none that I could see. I think he had a heart attack."

"And where are you in relation to the body?"

The body. So impersonal. "He's back in his cabin and I'm at the main house."

"All right, paramedics are on the way. They should arrive in a few minutes so you need to be available to meet them."

I hung up and sat down in the desk chair. How to break the news to Esther? She appeared so fragile at times. Would she be able to handle the death of a guest? While I didn't always get along with Gordon, I was suddenly glad he was manager of the farm. He'd be able to handle the day-to-day operations if Esther fell apart.

Heather walked past the open door, then popped back. "Dana, any trouble with the towels?" Her tongue ring glinted once more.

I stared at her for a moment, unable to process her question. What towels? Then my mind flashed on an image of a clean white towel on the rack just before I turned around and realized Maxwell was dead. I closed my eyes. When I opened them, Heather was watching me, one finger twirling a tendril of hair.

"What's wrong? You okay?"

I stood up. "Do you know where Esther is? I need to talk to her." I started for the door.

Heather untwined the hair and clutched my arm. "Can't you handle it yourself? You know how crazy she's been about the grand opening."

"No. It's important that I find Esther. Now." I brushed past her and walked out into the hall.

"Please, Dana. There are two sides to every story," Heather called after me.

What on earth was she talking about? A man was dead. That was the whole story.

In the distance, I could hear the wail of sirens. With the farm several miles from town, I hadn't expected them so soon. I had to find Esther before the emergency crew arrived.

The lobby was empty so I headed upstairs to Esther's living area. I'd only been up here on one other occasion, but I knew the basic layout. The first door led to an extra bedroom she'd converted to a sitting room, the next to a bathroom, and the master bedroom was at the end of the hall. I poked my head into the sitting room. A half-knitted green shawl and a basket of matching yarn waited by the wing chair. I continued to the bedroom door and knocked.

"Yes?" a voice called out.

"Esther, it's Dana. Something's happened."

The door flew open. Esther stood with one eyebrow drawn in, the make-up pencil clutched in her hand. Her gray hair was damp from her shower. "Oh, lord, what's wrong?"

I took Esther's free hand and guided her to the sitting room, patting the rose-colored divan and sitting down myself. The coils were stiff, the cushion too firm. She must not bring a lot of people up here.

I looked at Esther and her one eyebrow, trying to form the words. "I don't know how to say this . . ."

"Dana! Where are you?" Gordon's voice roared up the stairs.

Uh-oh. Based on his tone, the police had arrived.

Esther bolted off the sofa. "He sounds so angry. I'd better go, too." She ran for the stairs.

"Wait." I sprinted after her, surprised by her sudden speed, and bounded down the steps behind her.

Gordon stood at the foot of the stairs, flanked by two deputies, a duo of paramedics standing behind them. Both paramedics were men in their late twenties, one with blond hair and the other with black. The blond one held a medical kit. Out the window, I could see an ambulance in the lot, a fire truck parked nearby. Esther halted at the bottom and gasped at the group.

"What the hell are the police doing here?" Gordon asked, his arms crossed over his chest, wrinkling his suit jacket lapels.

Esther raised her eyebrows in alarm. "I have no idea. You didn't call them?"

Gordon stared at me. "Apparently Dana did."

Everyone turned in my direction. With six sets of eyes staring at me, my mind went blank. "Maxwell's dead," I blurted. So much for easing into it and not shocking Esther.

Esther recoiled while Gordon's mouth dropped open. "What?" he asked, his usual bravado gone.

One of the deputies pulled out a notebook and flipped it open. He was shorter than my five foot five inches and a good hundred pounds heavier, all muscle from the look of his biceps straining against his uniform. His name tag read WILLIAMS.

"Are you the one who called?" he asked me.

I nodded. "I was changing towels in the guest rooms when I found him."

Gordon stepped forward, blocking the deputy. "And he was dead? Sure he wasn't napping?"

Deputy Williams placed a hand on Gordon's arm, and he stepped back. "Please, sir, let me handle this."

Gordon pressed his lips together and nodded.

"Now, ma'am . . ." Deputy Williams said.

I was instantly distracted. Ma'am! I was only twenty-eight, for crying out loud. Hardly *ma'am* territory. *Focus, Dana, a man is dead*. He could call me *sir* or *hey you* for all it mattered. I tuned back in.

". . . where the body is," Deputy Williams was saying.

"I found Maxwell in his cabin."

The other deputy spoke up. Like a bad cop comedy, he was over six feet and rail thin, the exact opposite of his partner. I wasn't even sure how he held up his duty belt. "You need to take us there."

Not something I was looking forward to, but it'd make the cops' jobs easier. "Follow me." I led the way out of the house and down the path. My trip past the pool this time was met with silence and curious stares. I spotted

Tiffany and Christian but no one met my look. They were all eyeing the cops and paramedics.

I stopped outside Maxwell's cabin. The towel cart was where I'd parked it. Heather would need to finish the other rooms. No way would I walk into another cabin unannounced.

I gestured to the door and handed Deputy Williams the key. "This is it." I made no effort to unlock the door myself. I'd seen enough on my first trip. "Esther, let's wait out here."

Deputy Williams had opened the door, and now he turned back. "You all need to stay put."

Gordon tugged on his jacket lapels. "As the manager of the farm, I need to know everything that happens so I can deal with the guests and media appropriately."

"Sir, until we know what happened, you'll have to wait out here. This may be a crime scene."

Crime scene? I swallowed the lump that had suddenly materialized in my throat. Surely Maxwell had died of natural causes. This was Blossom Valley, for crying out loud.

The deputies disappeared into the room, the two paramedics following. Esther clutched my arm, and I patted her hand.

"I'm sure it's fine. Don't worry."

"Don't worry." Gordon snorted. "A man's died at the spa. I need to tend to the guests. Make sure the sight of these emergency vehicles isn't upsetting anyone." He turned and walked back toward the house, his jacket flapping as he moved.

Esther let out a whimper. "If only it wasn't opening weekend. People won't stay here when they find out a guest died. I'll lose the farm."

I loosened Esther's hold on my arm and hugged her shoulders, feeling more like a parent than an employee.

"People will understand. One man's death from a heart attack is not going to close the place down."

As I said this last bit, the paramedics emerged from the room, stripping off their latex gloves.

"Who said anything about a heart attack?" the blond one asked. "This man's been murdered."

4

Esther gripped my arm so hard that I winced.

"Murdered?" I said. "Are you sure?"

The paramedic pulled a cigarette out of the pack in his shirt pocket and stuck it between his lips. "Judging by the stab wound to his gut, it couldn't be anything else." He pulled a lighter from his pants pocket and lit the cigarette, exhaling a burst of smoke in my direction.

I barely registered the haze, instead picturing Maxwell as I'd seen him on the bed, in that odd position with his hands tucked under his body. He must have been gripping his stomach when he fell over and died. The poor man.

Two of the guests came around the corner at the other end of the cabins and glanced at us with obvious interest.

The woman fanned a hand before her face. "Smoking, at a spa," she said, loud enough to reach us. "The shame."

Her companion shook his head at us and they let themselves into their cabin. The paramedic kept smoking.

Deputy Williams popped his head out Maxwell's door. "Shut up, Carl, and stop blabbing about how the victim died." He turned his gaze on me. "And, you, ma'am. The detective will want to talk to you as soon as he gets out here. Go wait in the house."

I pressed my palms against my stomach. "Why do I need to wait in the house? Am I a suspect?" I could almost hear the clang of the cell door slamming shut.

The deputy scowled at me. "You can wait wherever you want. I just need to know where you are so I can tell the detective."

I felt myself blush at my overreaction. "Oh, then the house is fine." No need to call my lawyer just yet. Not that I had one.

I turned to go, Esther clutching my arm once more. I wanted to shake her loose, take a minute for myself, but one look at her drawn face and trembling mouth told me she was on the verge of hysteria. I patted her hand, a gesture I'd been repeating all day, and escorted her down the path.

On my way by the pool area, I glanced at the empty patio, marveling at how I'd seen Maxwell only hours before, attempting yoga. What had happened between then and now? Had someone entered his room and attacked him? I couldn't quite picture Maxwell stabbing himself in the stomach. I shuddered and kept walking.

"Dana?" Esther whispered beside me. "Do you think one of the guests killed him?"

"Let's let the police worry about that," I said, trying to sound soothing. But of course one of the guests killed him. Or one of the employees. After only a month on the job, what did I know about any of these people? But because killers didn't exist in my Pollyanna universe, a tiny part of me clung to the hope that Maxwell had tripped and fallen on the knife by accident.

I led the way back into the kitchen and deposited Esther in a chair. Zennia was washing dishes at the sink. When she saw us, she raised an eyebrow in query.

"Maxwell, that producer guy, died," I said.

She dropped the fork she'd been cleaning. It clanked in the sink. "Oh, Dana, no." She wiped her hands on her apron, her hair in disarray, springing out of her braid. "Esther, let me get you a cup of tea, my special herbal blend." She turned on the burner under the kettle and pulled a teacup off the hook on the wall. "Dana, would you like some?"

"Not right now, thanks. I don't feel like sitting."

I wanted to check on Gordon, see if he needed help. Dealing directly with the guests didn't fall under my normal job description, but this situation wasn't exactly normal either.

Knowing Zennia would keep an eye on Esther, I followed the sound of voices down the hall and found most of the guests in the lobby. A few sat on the blue-and-white checked sofa or in the matching blue wingback chairs. The rest stood in groups of two and three. I spotted Logan sitting in a corner alone, partially obscured by the ficus. He was texting on his BlackBerry, his white dress shirt now wrinkled. I wasn't sure why almost everyone had congregated here, but at least the only people near the cabins were the couple I'd seen earlier.

Gordon saw me enter the room and broke from his group to join me. "What the hell is going on? Have the police told you anything?"

I pulled him into the hall and kept my voice low. "Maxwell didn't die of natural causes. The police haven't said anything official, but he was probably murdered."

Gordon's face turned as red as a stop sign. "You'd better be kidding."

I stared at him. "I wouldn't joke about murder."

"How could he go and get himself killed during my opening weekend? What am I going to tell the clients?"

A man was dead and that was Gordon's first question? "I'm sure Maxwell didn't *plan* to be murdered. But I think we should tell the guests. The police will want everyone available for questioning. No sense making the cops chase people around the farm all afternoon."

"Fine, I'll tell them." Gordon whirled around and stepped back into the lobby. "Everyone, could I have your attention please?"

Conversations petered out and all eyes turned on Gordon.

"Unfortunately, there's been a death here at the farm." Several gasps emanated from the group. "Maxwell Mendelsohn." At this, Logan stopped texting and looked up, a lock of hair breaking loose and hanging in his eyes. "Please wait here until the police have a chance to speak with each of you."

Several people started talking to each other, the volume gradually rising. Gordon raised a hand and the room fell silent.

"I understand what a terrible inconvenience this is for everyone," Gordon said. "I'll make sure the police conduct their interviews as quickly as possible so you can get back to enjoying all the fine amenities the O'Connell Farm and Spa has to offer."

Enjoy the spa after a man was murdered? I could use a little of whatever spiked cider Gordon was sipping.

"In the meantime," he continued, "I'll arrange for some snacks and drinks to tide you over." With that, he walked past me and headed toward the kitchen.

The minute he moved, everyone started talking at once.

"Maxwell's dead?" Tiffany said, her hazel-green eyes wide.

"Which one was Maxwell?" a man I didn't know asked.

Guess his vacation wouldn't be too affected by the news.

I backed out of the room before anyone could ask me questions and bumped into someone from behind.

"Dana," Heather said. "What's happened? Why are the police here?" She was chomping on gum, the mint scent mingling with the fainter smell of cigarette smoke.

I studied her, looking for a spark of guilt. Why had she really asked me to change the towels?

"Maxwell was murdered," I said without preamble, just to see her reaction.

Heather's face paled, her bottom jaw dropping open, exposing her tongue ring and a wad of gum. Her surprise seemed genuine enough, and I felt a tinge of guilt myself at suspecting her of anything. But a man had most likely been murdered and someone was guilty.

"My God, do they know who did it?" she asked, fingering her T-shirt hem.

"Not yet." I looked Heather in the eye and hoped my voice wouldn't tremble with my question. "What were you doing when I was taking the towels to the rooms?" I held my breath as I waited for her answer, wondering if she'd ever ask for my help again. Probably not.

A shadow of emotion that I couldn't quite name flitted across her face as she broke eye contact, but then her gaze settled over my left shoulder and her expression was replaced with wariness. I turned to see what had caught her attention.

A man approached us from the lobby. His shoulder holster and buzz cut announced his status as a cop before he opened his mouth.

He stopped before me and cleared his throat. "You're Dana Lewis, right?" His voice was flat and businesslike.

I nodded mutely, my throat suddenly dry.

"I'm Detective Caffrey. I'll be questioning you. Is there somewhere private we can talk?"

"Let's use the office," I managed to choke out, my voice sounding scratchy. The room was only a few short steps away and I sank into the desk chair, suddenly unsure if my legs would continue to hold my weight.

Detective Caffrey remained standing, looming over me.

"You state that you found Mr. Mendelsohn's body when you entered his room with fresh towels. Is that correct?"

"He was lying on the bed. I thought he was sleeping." Once more, an image of Maxwell's prone body came to mind but I blinked it away.

"Doesn't the maid usually handle the towels?" Detective Caffrey asked.

"Right, but she had something else to do and asked me to help out. Apparently the towels weren't dry yet when she cleaned the rooms earlier." What had Heather been doing? She'd been so vague when I asked. Had she somehow known Maxwell was dead and wanted me to find the body? Had she killed him herself and wanted to point the finger at me? Ridiculous.

Detective Caffrey studied me, pen poised over his notebook, as those thoughts galloped through my brain. "Did you want to add anything else?" he asked. "The slightest detail may be important."

Perhaps Heather had a legitimate reason for not replacing the towels. No sense getting her in trouble with the police until I had a chance to ask her. I looked at Detective Caffrey's shoes, black and shiny, much like Gordon's. "No, nothing to add."

"Had you spoken to Mr. Mendelsohn on previous occasions?"

I thought back to his stay at the farm. "Not that I recall. I mean, I've spotted him here and there, but we never spoke. I did talk to his assistant, Logan, when he didn't show up for lunch."

"The assistant didn't show up for lunch or Mr. Mendelsohn?"

"Mr. Mendelsohn. I asked Logan if he was expecting his boss, so I could keep a plate of food ready, and he said yes." Had Logan been lying to cover his crime? Trying to create an alibi? Good grief, if I kept suspecting everyone, I'd drive myself batty.

Detective Caffrey jotted down a note. "Did you see Mr. Mendelsohn earlier in the day?"

"Around eleven. He was in a yoga class, although he was struggling with the tree pose, got angry, and left."

Detective Caffrey stopped writing. "He was angry with the tree pose?"

"Right. He almost fell over in front of the whole group."

"And that's the last time you saw him?"

I brushed at a patch of dirt on one knee that I had missed earlier. "He went back to his cabin after that."

"Did you actually see him enter his cabin?"

I thought for a moment, trying to picture the scene. "No, I was helping Esther catch Wilbur before he ate all the vegetables."

"Are guests restricted on the number of vegetables they can consume?"

"Wilbur's a pig."

Detective Caffrey frowned. "He can't eat that much."

If the detective had this much trouble following a simple conversation, Maxwell's killer could rest easy. "No, Wilbur is an actual pig. You know, the oink-oink kind."

A muscle pulsed below Detective Caffrey's eye. "Of course he is." He looked over his pages, then snapped his notebook shut. "If you think of anything else, please contact me immediately." He pulled a business card from his shirt pocket and handed it to me.

. I tucked the card under the keyboard on the desk. "What now?"

"I need to question the rest of the staff and the guests before they find out what's happened."

Uh-oh. "Um, the guests already know Maxwell died."

The tic under his eye beat faster. "How did they find out?"

I shoved the business card farther under the keyboard. "I explained to Gordon what had happened, and he told them."

"Who authorized you to release this information?"

"No one. Deputy Williams told me to wait in the house and I thought I'd do you guys a favor by keeping the guests in one spot." I swiped at my forehead, sure I felt perspiration forming. "But the guests don't know he was murdered. Only the staff does."

Detective Caffrey pressed his lips together, his only sign of annoyance. "How many are on staff here?"

"The maid, the manager, the yoga instructor, and the cook. And me, of course."

"I'll talk to the maid first," Detective Caffrey said. "Let's see if she's in the kitchen."

I stepped into the hall ahead of the detective and nearly bumped into Heather, her face flushed and glistening with sweat. Had she been listening at the door?

"Detective Caffrey wants to talk to you."

"Me?" Her entire body visibly trembled as she fingered the bump in her jeans pocket.

The detective gestured toward the office. "I'll need to ask you a few questions." He followed Heather into the room and shut the door, leaving me standing in the hall.

Had Detective Caffrey noticed Heather shaking? What would she tell him about her absence?

In the kitchen, Esther and Gordon sat across the table from each other. Esther clutched her teacup and stared into the porcelain bottom as if to read the leaves and find out what the future now held for the farm.

"Once the guests realize Maxwell was murdered, they'll demand an immediate refund," Gordon said, accenting the word *refund* with a sweep of his arm.

Esther shook her head slowly, whether in denial or defiance, I wasn't sure. "Not everybody will go. Some of these people traveled cross-country for their stay. That'd be a mess of trouble to change all their plans and book new flights."

"You make it sound like murder is a mere inconvenience," Gordon said. "We're not talking about a power failure or too much rain in the forecast. A man was killed. And the assailant is at large. People will run."

I sat down next to Esther. "Let's think positive. If the cops catch Maxwell's killer right away, people won't have a reason to leave."

Gordon snorted. "These cops are lucky if they see one murder a year. They won't solve it." With that, Gordon stood and walked out the back door. Amazing how he always disappeared when confronted with a dilemma.

But Gordon was the least of my worries. If they didn't catch the killer, no one would stay here. And no new guests meant no job for me. Which meant no paycheck. It felt like the air was being squeezed out of my lungs and I sucked in a mouthful. I didn't know how much longer my contract would be extended here at the farm, but I needed every day I could get. I'd depleted my savings before moving back home and couldn't afford to lose this job, not when Mom needed my help.

Esther sniffed. "This spa is my dream. I promised Arnold before he died that I would never sell the farm, but without any guests, I can't afford the upkeep. We have to keep this place open."

I studied the wrinkles in Esther's face, the gray in her hair, and wondered if she'd aged after her husband had become ill, as Mom had after Dad's passing. Esther shouldn't have to face more troubles when her husband's death was so recent.

I slapped my palm on the table. "Don't give up so fast. Have a little faith in the cops. And if I spot anything out of the ordinary while I'm working here at the farm, I'll tell

Detective Caffrey. I'm sure he'll appreciate the help." Or else tell me to butt out.

"That's sweet, Dana," Esther said. "But what can you do?"

Good question. But I owed it to Mom to help her friend. "You never know. Maybe I'll uncover some important detail for the police." I at least had to try.

The back door banged open and I wondered if Gordon had returned with more tales of doom. Instead, the reporter from the *Herald* stood in the doorway. Crisply ironed creases ran down the front of his Levi's, accentuating his height. His reddish-brown goatee, a shade lighter than his close-cropped hair, was neatly trimmed.

He pointed a finger at me. "You there. Who are you?" he barked.

Well, shoot, why'd he have to go and ruin his good looks by opening his mouth?

5

"If you're looking to talk to the police, try the lobby," I said, recognizing the local reporter who'd been covering the spa's opening. Here I'd been eyeing him all weekend, but now that Maxwell had died, the prospect of being questioned by the guy with the dimples had lost its luster.

I glanced at Esther to see how she wanted to handle the press, but she was staring at the rooster clock on the wall and appeared not to be listening. If I were her, I'd be trying to think up a magic potion to rewind that clock a few hours.

The man waved a notebook in the air, not unlike the ones carried by the deputies. "Forget the cops. The name's Jason Forrester. I'm a reporter for the *Blossom Valley Herald*, and I heard one of the staff found the body. Wouldn't happen to be you, would it?"

I stood frozen as he stared at me with his intense green eyes. What was wrong with me? Had I accidentally been hypnotized by the cover of a cheesy romance novel while standing in the checkout line? I never noticed men's eyes. But they sure were green. I shook my head to restart my brain.

"Sounds like you heard about the murder," I said. "But I don't think I'm allowed to talk to the press."

"So you *are* the one who found the victim. What can you tell me?" He held up his notebook and pen.

From her place at the table, Esther swung her head back and forth between us, as if watching a Ping-Pong tournament.

I raised my hands. "Hang on a minute. I should ask Detective Caffrey before I speak to you. I don't want to break any laws." I didn't recall this particular scenario being covered on *Law and Order*, but considering I'd already helped notify the guests of Maxwell's death when I wasn't supposed to, I didn't want to tick off the detective any more than I already had. The man did carry around handcuffs.

"You won't get in any trouble, trust me." He gave me a grin full of teeth and I suddenly felt like Little Red Riding Hood facing the Big Bad Wolf. "The paper comes out tomorrow and I can't afford to wait another week for your information."

Should I answer his questions? The police had only been here for roughly an hour, so surely they wouldn't want me talking to a newspaper reporter, even the local guy. But what about freedom of the press?

Detective Caffrey walked into the kitchen, saving me from my dilemma.

"Forrester! I don't remember saying you could bother people."

Jason straightened up. "I know you're new to the department, but I've got an understanding with the sheriff when a major crime occurs."

Detective Caffrey adjusted the holster strap on his shoulder. "This is an open investigation and I don't want you talking to anyone without checking with me first. I suggest you have the sheriff call me."

While the two argued, I inched back toward the hallway

and slipped around the corner into the dining room. The linens had been stripped from the tables and replaced with fresh tablecloths and polished silverware. Lunch was a distant memory, replaced by the horror of finding Maxwell's body.

I brushed my hand across my eyes as if I could wipe away the image and stepped out the side door that led to the patio. Tiffany walked past, heading in the direction of the cabins.

Even though I kept reminding myself that actors were just like everybody else, I felt my heart rate pick up as I opened my mouth to speak. Sure, she'd only starred in straight-to-video slashers, but Tiffany wouldn't be the first Hollywood success to get their start in horror films. She could be the next Renee Zellweger or Naomi Watts for all I knew.

I said a quick prayer that I wouldn't babble like a deranged fan. "Tiffany, did you talk to the police already?" I asked.

She stopped and looked at me, then back at the cabins, obviously torn. "Yep, all done."

"I hope you weren't too upset by what happened." As Gordon had pointed out, this was a vacation spa. People expected to relax, not be interrogated by the authorities.

"Nah. They really didn't ask a lot of questions, just if I knew Maxwell and when I'd seen him last. I told them how Maxwell had been in yoga with me and got all pissy." She glanced back at the row of buildings. "Now I gotta go change before the news crews get here. With Maxwell being so famous, I bet even *Entertainment Tonight* sends out a truck to cover the story. Or that *TMZ* show."

"I'll keep my fingers crossed," I said.

"Thanks," she said, completely missing my sarcastic tone. "It'll take a while for the crews to get up here once the story breaks, so at least I have some time. You wouldn't believe how long it takes to get camera ready." She turned to go. "Have you seen Logan anywhere?"

"No," I said, pleased that she at least cared about Logan, even if she didn't care about Maxwell. "But I'm sure he's pretty upset about his boss's death." I was careful not to use the word *murder* in case she didn't know.

Tiffany picked at a nail. "Logan's fine. I need to talk to him about who'll take over Maxwell's latest project. I know I'm the perfect fit for the role of Isabella. I tried talking to Maxwell about it, but he was running late for some appointment. Now he's dead. At least I didn't have to sleep with him first. That would have been a huge waste."

With that, she headed off to the cabins while I stood in place with my mouth hanging open. If Maxwell hadn't been murdered, would she have slept with him for a part in his next film? I thought those rumors about casting-couch affairs were exaggerated, but apparently Hollywood's sofa-sex tradition was alive and well. The sound of my name interrupted my musings about which of today's stars likely slept their way to fame.

"Dana!" Gordon emerged from the dining room, clipboard in hand. Knowing him, he probably counted the silverware after every meal to make sure guests and staff members didn't pocket the spoons. "What are you doing out here?"

"I, um, I'm just gathering my thoughts."

"Well, get back inside. We have a farm to run and we can't have the staff sitting around doing nothing."

I felt the heat rise up in my cheeks. "I'm not sitting around. I talked to the police and was comforting Esther for a bit." I took a step closer. "Speaking of Esther, she's my boss, not you."

Gordon leaned in, his breath hot on my face. "We both know Esther can't handle anything right now, so I've taken it upon myself to keep things running smoothly. And we need those marketing brochures now more than ever." He stepped back and looked me up and down. "Unless you're not up to the task."

I straightened up and stuck my chin out. "Why don't you go count the chickens? To make sure they're not bothering the guests, of course." I brushed past him and reentered the house, my cheeks still flaming. What a twerp. But he was right, much as I hated to admit it. Once word got out about the murder, I'd need to produce one heck of a brochure to convince people to stay here. Of course, if Gordon whined enough to Esther about my backtalk just now, I might not be creating brochures much longer.

I sat down at the desk in the office and jiggled the mouse to activate the screen. My half-finished document that I'd started hours ago still waited. I stared at the picture of the herb garden with the pool in the background, but the only tag lines I could produce were too macabre to print. "Come splash in the pool, mere yards from where a man was knifed." "Try our organic vegetables, but keep your doors locked."

Doors locked. Had Maxwell locked his door when he left yoga? The cabin hadn't been secure when I arrived, but that meant the killer hadn't locked the door on his way out. Had Maxwell let someone in, not knowing their intent?

I shuddered. Let the police worry about Maxwell. I needed to focus on the brochure. I studied the cracks in the ceiling, tapped my fingers on the keyboard, then forced myself to type a few words to at least feel like I was accomplishing something.

I removed my hands from the keyboard and set them in my lap. What I needed was a glass of Zennia's lemonade to help the creative juices flow, or at least provide a distraction until I could think of something to write. I saved the file and went into the kitchen, feeling momentary angst that Jason might be waiting to pounce. He didn't seem like the type who would give up easily.

But only Zennia and Esther were in the kitchen. I wasn't sure Esther had even moved since she had first sat down. Zennia had freshened Esther's cup of tea and now held a mug herself.

I took down a glass from the cupboard and grabbed the lemonade pitcher from the fridge. "How're you holding up, Esther?"

She looked at me, twining her fingers together and squeezing them until the knuckles turned white. "What's going on out there? Are the guests terribly upset?"

I poured a glass of lemonade and took a sip, my lips puckering at the tartness. "I've only seen Tiffany. She was about to doll herself up in anticipation of the paparazzi arriving."

"The devil's in that girl," Zennia said. "I bet she eats trans fats and drinks alcohol all day. She needs a cleansing of both her body and spirit."

"She's young and ambitious," I said. "I'm sure she'll use Maxwell's death as an opportunity to plug her new movie."

Esther sniffed. "At least she's staying."

"Tiffany may be the only one," Gordon said as he walked into the room. He eyed me with my glass of lemonade and frowned.

I reminded myself that he wasn't my boss and smiled at him.

"What do you mean?" Zennia asked.

"Two couples have requested refunds and are planning to leave as soon as the police give the okay."

Esther gasped. "Already?"

"Apparently murder wasn't part of their vacation plans," Gordon said.

"Do the guests know it was murder?" I asked. "I thought the police would want to keep that part quiet."

Gordon refastened a cuff link. "One of the deputies let it slip. Not that they could have kept it secret for long. You know how this town is."

I sure did. Info traveled fast in Blossom Valley. Of course, since I'd had the audacity to move away for college, I was considered an outsider and thus was shunned when the locals shared gossip. But the waitresses at the Breaking Bread Diner would be spreading tidbits faster than the patrons could spread cinnamon butter on their famous honey rolls.

"What should we do?" Esther asked.

"I've got a plan," Gordon said. "I'm going to spread a rumor that Maxwell was the victim of a mob vendetta. If people think the crime was targeted, they might feel safer and stay."

"You think a mob attack will make people feel safe?" I asked. "Besides, lying to guests is a bad policy."

Gordon glared at me. "It's either that or kiss this whole operation good-bye." He turned to Zennia. "Dinner's not for a couple of hours, but you'd better be prepared. Some of the guests are bound to be hungry, even with this murder."

Esther stood, seeming to gather her strength as she rose. "Gordon's right. We need to get back to work. It'll do us all some good." She touched my arm. "Except you, Dana. You should go home and rest."

"Nonsense," Gordon said. "She needs to finish those brochures."

"Don't be silly. Dana found the body, poor girl."

Much as I wanted to stay and help Esther, I could feel my energy sagging. Just holding my head up suddenly felt like too much work.

I set my glass on the counter. "I'll be back first thing

tomorrow," I told Esther, resting a hand on her shoulder for a moment and giving it a squeeze.

Saying a quick good-bye to the others, I retrieved my purse from the office, updated my time sheet, then slipped out the kitchen door. I took the back path past the pigsty and cabins to reach my car on the far side of the lot, hoping to avoid questions from the guests or the police. No one stopped me, not even Jason.

Once in my Honda, I locked the door and sat for a moment. People were checking out. And who could blame them? But if we ran out of customers, Esther would have to shutter the farm. I'd be out of a job.

Again.

Then what would I do?

6

I took the on-ramp for the highway and drove toward home. As usual, traffic was light yet slow, a sharp contrast to the Bay Area freeways that I'd been navigating up until six weeks ago. A lingering memory of fast-paced Silicon Valley encouraged me to press the gas pedal a little harder but I immediately let up to stay with the flow of traffic. The highway patrol was notorious for ticketing along this stretch.

Exiting at Main Street, I cruised through the two blocks of downtown. Vacant shops were interspersed among the open but clearly struggling stores. Leaves on the oak trees lining the street drooped as if in despair, a sharp contrast to the rainbow balloon arch over the door of the Get the Scoop ice cream parlor. At least the parking lot of the nearby Breaking Bread Diner was half full, even at this early dinner hour. I'd have to stop for a grilled cheese sandwich one of these days.

Seeing the now-defunct video rental store, I wondered if nearby Mendocino was suffering as well. Probably not. Tourists flocked to the town's whale-watching events and music festivals. But without the stunning coastal views and artist atmosphere, Blossom Valley was merely another stop-off for gas and Big Macs on the way to the ocean.

I hung a left on Orchard Street and studied the houses. When I was growing up, children had filled the streets on warm evenings, running through sprinklers or playing impromptu games of tag. Now, once pristine houses showed cracks in the paint, the lawns in front slightly overgrown, the aging owners finding it harder to keep up appearances. Long gone were the kids running around the yards. We'd all grown up and moved on.

Unfortunately, some of us, namely me, had moved back.

My sister Ashlee's red Camaro occupied the driveway, so I flipped a U-turn and pulled to the curb in front of the light blue single-story ranch-style house where I'd spent my childhood. A dogwood tree sat at the edge of the rectangular lawn, its delicate pink blooms beginning to brown. African daisies and peonies waved hello from the red brick planter box that stretched across much of the house front. I stepped out of the car, reached back for my purse, and headed up the walk. Before I reached the porch, the front door flew open.

Mom bounded down the steps in dark blue slacks and a simple cotton blouse. She hugged me in a tight squeeze. "Dana, thank God you're all right. Tell me what happened."

She released me and I took a step back to regain my balance, clutching my purse to my chest. I studied Mom in the afternoon light. Since Dad's death last year, she'd aged a good decade, her once salt-and-pepper hair now a solid gray, new wrinkles visible every time I visited. But now that I was here to stay awhile, maybe I could stunt the aging process.

"Are you talking about one of the guests dying?" I asked. "How did you find out?"

"Everybody knows about the murder," Ashlee said as she popped out the front door and joined us on the walk.

Her blond hair gleamed and her baby blues sparkled. We shared the same eye color, but hers always appeared a shade bluer, aided by the ever-present eye shadow and liner.

Ashlee blew a bubble, then plucked bits of gum off her bottom lip as she continued. "Lucy at the salon has a daughter who's dating the cousin of the 911 operator and she heard you found some dead guy riddled with holes and bleeding all over the place. What was that like? Was that totally gross?"

I reminded myself that my younger sister had never found a dead body. Her only experience with murder was from watching *NCIS*.

"As a matter of fact, Ashlee, the whole thing was pretty horrible. A man was killed, you know."

"But you didn't know the guy, right?"

Did that really matter? "No."

Mom glanced around. "Girls, let's get in the house before the neighbors see us out here. We don't want them gossiping."

Gossiping about what? That we were talking on our own porch? I looked across the street at the closed windows, no crack in the blinds where an evil neighbor gossiper might be peeking through the slats.

With a last look around, I followed Mom indoors, Ashlee practically bouncing on my heels in her eagerness to find out more about my grisly discovery.

"Was his skin all pale?" she asked, stalking me as I walked into the living room.

I sat down in the recliner and settled into the familiar contour of the thinning cushion. I released a sigh, some of the tension escaping with my breath. Though the brown corduroy seat had a bald patch and I had to use two hands on the footstool release lever, the recliner had been Dad's favorite and Mom refused to replace it.

Ashlee perched nearby on the edge of the brown and

beige floral couch, almost sliding off the chenille surface as she leaned toward me. She lowered her voice to a whisper, even though Mom was in the kitchen and out of earshot. "I heard that when someone dies, they, you know, poop their pants. Did he?"

"Ashlee, please!" I snapped. "I'm not going to talk about it."

Ashlee put a hand over her chest like I'd stabbed her with her mascara wand, just as Mom walked into the room with a glass of iced tea, the ice cubes stacked in a neat pile.

"Now, Dana, don't yell. It's perfectly natural that your sister is curious. No one ever gets killed in this town. People are bound to have questions." She handed me the glass. "Drink this tea. You look thirsty."

How exactly did one look thirsty? Were my eyes bulging? My lips cracked? Man, was I cranky. I sipped the tea and instantly felt better, though I kept that info to myself.

"I never would have gotten you that job if I'd known how dangerous it was," Mom said.

"You couldn't know someone would be murdered," I said, pressing the glass against my temple, the condensation cool against my warm skin. "Odds are better that I'd win best tap dancer at the Blossom Valley talent contest, and I don't even know how to tap dance."

Mom took the glass from me and set it on a ceramic coaster on the oak end table. "But Esther must be beside herself. First, Arnold passes away, now her dream spa is home to a crime as ugly as murder."

"Sure, she's upset. Gordon, that manager she hired, convinced her that people would run screaming when they heard about the murder."

Ashlee shivered. "I wouldn't stay where a man was killed. Talk about creepy."

"Poor Esther," Mom said. "I wish I could help somehow."

Too lazy to bend down, I used the toe of one Ked to shove the heel of the other off my foot. It thunked on the floor. I wiggled my free toe into the heel of the other shoe and it dropped down to its partner. "Don't worry. I told Esther I'd try to find out information to pass along to the police, help with their investigation."

Ashlee popped another bubble. "Just like that *Mentalist* guy."

Mom picked up my shoes and placed them to the side of the recliner with only the tiniest of frowns. "Isn't that dangerous? Someone was murdered, Dana. I don't like the idea of you poking around."

"I'm not going to sneak into guests' cabins at night or rifle through their luggage. All I'm doing is paying extra attention, looking for anything odd or out of place." Well, I'd do a bit more snooping than that, but no need to worry Mom.

"The killer might get suspicious, you eavesdropping like that. You could get hurt."

I straightened in the chair. "You want to help Esther, and I'm in a position to do so. The faster the police solve the murder, the sooner Esther can get back to business." The more I talked, the more I was warming to the idea that I could really help the police. And Esther.

So far, I knew little about Maxwell other than his Hollywood background, but both Logan and Tiffany knew him. They'd be first on my suspect list, along with Heather since she'd conned me into changing the towels. And I'd seen enough *Castle* episodes that I'd recognize a clue when I found one. Probably.

"Dana's right, Mom. Let her help." Ashlee leaned toward me. "Now tell me about the murder."

"Lay off, would you?"

A hint of color tinged Ashlee's cheeks. "I know finding

him must have been awful. But everyone at the vet clinic will be pestering me for information tomorrow."

"Tell them you don't know anything."

"Are you kidding? When my own sister found the guy?"

"Can't help you." Technically, I could, but rehashing the details again about finding Maxwell's body had about as much appeal as eating one of Zennia's faux fish sticks.

Mom patted Ashlee's head like one of the dogs at the vet clinic where Ashlee worked. "Let's go easy on Dana. She's had a rough day."

"All right," Ashlee said. "But tomorrow morning, I want a full report."

My stomach growled and I clapped a hand over my belly. "Need any help with dinner?" I asked Mom. Anything to get away from all this talk about a murdered man.

"No, but I'm glad you mentioned eating." She sat down on the couch next to Ashlee, the cushion sagging from years of use, and smoothed her cotton slacks.

The fake Tiffany lamp on the end table cast light on Mom's face, accentuating the now permanent frown lines.

"Ever since your father's heart attack," she said, her voice soft, "I've been thinking about how we could have saved him."

This was the first time in a year that Mom had even mentioned the cause of his passing.

"Mom, don't," I said, wanting to reach out and touch her. Ashlee must have read my mind because she stroked Mom's hand with her own. "The doctors said it was one of those things. You couldn't have changed what happened."

"Nonsense," Mom said. "We ate fried foods and sweets for years. That must have contributed to his death." She choked out the last word and covered her mouth with her hand.

Ashlee put an arm around her, while I rose from the

chair and bent down to give her a hug before returning to my seat.

Mom grabbed a Kleenex from the box on the coffee table and dabbed at her tears. "I've made a decision. Starting today, we improve our eating habits."

My stomach dropped, most likely from sheer disappointment. More healthy food? That's all I ate at the spa. Mom's home dinners of fried chicken and mashed potatoes with gravy had been my oasis in a desert of quinoa and tofu.

"Great idea, Mom," Ashlee said as she pinched a bit of skin on her thigh. "I've been meaning to drop a few pounds."

I glanced at her size 0 frame and rolled my eyes.

"Wouldn't hurt Dana to slim down either," she added.

"Hey, keep an eye on your own weight." Just that morning I'd noticed a bit of flab hanging over my jeans, but I certainly didn't need to hear it from ol' stick figure over there.

"I'm trying to help you get a man, Dana. You haven't dated since you moved back."

"You're dating enough for the both of us," I said.

Ashlee stuck her tongue out at me.

"Girls, could we focus on what I'm saying?" Mom asked.

I felt myself blush. When would I grow up—and Ashlee, too, for that matter?

"No more fatty foods. No more hot fudge sundaes," Mom said. "I want to be around to see at least one of you girls get married." Mom looked out the window at the neighbor's cat grooming himself atop the cross-rail fence.

Ashlee pointed to herself and mouthed the word "Me."

Mom turned back and Ashlee dropped her hand.

"Our first menu is braised chicken breast with brown rice." She rose. "I'll get started."

Chicken and rice, not the most exciting food, but it beat tofu fish sticks any day.

I jumped up from the recliner. "I'll help." I walked with Mom down the hall and into the kitchen. The white stove gleamed under the fluorescent ceiling fixture. Ancestors long dead peered out from the framed pictures on the wall. Out the window over the sink, I saw a squirrel run up the pine tree.

"How about a green salad on the side?" Without waiting for an answer, I grabbed a head of lettuce and a bag of shredded carrots out of the fridge.

I set the carrots on the counter and the lettuce on the cutting board and slid a knife out of the block. "I see the video store went out of business downtown. That's the third store since I moved back."

Mom pulled a copper pot off the rack and set it on the counter. "Ever since the lumber mill closed a few years back, people have been struggling. Recovery has been slow, and now with this economy, no one can afford to shop."

"Is Mendocino having the same problem?"

Mom shook her head. "What better way to forget your troubles than to stay at a nice bed and breakfast overlooking the ocean? And browse in those cute boutiques? Business may be down a bit over there, but nothing like here."

I shoved the knife tip into the lettuce and cut the head in half. "This town needs more ways to attract the tourists."

"Esther's spa should help some. That's why I'm so happy you're working there. Some townspeople are convinced her place will create all sorts of new jobs as out-of-towners sign up to stay there. I don't think the impact will be that great, but every little bit helps." She stepped around me to pull the chicken from the refrigerator.

I hadn't considered myself a Blossom Valley resident since I'd gone away to college, but seeing the place crumble was unsettling. The O'Connell Farm and Spa couldn't revive the entire town on its own.

I chopped up the lettuce, tossed in some carrots, and

diced up a tomato. I put the bowl in the fridge to chill, noting that low-fat vinaigrettes had replaced all the creamy dressings. My stomach grumbled in protest.

While Mom dumped the rice into the pot of water on the stove, I flipped through the stack of mail I'd spotted on the kitchen table. My forwarded bills were trickling in, a last remnant of my high-tech life in San Jose. I never thought I'd treasure my bills.

Auto insurance ads. Credit card offers. My hand settled on the fourth envelope, addressed to Mom. The return address was Bank of America Home Loans. Across the envelope, FINAL NOTICE stretched out in scarlet red.

I glanced at Mom. She was seasoning the chicken. I studied the outside of the envelope, then held it up to the light, squinting at the letters struggling to shine through the thin paper.

"Dana!" Mom had approached without my noticing.

The envelope fell from my hand and landed back on the stack.

"That's my mail."

I willed myself not to wince under her glare. "But what's this about a final notice? Are you behind on your house payments?"

"None of your business. Quit snooping."

I knew Dad didn't leave much, but I never imagined Mom's house might be in jeopardy. "We should talk about this. Now that I'm working again, I can pitch in more on the bills."

Mom pointed a finger at my chest, poking the air with each word. "It's just a misunderstanding. I'll take care of it." She turned and stalked to the stove. The poor rice didn't stand a chance under her whip-like stirring.

I stared at her back for a moment. Was she really going to lose the house? No way could she get a new mortgage at her age with no job.

That left me. At least for however long my marketing skills were needed after a man had been murdered at the farm.

The next morning, I studied the clothing options in the closet. I pushed all the business clothes from my last job to the side and grabbed a green-and-white-striped hoodie. Done with dressing, I dug around the pantry for my usual box of Fruity Pebbles, then gave up and put on the kettle to make a package of instant oatmeal. Sugar-free oatmeal. Yech.

While I waited for the water to boil, I flipped open the morning paper. MURDER AT O'CONNELL FARM AND SPA screamed back at me in bold black letters, Jason Forrester listed in the byline. I read the article, my stomach clenched in anticipation. Jason started right off with the murder itself, mentioning the dark pool of blood on Maxwell's shirt that, thank God, I'd missed, the hands clutching the wound, the yoga pants. My mind immediately flashed back to the scene and I wondered if he'd managed to sneak in and see the body before it was taken to the morgue.

The one bright spot in the article was that while Maxwell was indeed a Hollywood producer, low-budget horror films made up the bulk of his credits with an occasional attempt at more dramatic fare. I'd even seen one or two of his films, but hadn't recognized his name when he'd checked in at the farm. With any luck, he'd merit a brief article on *Entertainment Weekly*'s web site before the latest Mel Gibson or Lindsay Lohan antic displaced him; people would soon forget that Maxwell had been killed at my place of employment.

With a sense of relief, I finished the article, noting my name was absent. Jason had only written that a staff member had found the body. Granted, everyone in town knew I was the staff member, but until I saw my name in print, I'd live in denial.

The kettle whistled as Mom entered the kitchen.

"Oh, good, you found the oatmeal. I threw out that disgusting cereal you insist on eating. All that sugar is horrible for you."

I poured the hot water into the bowl and stirred the oatmeal mix. "I like that cereal. I finally collected all four glow-in-the-dark yo-yos."

"Oh, for heaven's sake, a free yo-yo isn't worth your health." Mom dropped a piece of whole-wheat bread into the toaster and pushed down the lever.

I carried my bowl to the table and flipped through the rest of the paper. The bowling alley was adding new arcade games. The mayor's cat, Milly, had produced a litter of eight kittens. Applications were now being accepted for entry into the Fourth of July parade in six weeks. Would the madness never end?

"Did you sleep okay? No bad dreams from yesterday?" Mom asked.

I folded up the newspaper and set it on the table. "Nope. 'Course it helps that I didn't know Maxwell."

Mom grabbed the paper. "Sue Ellen called this morning, snooping for information, so be prepared for questions from people. But I imagine you'll stay home today after what happened."

"Actually, I'm off to the farm as soon as I'm done with this oatmeal. See if I still have a job today. All the guests may have fled overnight, forcing Esther to let the staff go."

Mom walked over and put a hand on my shoulder. "Oh, Dana, do you think you'll lose your job? It took you so long to find one."

She didn't need to remind me of that. I was well aware of my lengthy unemployment.

"We'll see what Esther says. My contract is almost up anyway, but I was hoping to stay on for a bit longer."

I scarfed down the rest of my oatmeal, then rinsed my bowl in the sink and put on my Keds. Might as well get this over with.

On my way to the farm, I spotted the sign for the Daily Grind and swung into the lot. One packet of oatmeal was not enough sustenance for me to face Zennia's cooking. I might suffer a weak moment and eat one of her wheat-germ muffins.

With the nearest Starbucks fifty miles away, the Daily Grind had a steady business. I parked in the only vacant slot and pulled open the door to the coffee shop, a wave of conversation hitting me as I stepped inside. Half a dozen people waited for their turn at the register, hemmed in by display stands touting vinegars and jams from nearby farms, several jars acting as bookends to hold up poetry anthologies and novels by local authors.

In San Jose when I ventured out of my cubicle for a coffee break, lone java drinkers occupied half the café tables, hunched over their laptops, updating their Facebook status. But here, at least two people occupied every table, chatting over their morning coffee.

I took my place in line behind a man in jogging shorts and a tank top. To my left, the mayor sat at the counter that lined the plate-glass window. I thought about congratulating him on his kittens, but he was talking with the man sitting next to him. In the tiny coffee shop, I had no trouble hearing their conversation.

"And now someone's been killed," the man I didn't know was saying. "I knew that spa was a stupid idea. Bringing in those crazy Hollywood types with their liberal agendas."

The mayor put a hand on his shoulder. "Now, Jim,

anything that brings folks into town is a godsend. You know we don't have enough residents to keep some of these businesses afloat. The downtown's starting to look like a ghost town. We need the revenue."

"Wouldn't be so bad if it weren't for that organic nonsense. You know those vegetables are dirty. You gotta use pesticides to make the food safe. Won't catch me eating that hippie food."

The mayor drained his coffee cup and glanced at his watch. "I need to prep for my TV conference. A few of the Bay Area news stations, and even *Entertainment Tonight*, have sent crews to Blossom Valley, thanks to this murder. Great opportunity to plug our little town." He slid off the bar stool, took a moment to shake hands with a couple of guys in suits at a nearby table, then made his way to the door.

Tiffany would be thrilled to hear that the press had arrived. Of course, she probably knew by now and was dressed and ready for her close-up. I ordered my mocha, then watched the crowd while I waited. I spotted my old dentist and his wife in the back corner and felt a flash of guilt that I hadn't gotten my teeth cleaned since I'd lost my dental insurance.

In the corner, Mrs. Harris, my freshman English teacher, nursed a cup of tea while an older gentleman sat in the other chair, reading a newspaper. The year after I graduated high school, a group of students had disassembled her old VW Bug and reassembled it on the science building roof, prompting her early retirement. Good to see she was still around.

The barista called my name, the tattoo of a mermaid on his cheek moving as he spoke. I'd noticed since my return that anyone considered renegade in Blossom Valley worked at either the coffee shop or the pot dispensary. I grabbed the cup he offered and hightailed it out of the building before my dentist could question my flossing habits or Mrs. Harris asked me to diagram a sentence.

With no commuter traffic on the highway, I arrived at the farm in minutes. Turning into the lane, I took a swig of coffee, then looked at the road ahead and almost dropped my cup. The parking lot was full of vans, giant satellite dishes propped up on their roofs. People with mics and cameras milled around in front of the main house, chatting amongst themselves.

As one, they turned toward my little Honda Civic, squinting against the morning sun and trying to see through the windshield. I felt like a panda at the zoo. Where was a thick clump of bamboo to hide behind when you needed one? No way did I want to talk to these people.

I pulled into the spot closest to the side path, then bolted out of my car, leaving my half-drunk coffee behind.

"Do you work here?" a chesty blonde with a microphone hollered while a cameraman trailed behind her.

"Did you know Maxwell Mendelsohn?" a man in a polo shirt and khakis called.

I waved to them as I hurried down the path. "Sorry, can't talk. Late for work." I glanced over my shoulder and saw the blonde trotting after me. I increased my pace, darted around the cabins, and stopped, listening. No click-clack of heels on the pavement behind me. She must have given up running in those shoes.

I glanced to my left and realized that I'd stopped directly outside Maxwell's cabin. Yellow crime scene tape blocked the door, an official notice to keep out taped to it. My coffee churned at the reminder and I turned away.

Avoiding another glance at the door, I walked down the path, rounded the corner of the last cabin, and found Jason directly before me.

His hands clamped down on my shoulders. "You're not slipping away this time."

7

I jerked out of Jason's grasp. "Get your paws off me, buster!"

He held up his hands. His striped button-up shirt lay flat against his stomach, hinting at a six-pack. "Hey, sorry. I was excited to find you. Your disappearing act yesterday didn't go over too well with my boss."

Jason looked so contrite that I felt heat rise in my cheeks. "Guess I'm a little on edge."

"Who could blame you with what happened yesterday?"

"Yeah, finding a dead guy was the last thing I expected."

I started to walk toward the main house again and Jason fell into step beside me. We passed the pigsty, and I'd swear Wilbur snorted his approval of Jason. I brushed my hair behind my ear and wished I'd thought to apply lipstick this morning.

"What were you doing in his cabin anyway?"

I caught a whiff of mint as he spoke and wondered if he could smell my coffee breath. "What? Oh, just changing the towels."

"I thought you were the marketing person."

The hairs on my arm prickled. "I am."

"Then why were you replacing the towels?" Jason's words came out a little too quick and a warning light flashed in my brain.

"Heather was busy."

"What was she doing?"

The warning light flashed brighter and faster, and I felt my defenses rise. "Picking her nose? Learning to belly dance? She didn't say."

"Really," Jason murmured.

Out of the corner of my eye, I saw him pull a notepad and pen from his shirt pocket and jot something down.

I stopped and faced him, crossing my arms over my chest. "What are you doing?"

"Taking notes. I may need this information for my next article."

"Forget it. You can't use what I said in the paper."

Jason held up his hands. "I'm a reporter. That's my job."

"But people will read it. And gossip about me."

A gust of cool wind blew past, rustling the camellia bushes, but not helping at all with the heat from my sudden ire.

"Trust me," Jason said. "They're already gossiping about you. You're the one who found the body."

A memory of my college roommate being misquoted in the press, ruining her chances for an internship with a senator, flashed through my mind. Was Jason any different? Unlikely.

Without another word, I stomped off through the herb garden, squashing the cilantro.

"Hey, I'm not done," Jason called after me.

"Oh, yes you are." The scent of cilantro followed me as I strode into the kitchen. I slammed the back door behind me.

Zennia glanced up from where she was preparing a fruit tray. She wore an embroidered smock and gauzy pants, a handkerchief tied around her head that made her look sixty rather than her true age of forty-two. "Everything all right?"

"That reporter, Jason, was pestering me again. I thought we were having a perfectly nice conversation but he was secretly digging for details about the murder."

Zennia peeled a banana. "That is his job, Dana. But he's a good man. He wrote a whole series of articles in the paper about the plight of the polar bears due to global warming."

"I don't like feeling used."

Truth be told, I was a little mad at myself, not Jason. I'd been so busy avoiding his questions, I hadn't thought to ask him any of my own. He must know more than me about the murder by now. The cops sure wouldn't share any info, so he was my best shot, and I'd blown it.

I plucked an apricot slice off the tray and popped it into my mouth. The sweet juice alleviated my gloomy mood. "How do things look this morning? Any more guests leave?"

"Most have packed up by now," Zennia said. "The film crew is heading out this morning. No sense looking for movie locations with no producer. I heard one of them say the project is officially on hold."

My breathing stopped for a moment, the apricot slice sitting on my tongue. Time to dust off my résumé? Not that I'd even been here long enough for it to collect dust.

"Fortunately, they've all been replaced by new reservations," Zennia added, slicing the banana into chunks. "In fact, we're booked solid, with a waiting list."

"You're kidding me." My breathing returned, as if my

brain had been waiting for a sign that inhaling oxygen was worth the effort.

"Seems people want to stay at the spa where a Hollywood producer was killed. 'Course they have no interest in our many health benefits. But perhaps a few days of my cooking will enlighten them."

"Was Maxwell really that famous?"

"I don't know, but he did those horror movies, and now, instead of plotting ways to kill people, he's become a victim. His fans are fascinated by his death."

Some fans. They should be mourning his passing, not fighting over room rentals.

"What is wrong with people?" I asked as Gordon walked into the room.

Today, he sported a diamond-patterned gold and black vest under his dark suit jacket, shiny gold cuff links winking in the fluorescent light as he rubbed his chin.

"Whatever is wrong with those people is right for this farm. I certainly won't turn away business because some guest gets his jollies from dead people."

He stretched his arms out and compared his two cuffs to make sure they were even, then looked at me. "That makes those brochures hot commodities right now. I'd even include a picture of Maxwell with a comment about how guests should visit to pay their respects to one of Hollywood's great producers."

My stomach twisted like a bow. "The man was murdered. We shouldn't exploit it."

"At least give it some thought. I'm running a business here."

Gordon reminded me of a CEO at one of those banks that had passed out mortgages like they were passing out two-for-one coupons for the ice cream parlor. Anything for a buck.

Without answering him, I walked out of the kitchen. I

really did need to work on the ads. Esther was paying me to market the farm, at least until I finished the last brochure.

I sat down in the desk chair and hit the power button. The computer whirred and beeped, then the Windows loading sign appeared.

Through the open door, I could hear Esther and a man talking.

"But I want to stay in his room," the man was saying.

"Young man, the police haven't finished looking for clues. The room is closed until they give the okay," Esther said.

"Well, as soon as it's available, I want to be moved. Imagine the looks on my friends' faces when I tell them I stayed in the same room where Maxwell Mendelsohn was murdered."

Tuning out Mr. Death, I opened the brochure file. After staring at the ceiling for a moment, inspiration struck and I added the necessary lines to the brochure. One down and one to go. Now what to put in this last one? A walk around the farm might give me fresh ideas.

I exited out the back door in case the news vans were lurking out front again and wound through the herb garden, stopping to sniff the lavender. At the pigsty, Wilbur and his fat, pink buddies were happily rooting around in the mud, their snouts oozing slime and brown bits I wasn't quite sure were mud. I'd leave that part out of the brochure.

The chickens were clucking over in the hen house and I wandered over, the sun already making the top of my head hot. A cluster of hens pecked at the ground inside the chicken wire while the rooster strutted. I stopped for a moment and studied the birds as they hunted for leftover feed. Chickens had such an easy existence. Sure, some farmer came by and stole an egg out from under your butt every morning, but otherwise, you got to eat all day and sleep all night. No job, no bills, no worries until the farmer showed up with an ax. And then the end was quick. Not a bad life at all.

With a last look at the chickens, I cut past the wide trunk of the redwood tree and emerged through the shrubbery onto the little side patio that ran by the pool. Only two people lounged by the water, both strangers. Christian must not be teaching a class until later. I nodded to the sunbathers, then approached the French doors to the dining room, ready to finish my last brochure and work myself out of a job. Well, *ready* wasn't the right word, but I could only stall for so long.

As I touched the door handle, I heard a voice behind me. "Dana? Dana Lewis? Is that you?"

I turned to see a woman about my age hurrying toward me. She wore brown knee-high boots, skinny jeans, and a tank top that fit her like shrinkwrap on a package of hamburger. Her red hair was accented with lighter streaks a smidge too symmetrical to be natural. With her designer sunglasses and perky bust, she was a walking *Glamour* ad.

"I'm sorry, do I know you?" I asked.

She removed her sunglasses and smiled, revealing perfectly straight, perfectly white teeth. "It's me, Kimmie Wheeler, well Kimmie Peters back then."

I stared. Under the layers of makeup and self-tanner, I spotted a glimpse of the cheerleader I'd known in high school. But her hair had been brown, her teeth crooked, and her chest smaller. Much smaller.

"Wow, I didn't recognize you."

She held a hand up. "Oh, stop. You're too kind. Thank you."

I hadn't actually been complimenting her, but she could think what she liked.

She stepped back and eyed me from the soles of my battered Keds to the roots of my dishwater blond hair. "You look exactly the same."

Definitely not a compliment.

"I didn't realize you still lived in town," I said.

"Oh, God, please. I would never stay in this dump. I married Bob Wheeler, a plastic surgeon. We live over in Mendocino, although his work takes him all over the state, mostly to help the Hollywood clientele." She looked pointedly at my chest. "Say, he'd give you a great deal if you wanted to get some work done."

I glanced down at my modest frame. "Happy with the ladies, thanks."

"If you say so."

Now I remembered why I hadn't hung out with her in high school. "So what do you do while Bob is turning back the clock for those aging actresses?"

"I don't like to brag." She brushed her hair back, the sparkle from her diamond ring almost blinding me. "But Bob and I opened a restaurant, Le Poelon, in Mendocino a few years back. Michelin recently awarded us three stars. You probably read about it in the paper. The French Laundry is the only other restaurant in Northern California to have that many."

"Congratulations."

Kimmie touched my arm and lowered her voice. "How about you? Do you live here?"

"Moved back a few weeks ago. In fact, I'm a marketing consultant for the spa." Somehow, telling her I created brochures didn't seem impressive enough.

A look of pity flitted across Kimmie's face. "Laid off, huh? A lot of my friends couldn't find work either and became consultants."

"And what brings you to the farm?" Hopes of getting on camera? A desire to tell your friends you'd visited the scene of the crime?

"I'm checking on a friend. She's been dreadfully upset about the murder. She wants to leave, but I think the best thing is to stay here and relax, recover from the shock."

That plan was definitely good for Esther and her business. "What's your friend's name? I've probably met her."

"Sheila Davenport." Kimmie looked at me expectantly.

Visions of beads and baubles popped into my head, dangling earrings accentuating a slender neck and short auburn hair. "The jewelry designer. She's nice."

Kimmie wrinkled her nose. "Too nice, if you ask me. But these artists live and work through their emotions. And when any type of tragedy occurs, the artistic types suffer more than us normal people."

Oh, gag. "Did Sheila know Maxwell? I don't recall seeing them together except at a yoga class."

Kimmie raised one professionally plucked eyebrow. "You mean you don't know?"

"Know what?"

"Sheila is Maxwell's ex-wife."

8

I took a step back and bumped into the French doors. "Sheila is Maxwell's ex-wife? Are you sure?" Or was Kimmie making that up? Trying to sound important?

"Of course I'm sure. I was maid of honor at their wedding. And I helped Sheila finish off the second pitcher of margaritas when Maxwell dumped her for that twenty-year-old bimbo he cast in one of his ridiculous movies." Kimmie ran a finger down the crease along her mouth. Time for another Botox injection. "Not that I've ever seen one of his films myself. I only watch movies with value."

"Maxwell sounds like a jerk," I said, then remembered the man was murdered and felt myself flush at my comment.

"Rumor had it he only married her for her family's money to start his career, so no surprise things didn't work out. But Sheila's the emotional type that will be devastated by his death."

She might be even more upset if she was the one who had killed him. Ex-wives made the perfect murder suspects, with those unresolved feelings of love and bitterness. Sheila had just claimed the top spot on my suspect list. "Any chance she still loved him?"

Kimmie waved a manicured hand. "No. She told me last month over cocktails that the divorce was the best thing to ever happen. She wasted years focusing on Maxwell's happiness instead of her own. With the jewelry business, she's realized how fulfilled her life is now."

"Glad she got over the two-timing bum."

"'Course her grandfather's trust fund helped. I'd be fulfilled, too, if I were sitting on a few million. Although, between the restaurant and Bob's plastic surgery business, we're not exactly hurting."

I almost choked on my own saliva. "Did you say a few million?"

Kimmie glanced at her diamond-encrusted watch. "Gotta run. I want to see Sheila first, and then I have to visit my mom. We keep inviting her to move in with us, what with her poor health. We've got plenty of room in that giant house in Mendocino, but she likes it here. God only knows why anyone would choose to stay in Blossom Valley." I cleared my throat and she blushed. "No offense."

"None taken." Gee, I sure hoped she didn't accidentally scratch her eye out with those nails of hers. Blood was so hard to remove from acrylic.

With a "ta-ta" and a wave, Kimmie strolled down the path, heels clacking on the pavement.

I watched her go, marveling at her revelation. Sheila and Maxwell had been married. Until Maxwell left her for a younger woman. Did that have any bearing on his murder? Why had he been staring at Sheila in yoga class yesterday? His gaze had been more amorous than acrimonious, but she hadn't even glanced in his direction. Was the note on the nightstand from her? Did the police know about their history together? Surely they'd done a background check on Maxwell and knew about any previous marriages.

With questions swirling around my head, I entered the

farmhouse through the French doors and found Esther in the office. I'd had an epiphany about my job last night while staring into the dark and trying to quiet my inner voice that kept babbling about money issues and mortgage payments. Now was my chance to run my idea past Esther.

She was shuffling through a pile of bills, her checkbook open. She glanced up when I entered. "Hi, Dana, am I in your way? I'm trying to figure out these numbers, but I'll be done in a minute." She punched buttons on a calculator, squinting at the display.

"Take your time." I sat down in the extra chair by the bookcase and craned my neck around to study the titles: *Small Business for Dummies*, *How to Go on Living when Someone You Love Dies*, *Learning Hip-Hop Moves in Twelve Easy Steps*.

I was still staring at that last book when I heard Esther move behind me.

She stacked together the loose papers on the desk and put the calculator in a drawer. "All yours."

As she started to rise, I put out a hand to stop her and she settled back in the chair.

"I wanted to tell you that I'm almost finished with the last of the brochures you requested. Which means I've nearly completed my contract."

A frown appeared on Esther's face. "Oh, Dana, are you leaving us? Did you line up a job with someone else?"

"No. In fact, with the sudden spotlight on the spa thanks to Maxwell's death, I thought now would be a good time for a marketing blitz. Magazine ads, a full-page spot in the *Herald*, or even a commercial."

Esther patted my knee. "Oh, goodness me, we don't need such a kerfuffle. With all these cornballs staying here, I have more business than I can handle at the moment."

Ugh. Not the response I wanted to hear. "Even if you're

booked solid now, we need to think about future business, after the interest in Maxwell dies down," I said.

"I don't know. It's so hard to think months, or even weeks, down the road with his murder hanging over the farm."

I scrambled to think of a new selling point. No way would I accept the end of my contract so easily.

"But I've been thinking," Esther said before I could speak, "I do have this pesky Web site Gordon insisted I set up. Well, one of the local teenagers did it. I have no idea how these computer things work."

"Everyone needs a Web site these days," I said, gripping my St. Christopher medal as my hope meter rose a few degrees.

Esther glanced at the necklace, then shrugged. "If you say so. But Gordon said we need to change it every now and again, to keep people coming back. He mentioned something called a frog? Or was it flog? I know I want to flog my computer sometimes."

I bit down on my lip to hide my smile. "I think he meant a blog. And I could easily write one for you. How often were you thinking?"

"Heavens, I don't have the first clue. Once a month? Every week?"

"A weekly blog's good, but with all the attention on the farm right now, a daily blog might be better." And a daily commitment would at least keep me partly employed.

Esther patted my knee. "Every day, then."

I sat up a bit straighter, ready to push the matter. "But a blog won't keep me busy all day," I said. "Are you sure there's nothing else? *Sunset* magazine prints a weekend getaway section in every issue. I could submit an article about the spa."

"We'll worry about that another day. But I would love for you to stay on." Esther chewed on her lower lip, getting lipstick on her teeth. "Besides that web thing, you could be a general assistant around here. You know, help Zennia serve meals, run the front desk when Gordon's busy, that sort of thing."

My momentary high slowly lowered, like a helium balloon with a pinpoint leak. I'd built my entire career around marketing, from the moment I'd graduated college. I had a damn good résumé now, minus that little yearlong unemployment spell. Did I want to be the rural version of a Girl Friday?

I thought again of the red letters on Mom's mortgage payment and her defensive anger at my questions. She needed my help, whether she'd admit it or not. And I couldn't live off her while I looked for another marketing job, considering how long it'd taken me to land this one.

Esther was staring at me, hands clasped.

"Of course," I said. "I'd love to stay and help out."

Esther beamed. "Fantastic. We can work out a new contract when you're done with this one. And don't you worry, I'm sure we'll need to advertise the spa again soon. We can't count on another murder to keep our name in the limelight." I stared at Esther, and she clapped a hand over her mouth. "Shame on me for saying such a thing."

She bent down, opened a bottom drawer, and extracted a petty cash box. From her slacks pocket, she withdrew a key and unlocked the box, revealing a stack of small bills. She pulled out two tens and handed them to me. "For your first task, be a dear, and go pick up some honey from Queenie."

I folded the bills and stuffed the money in the back pocket of my jeans. "Who's Queenie?"

Esther shut the lid, locked the cash box, and set it back in the drawer. "She lives in a trailer on land that butts up to the back of the farm. After her husband ran off with her brother, she turned nuttier than that almond butter Zennia sells at the farmer's market. They say she beat a guy to within an inch of his life when he made a wisecrack about it. But she found the Lord while in jail. Now that she's out, she pretty much sticks to herself, except for the occasional run to Taco Bell and delivering honey to the food bank."

In the vast collection of gossip Mom had shared over the years, she'd somehow missed this tale. "Has she lived here long?"

"A year or so. Came from down south and moved onto Old Man McGillicuddy's land after he passed. He and my Arnold loved to have coffee at the Breaking Bread Diner, chewing the fat, talking about the old days before the highway got built."

I remembered Old Man McGillicuddy. He used to sit outside the post office and whack the children on the legs with his cane when they walked by. In return, the kids would throw rotten pears from the nearby orchards onto his front porch. Or maybe the rotten pears caused him to whack the kids. Must have been one of those chicken-and-egg situations.

I stood and pulled my car keys from my pocket. "His farm is off Pine Cone Road, right?"

"From here, it's more trouble than it's worth to drive all the way around. Follow the Hen House Trail back through the farm property. When you get to the bench under the elm tree, you'll see the trailer."

I stuffed the keys back in my pocket and moved toward the door. "I'll go right now and be back in time to help Zennia with lunch service," I said, already accepting my new role.

Esther put a hand to her lips. "I should probably mention that Queenie is a bit skittish of strangers so make sure you call out before you reach the trailer."

"Does she have a guard dog?"

"No, just a shotgun."

I jerked my head back. "And you're sending me out there without a bullet-proof vest?"

Esther waved a hand. "She won't shoot at you, silly. Not after the last time when she almost hit a guy."

Well, that was comforting. I exited the house and headed through the herb garden. As I walked down the path toward the trails, I wondered how I'd gone from a high-tech career in Silicon Valley to buying honey from a crazy beekeeping Bible-thumper with a shotgun. I could only imagine what the Kimmies of the world would say about my slide.

The temperature had heated up and the sun beat down on me, reminding me more of August than May. I slipped into the shadows of the oaks with relief. Sparrows chirped and dragonflies buzzed as I turned onto Hen House Trail, which was nowhere near the actual hen house.

I knew from Esther's comments that while the majority of the O'Connell land had been used for farming, several acres near the base of the foothills had been left unplowed. Esther had hired a crew to remove underbrush and create a series of paths throughout the property, adding a bench here and there. While Queenie's property must meet up with a small piece of Esther's farm, the rest of the land merged with the nearby hills, nothing but trees and dirt for miles.

I hadn't seen any guests venture onto the trails yet, but I spent most of my time at the house, the view of the trail entrance obscured by the camellia bushes.

Then I noticed faint shoe prints in the soft dirt. Guess I wasn't the first person after all on the path, but I was currently the only one.

A tree branch cracked nearby and I jumped, then whirled

around and peered through the shrubbery. I couldn't see anything, but I grabbed a large stick lying off the path anyway.

Stick in hand, I followed the dirt track, passing pine trees and manzanita bushes until I reached the wooden bench under the elm tree. With its plethora of branches and broad leaves, the tree was a perfect umbrella to block out the sun.

Behind the bench, something bright pink at the base of the tree caught my eye. I leaned in, brushing my arm past a small clump of leaves, and picked it up, the material smooth against my fingers. I recognized the Y-shape at the waistband. A thong. Yuck.

I dropped the underwear in the dirt, kicked it under the bench, then wiped my hands on my jeans. What was a fluorescent pink thong doing out in the woods? Better yet, what had the owner of the underwear been doing?

I made sure the thong was bunched up against the leg of the bench, not wanting any guests to find it, then looked for the trailer Esther had mentioned. Through the overgrown foliage behind the tree, I spotted the trailer about five hundred yards away in the middle of a meadow. I pushed through the underbrush and broke out into the field, the knee-high grass brushing against my jeans. Better not be a rattlesnake in this here grass.

A field mouse ran over my foot and I shrieked. I threw the stick at it, missing the tiny creature by a mile. How pathetic. Terrified by a mouse. I'd definitely been living in the city too long.

The door of the trailer banged open. A woman in a faded peach peasant top, brown sweats, and no shoes barreled down the steps, shotgun in hand. Her thick black hair was snarled, bringing to mind pictures of Medusa in my old mythology textbooks.

"Who is that? Who's yelling?" she demanded, her hoarse voice suggesting a two-pack-a-day habit.

But I didn't have time to worry about her nicotine habit.

With a snarl, the woman raised her arms and pointed the shotgun straight at me.

And with the farm being the closest property, no one would hear me scream.

9

With exaggerated slowness and a sick feeling in my stomach, I raised my arms as the woman with the crazy hair continued to point her shotgun at me. Good thing I'd gotten rid of that stick a moment ago. No sense in antagonizing her.

"I asked who you are," she said.

"I come in peace." What the heck made me say *that*? I wasn't Buzz Lightyear.

The shotgun didn't waver. "What do you want?"

Frankly, I wanted to turn around and run. "Esther sent me to buy honey for the spa," I said, tilting my head toward the trees that marked the property line. "You're Queenie, right?"

She pursed her lips. "How do you know that? Did the devil tell you?"

"No, Esther did."

Queenie lowered the shotgun an inch or two.

In return, I dropped my right arm and reached in my back pocket. Queenie watched me, the shotgun still aimed in my general direction but without her finger on the trigger. I pulled out the folded money and held it toward her. Licking her lips, she snatched the money from my hand

and reached down her shirt to stuff the bills in her bra. I could see where the strap was frayed, almost ready to snap, much like Queenie had apparently snapped.

I must have smirked because she immediately glared.

"Don't be looking all smug, honey. I use this money for God's work."

"Good for you." The honey money might be better spent at the hairdresser. Up close, I could see bits of leaves and grass clinging to her matted mane.

"If it weren't for donating my money to buy harnesses for those one-legged puppies, I wouldn't even accept a penny from that spa."

I got caught up on the vision of a one-legged puppy and it took me a second to process her comment. "What's wrong with the spa?"

"Let's just say that 'Whoever sheds man's blood, by man his blood shall be shed.' That feller might want to keep that in mind."

"What feller, I mean fellow, are you talking about?" And what about shedding blood? An image of Maxwell popped into my head. Had Queenie seen something related to his murder?

"I don't know what he was up to, but that place is a modern day Gomorrah, if you ask me," Queenie said, not answering my question.

Now I was really confused. The spa had only been open three days. "What on earth are you talking about?"

Queenie leaned in close and smiled, exposing brown teeth, one canine missing. "The wanton enjoyment of flesh right out here in front of all His little creatures."

Looking at her muddy bare feet and snarled hair, I couldn't help but wonder if Queenie'd been sipping a little fermented honey. Of course, I *had* found a pair of underwear under the bench, so perhaps she wasn't as delusional as I'd like to think. "What exactly did you see?"

"A golden-haired temptress writhing and moaning in ecstasy."

Yikes. I resisted the urge to fan myself, wondering why Queenie felt compelled to tell me these dirty details. "Did you recognize her?" If someone had really been on the bench and not just in Queenie's imagination.

Queenie scowled at me. "I will speak no more of such evil. It is not for me to judge, but rather our Maker."

"Wondering if it's anyone I know." The only woman I'd met at the spa who could be described as a golden-haired temptress was Tiffany, with her blond hair and short skirts.

"'For we must all appear before the judgment seat of Christ, so that each one may receive what is due for what he has done in the body, whether good or evil,' as it says in 2 Corinthians 5:10."

Guess she wasn't coughing up any more information. I glanced at my watch. Lunchtime was fast approaching and I didn't have time for a Sunday school lesson. "Could I get the honey now, please?"

I expected Queenie to throw a bit more scripture my way but she said, "Wait here."

She disappeared inside the trailer, a decent-sized Prowler with orange and brown stripes on the side, the paint on the aluminum siding peeling in patches. Two metal poles ran up each end of the side with the door, holding a rolled-up awning in place. In this heat, I'd have that puppy unrolled, but she might like the sunshine.

The trailer door swung back open and Queenie tramped down the metal steps, a mason jar of thick amber liquid in place of the shotgun. The jar carried no label. A long trail of honey ran down one side. Definitely a home business.

I accepted the jar, adjusting my grip so I didn't end up with honey all over my hands. "Thanks." For the honey *and* for not shooting me.

I walked back across the field, then turned around when

I reached the tree. Queenie stood in her trailer doorway, watching me.

"'Let the sinners be consumed out of the earth, and let the wicked be no more,' so sayeth the Lord in Psalm 104:35," she called, the words easily carrying in the open air.

Wasn't there something in the Bible about casting the first stone? If she almost beat a man to death over a joke, she should calm down over a little nooky in the woods.

I held the jar of honey aloft, then turned my body to more easily break through the bushes, the twigs snagging at my hoodie, scratching at my jeans. I took one last look under the bench to make sure the underwear was out of sight, then followed the dirt path back toward the house. The sun felt even hotter on the return trip and I quickened my steps as I passed the pool area.

On the small patio, Christian led a group of six in yoga, Sheila one of the students. Guess Kimmie convinced her to stay after all. Or she wasn't as delicate as Kimmie seemed to think.

I entered the kitchen and set the mason jar on the table, next to an array of filled salad plates. I recognized romaine lettuce and chopped apple pieces, but the other ingredients were a mystery.

Zennia was frying a large battered object in a skillet, the long sleeves of her shirt rolled up. I inhaled the familiar smell of hot oil, my head filling with visions of fried shrimp and onion rings.

"Esther had me pick up honey from Queenie."

"Perfect. I ran out yesterday and want to make granola for this afternoon's snack." She turned back to the stove and used a slotted spatula to break off a piece and lift it out. She held the spatula out to me. "Try this."

I eyed the golden concoction, unsure what she was offering me. Unless Zennia's body had been taken over by aliens in the night, this was bound to be healthy. "What is it?"

"Stuffed squash blossoms."

The giant hole that had opened up in my belly to accommodate a naughty treat shrank a little. "You're serving flowers for lunch?"

"Filled with ricotta cheese, herbs, and flaxseed."

"I'm surprised you fried them."

Zennia looked back at the pan. "Not my first choice, but I used peanut oil, which is high in monounsaturated fat, and I'll drain them thoroughly before I serve the dish."

I accepted the piece, holding it up to the light. The thin batter lightly coated a large orange petal. Flowers. Sheesh. I closed my eyes and popped it into my mouth, chewing quickly. Then I opened my eyes.

"Delicious. I don't believe it."

Zennia smiled. "I'll take that as the compliment you intended." She glanced at the wall clock. "Do you have time to help me serve lunch?"

Guess Esther had shared the game plan with Zennia about my new role as a Jill-of-all-trades. "You bet." I grabbed the first two salad plates.

The dining room was bustling, people chatting and plucking raspberries from the bowls on the tables. Zennia had swapped out yesterday's daisies in the center vases with violets, the purple complementing the red of the fruit. I dropped off the salads and headed back for more. When I'd served everyone, I stood to one side, waiting for people to finish before bringing out the main course.

In the far corner of the room, Logan, Maxwell's assistant, sat alone at a table, texting with one hand and eating his salad with the other. Now was my chance to question him. I wandered over, noting where salad dressing had dripped on his white dress shirt.

"Logan, I wasn't sure you'd be staying."

He glanced up in surprise, his fingers convulsing on his BlackBerry. That should make for an interesting text. He flipped his smartphone upside down on the table to block the screen, and I had an impulse to snatch it up and see what he was hiding.

"The room was paid in advance for the full week, so I figured I'd take a little vacation. I deserve it after all the work I've put in the last few months."

"But your boss was murdered. Aren't you upset?"

Logan shrugged. "Upset that I'm out of a job. But Maxwell was a slave driver. Calling me at two in the morning for a glass of warm milk, demanding I pick up jewelry he ordered, expecting me to iron his clothes every Sunday for his Monday morning meetings. No one should put up with that."

"Then why did you?" I blurted. I'd read stories about how Hollywood assistants worked grueling hours for little pay and no respect and always wondered why someone would tolerate such conditions. Had Maxwell's demands pushed Logan over the edge?

"Connections. Maxwell knew a lot of people in Hollywood, and whenever he had meetings with the bigwigs, I was right there in the background. In fact, Nathaniel Wilcox of Tiger Shark Studios has contacted me about working for him."

Boy, the film industry didn't waste any time. "What would these connections do?"

Logan rested his hand on his BlackBerry and leaned toward me. A lock of his brown hair broke free of its gel prison and fell across his forehead. "I'm a scriptwriter. Once I've built up enough trust, I can pitch my story to Wilcox, and he might option it. If I can write one blockbuster, I'll have my pick of the projects."

A man cleared his throat behind me, but I stayed focused on Logan.

"Any idea what happened to Maxwell yesterday?"

Logan picked up his BlackBerry, checked the screen, and laid it back on the table, face down. I was dying to know what was more interesting than the topic of his murdered boss.

"Not a clue," he said. "Like I told the police, I barely saw Maxwell that morning. But when I stopped by his cabin before his yoga class, he was all wound up about something."

I leaned forward and rested my hand on the cream tablecloth. "Did he tell you what?"

Logan's hand twitched toward his BlackBerry but he managed to drag his gaze away from the device. "No, but he was ranting and raving about how someone would pay, and how he was going to be there to collect."

"You don't know who he was talking about?"

"Nope." He picked up his PDA once more and began texting, careful to keep the screen turned so I couldn't read it.

The throat clearing came again. "Uh, miss?"

I turned around to find a tableful of people looking at me.

The man pointed to his empty salad plate. "Could we have our entrees now?"

Oops. "Right away." I stacked up their plates and fled to the kitchen where a row of fried squash blossoms waited.

"Better hurry before these get cold." Zennia said, sliding a blossom onto a vacant plate.

I hustled back out, making several trips until everyone was served. I positioned myself by the door while people ate their flowers.

Who had Maxwell been talking about when he said someone would pay? Did it have anything to do with his murder? Maybe another producer stole a project. Or an actor had dropped out of his latest movie. But if that were the case, he'd have mentioned the details to Logan.

As I was musing, the dining room emptied out and I began schlepping plates to the kitchen. When all the guests were gone, I cleared the rest of the tables, set the dishes by the sink, and prayed that "dishwasher" wasn't part of my new job description.

One squash blossom remained in the skillet and I gestured to it.

"Mind if I eat that?" I asked Zennia.

She wiped her hands on a dish towel. "I'd love it. I thought you weren't too fond of my culinary creations."

I felt my face heat up. Guess I needed to work on my acting skills. "You cook with a lot of unfamiliar foods, but all your meals are delicious." Let's hope Zennia didn't strap me to a lie detector machine and make me repeat that last statement. I sat down at the table with the blossom and took a bite. Zennia filled the sink with water, added a few drops of dish soap, and scrubbed the first plate.

As I was scraping up the last of the cheese, I heard voices in the hall, increasing in volume as they approached the kitchen.

I recognized Gordon's voice. "You know that committee is absolutely worthless. Why you insist on belonging is beyond me."

Gordon and Esther entered the kitchen, both red in the face. Gordon had removed his vest sometime during the day and now looked rather plain with just a white dress shirt under his jacket.

"Nonsense. Arnold and I helped found that committee. It's been a tremendous benefit to Blossom Valley. But I'm not sure I can attend the meetings right now with the murder. All this hoopla might make people forget our group's mission."

I washed down my fried flower with a sip of water. "What committee are you talking about?"

"The Blossom Valley Rejuvenation Committee," Esther said, patting her gray curls in obvious pride. "We organize local events to draw in tourists or raise money for worthy causes."

Gordon snorted. "The whole thing's a crock."

"Stop that," Esther said. I'd never seen her so worked up before. I expected beads of sweat to literally pop out on her forehead. "Our little group does a lot of good for the town. Mostly, anyway. The earthworm races didn't really pan out."

I raised my eyebrows at her.

"We held the race early in the morning this past March and didn't provide any cover for the worms," she said. "The robins and blue jays ate most of the contestants."

"Well, you know what they say about the early bird and the worm," I cracked.

Gordon kept his usual glower, but Zennia chuckled. Esther frowned. Too soon for jokes, apparently.

"People drove for miles to watch the worm races," Esther said. "Imagine how horrified the children were when the birds swooped in."

"It must have been traumatic," I said quickly. Where was my trophy for keeping a straight face?

Esther clutched one hand with the other. "But now our monthly meeting is this afternoon, and I'm not sure I can face all the questions about Maxwell. The committee was so supportive of my decision to open the spa, I couldn't bear to see their looks of pity. I should skip this one meeting."

"For once, you and I agree," Gordon said. "Attending the meeting is a terrible idea."

"But it's the last meeting before the cricket-chirping festival. They may need my help."

I choked back a laugh. "Cricket chirping?"

Gordon rolled his eyes. "The most asinine idea ever."

"Nonsense," Esther said. "George from the committee thought of it one evening a few years back while listening to the chirping in his backyard. He reckoned he wasn't the only one who enjoyed crickets. Why not have people bring their pet crickets together and hand out a prize for the loudest chirper?"

Pet crickets? Did people take them for walks on itty-bitty leashes? Teach them to fetch a grain of rice? "And enough people have pet crickets to organize an entire contest?" I asked.

"We have twenty entries lined up."

Esther eyed me a moment, and I held back a groan, well aware of what she was about to propose.

"Say, Dana, could you attend the meeting for me?"

Another random job for this Girl Friday? But Esther looked so darn hopeful. Plus, she was the boss. "Where and when is it?"

Esther clapped her hands together. "Four o'clock at the town hall."

"Doesn't Dana have marketing work to do?" Gordon asked.

"I'm almost done, but Esther has asked me to stay on as more of a general helper, serving meals for Zennia, covering you at the desk, running errands . . ." My voice trailed off and died away.

Gordon glared at Esther. "Do you have the extra money for that? If Zennia used her time more efficiently, she could cook as well as serve."

"I'm a hard worker," Zennia said, gripping the kitchen sponge. "These meals take time."

Gordon continued as if she hadn't spoken. "And we're not exactly the Holiday Inn Express. We don't need someone covering the desk at all times."

This guy sure had a habit of forgetting who was boss around here.

"I like knowing we have backup if needed," Esther said. "And there's always a hodgepodge of chores that I don't have time for. Besides, you know we're booked for the next six weeks, so money isn't a problem."

Gordon grunted in reply, then turned on his heel and strode out. Poor sport. Remind me not to play Monopoly with him. But I felt like hugging Esther. When she decided on something, she didn't back down, even with Gordon questioning her every decision.

I glanced at the kitchen clock. With a couple of hours to kill before the meeting, now was my chance to find Heather. Under the pretext of helping her clean rooms, I wanted to ask her about where she'd been yesterday. And her strange comment about two sides to every story.

If she'd known Maxwell was dead and was using me as her alibi, I was going to find out. I was no one's patsy.

10

I swept open the door to the laundry room, looking for Heather. The maid's cart was tucked in the corner, the top empty of towels. But the washing machine vibrated and clanked through its spin cycle. Heather had to be on the grounds somewhere.

I checked the front lobby and earned a glare from Gordon as he filled out paperwork at the counter. Must be smarting over Esther's refusal to quit the committee or her insistence on keeping me on as a staff member. I stepped out the front door to see if Heather's car was parked, forgetting my encounter with the press when I'd arrived this morning. Within seconds, four reporters with microphones descended on me.

"Who are you? Are you staying here? Did you know Maxwell Mendelsohn?" The questions hit me like paint balls at a corporate team-building event.

I held my hands before my face as flashbulbs blinded me. "I didn't know him. I only work here." I darted back inside, the front door whacking me on the behind.

"What a zoo," I said to Gordon.

He kept writing as if I hadn't spoken.

Stick my tongue out at him or try for maturity? If I was

going to work with the guy, I might as well extend the proverbial olive branch.

"Having the media camped out front will sure help draw attention to the spa," I said.

He looked up, pen poised over paper. "Great publicity. We probably don't even need your brochures at this point."

Should have extended a rose bush branch instead, nailed him with a few thorns.

"Still," I said, "once the rubberneckers check out, those brochures will be crucial for attracting new customers."

"We'll see," Gordon said. "The townspeople are already using the extra media attention to their benefit. Mitchell at the Get the Scoop ice cream parlor has bumped up prices by a good fifty cents per cone. And Clyde, over at the kitchen store, has all knife sets at half off."

"That's horrible! Maxwell only died yesterday."

"Savvy business people jump at any opportunity."

"When did murder become an opportunity?" I said.

Gordon shook his head, as if he pitied my lack of cut-throat instincts.

"Have you seen Heather?" I asked. "I was going to help her with the rooms this afternoon."

"Not for a while." He scribbled on the top-most paper. "I never did understand why you were taking care of towels yesterday instead of her."

Was it any of his business? "She'd cleaned the rooms but the towels weren't dry, so she asked me to finish up."

"Why didn't she do it herself?"

The very question I planned to ask Heather when I found her. To Gordon, I said, "She mentioned other obligations."

Gordon put down his pen. "What obligations? I saw her smoking out back right before the police arrived."

"You sure?" Why on earth was I doing her job while she took a cigarette break?

"I've told her a million times not to smoke on the grounds. This is supposed to be a health spa, for Christ's sake. I was about to speak to her when I heard the sirens."

"Odd," was my only comment. Why couldn't she finish the towels and then step out back? Or if her craving was so strong, she could have smoked a quick cigarette, then done the towels. Why pawn the job off on me? Unless, of course, she'd wanted me to find Maxwell's body. Right where she'd left it when she'd killed him. Heather had only started work on Friday. I knew almost nothing about her.

Gordon picked up his pen and flipped through the pages. I hurried outside, careful to use the dining room exit and avoid the drooling, snarling pack of paparazzi.

Heather was nowhere near the pool area, and I quickened my pace, even more intent on asking what she'd been up to yesterday afternoon.

I rounded the corner of the closest cabin and ran smack dab into Tiffany. She was wearing a piece of shiny silver material that appeared to be a dress, though it was cut too low on the top and much too high on the bottom.

"Sorry, Tiffany. Guess I need to watch where I'm going."

Behind her, I could see a woman in shorts and a tank top taking pictures of Maxwell's closed door, the crime scene tape still plastered on the outside. A man in a tie-dyed T-shirt and cargo pants sat on the ground nearby, unlacing his shoes.

"No worries," she said, bringing my focus back to her micro dress. "I'm taking a little walk."

I glanced at her four-inch red stiletto heels. "Get a lot of walking done in those shoes?"

She blushed. "I needed some fresh air. The cabin smells funny, like old people."

"You could open a window."

She tugged at the bottom of her dress without replying.

"I figured you'd be packing up and heading back to L.A. like the rest of the film crew," I said.

"Why would I do that?"

I glanced again at Maxwell's cabin. The man who'd been unlacing his shoes now lay prone on the ground in front of the door, arms crossed over his chest. The woman snapped several pictures. Talk about tasteless.

"Aren't you with the group that was scouting locations for the new movie?" I asked Tiffany after I could force my gaze away from the ridiculous scene behind her.

Tiffany put a hand over her heart. "Don't I wish. I came up on my own to celebrate that movie role I landed. Remember? I'm in *Octogiant Meets King Crab*."

"Guess I assumed you were with the production group." Tiffany was an actress, Maxwell was a producer. Seemed like a logical leap. "So, if you weren't working for Maxwell, then you probably don't know why anyone would want to kill him."

"Must have been some wacko." She glanced around like a crazy man might be lurking in the bushes as we spoke. "Maxwell was such an awesome producer, you know?"

I nodded noncommittally, distracted by the man now pretending to fight off an unseen assailant while the woman took more pictures. Maybe we should create a screening process for potential guests.

"Did you see him after yoga yesterday?" I asked Tiffany. "I saw you two were in the same class."

Tiffany took a step back, wobbling on her heels. "What? Me? No. Why would I see him?"

"No reason. I was just curious if you'd noticed anything strange yesterday. What did you do after yoga?"

"I went straight to my room. Where else would I be?" She pointed toward the main house and parking area.

"Now I need to go. As an actress, I have a duty to tell those news people everything I know about the murder." She wobbled off down the path, one cheek peeking out the bottom of her hemline, a rash plainly visible. As I watched, she reached down and scratched it.

I didn't know what she was hiding, but it wasn't under that skirt. Obviously she'd gone somewhere else after yoga, and I needed to find out where.

Turning back, I spotted Heather at the other end of the row. She was stepping out of the last cabin, a basket of cleaning products dangling from one hand.

I raised an arm. "Heather!"

She looked in my direction, then darted back inside. I broke into a trot, running right between the woman taking pictures and the man who now posed beside the crime scene tape.

"Hey," the woman said, but I ignored her.

I stopped in the doorway I'd seen Heather enter. She was straightening a couple of magazines on the coffee table, the basket now at her feet.

"Heather, why did you run like that?"

She focused on lining up the magazine bindings, her long brown hair hanging in tangles, partially covering her face. "I wasn't running. I remembered that I hadn't finished cleaning this room, that's all."

I stepped farther inside and glanced around. The bed was made, the cover smooth, the pillows fluffed. Random bottles and jars sat in a tidy clump on the bathroom counter. The television remote control was perfectly lined up with the nightstand edge.

"Looks finished to me," I said.

Heather's hand settled on top of the magazines. "I like to double-check my work. I take a lot of pride in my job."

"I've noticed. That's why I wanted to ask why you needed me to change the towels yesterday."

I'd swear Heather's skin turned a bit paler under her thin layer of makeup. She continued lining up the magazines. Who knew fixing two magazines could take so long?

"I told you, I had other things to do."

Okay, enough beating around the bush. "That's what you said, but Gordon saw you smoking out back. Seems if you had time to suck on a nicotine stick, then you had time to change a few towels."

Heather knocked the magazines to the floor, providing a flash of anger that belied her usually quiet demeanor. "Why are you checking up on me? You're not my boss."

Good question. Why was I suddenly the work police? Oh, right, a man was murdered. And I'd found him.

"Heather, you make it sound like I was spying on you. But the police are going to ask me the same question about why I was doing your job, and I'd like to know the reason."

At the mention of the police, Heather's face went from merely pale to ashen and she sank onto the edge of the bed.

"Oh, God, don't tell the police. Please."

She huddled on the bed, her shoulder blades protruding under her thin cotton T-shirt.

I sat down next to her. "Why didn't you want to finish the rooms yesterday?"

Heather eyed the magazines on the floor.

She'd better not straighten them again, or there would be two murders at the farm.

Instead, she pulled on a thread hanging from her frayed denim shorts. "Because of Maxwell."

My pulse quickened, and I tried to keep from rushing my words, as I wondered if Heather was about to offer up a clue to Maxwell's death. "What about him?"

"He came back from breakfast as I was finishing his room. He caught me looking at some jewelry."

"No biggie," I said.

She tugged a little harder on the loose thread. "All right,

I wasn't just looking. I was holding the necklace up to my throat and admiring myself in the mirror."

Uh-oh. "And Maxwell caught you?"

Heather yanked the thread off. "I've never owned anything as pretty as that necklace in my life. I'm sure those diamonds and rubies were real. But I would never steal it."

"I didn't say you would."

"But Maxwell did. Called me a thief and threatened to report me to Esther."

Typical jerk response.

Heather sniffed. "I didn't know what to do, so I ran out. When I remembered that I hadn't finished with the towels, I asked for your help. I couldn't go back in his room and risk seeing him again."

Her story sounded plausible. But now I had something else to consider. What were the odds two diamond and ruby necklaces were floating around the spa? If Heather found the necklace in Maxwell's room, how did I see it in Sheila's room only a couple of hours later?

"Oh, Dana, you wouldn't believe how freaked out I was yesterday when you came back from replacing the towels and said you had to report something to Esther. I figured Maxwell had complained to you and you were going to rat me out."

She really thought I was the ratting-out type? "So that's what you meant when you said there were two sides to a story."

Heather nodded.

I patted her knee and rose from the bed.

"You're not going to tell the police about the necklace, are you?" Heather asked.

I paced a moment and pulled at my lip. "I don't know yet."

"Dana, please. I can't afford to lose this job. It's my first real one." She stood up. "I've got two kids to take care of."

She couldn't be more than twenty-two. And she'd never mentioned a husband. This job was most likely her only means of support. But the necklace might be a factor in Maxwell's murder. The police needed to know.

"Heather, you're the one who should tell the police what happened."

Without looking at me, she bent down, picked up the magazines, and set them on the table. Not exactly the confirmation I was hoping for. Could I count on her to be honest? Her fear of the police seemed a little irrational. Was she hiding something else?

But more importantly, what exactly was Sheila hiding? Sheila could have killed Maxwell as payback for when he walked out of their marriage, and then stolen the necklace as a souvenir.

If I didn't tell the cops about seeing the necklace in Sheila's cabin, they might not discover the information on their own. And Sheila might get away with murder.

11

I left Heather arranging the magazines and stepped outside, inhaling a lungful of late spring air. Should I mention to the police what Heather had told me about the necklace? Or would that get her into trouble she didn't deserve? My idea that Sheila had killed Maxwell and stolen the necklace was speculation at best and lunacy at worst. I'd see what else I could discover before I decided.

I dug my cell phone from my pocket and glanced at the time. If I left now, I could stop for a quick bite at McDonald's before the committee meeting at four. The stuffed squash blossom had temporarily sated my empty stomach, but I could sense the rumblings. And after all this healthy eating, nothing sounded better than an artery-clogging, sugar-laden treat.

Back in the house, I grabbed my purse from the office desk, filled in my time sheet, and then peeked out the front door to recon the media situation. In a corner of the lot, a group stood in a semicircle, their backs to me. In between their shoulders and hips, I could see Tiffany speaking into a cluster of microphones, her silver micro dress making her glow like a spirit in the afternoon sunlight. At least she hadn't risked a sprained ankle in her four-inch stilettos for nothing.

I slipped out the door and sidled down the sidewalk toward my car, glad I'd worn my silent Keds as I stepped across the concrete. All eyes stayed on Tiffany. She twirled a lock of hair and pouted her lips as she spoke. I slid into my car and pulled out of the lot without interruption.

I motored to town and swung into the McDonald's parking lot, where I had the pick of parking spaces at three thirty in the afternoon. After wolfing down some Chicken McNuggets and a chocolate shake, I drove to the town hall.

On this end of town, business was faring no better than the main strip. Father Time Antiques had folded, along with the Here's to Your Health natural foods store. Zennia had probably wept over that closure. At least the Going Back for Seconds clothing store was still open.

Growing up, I'd been accustomed to all the cute store names the town council insisted on. Now, hearing the names as an adult, they were starting to sound downright silly. And creative names brought in no additional business, as far as I could see.

On a Sunday, the town hall parking lot was about as busy as McDonald's and I parked in front. A blue jay squawked at me from a twisted pine as I walked up the path to the entrance. I pulled open one of the double glass doors and stepped inside. The door swished shut behind me, effectively blocking out the small amount of street noise.

The town hall was Blossom Valley's pride and joy. Marble flooring shone in the overhead lights. A double staircase rose up on either side of me. A plaque atop an oak stand in the middle of the lobby announced that the town had been founded in 1857 by William Kendall, who named it after the acres of flowers he first spotted upon cresting the nearby hills and discovering the valley.

I took the stairs on the left and found myself in a dimly lit hallway. At the end, a doorway glowed, as if welcoming my approach. Inside the room, two long folding tables ran down the center, surrounded by metal chairs. The thin carpet under my feet was splotched with coffee stains and occasional rips and tears. Apparently the adoring public was only supposed to see the lobby. The town hadn't bothered to dress up the conference rooms.

In one of the chairs at the end of the table, an older woman doodled on a tablet. Her graying hair was swept up in a bun, a garland of daisies encircling the base. An orchid sat behind her ear.

The woman caught me studying her flora. "Hi, I'm Bethany. I own the Don't Dilly-Dahlia flower shop."

I held out a hand and we shook. "I'm Dana Lewis. I'm filling in for Esther today."

She tilted her head to study me, the orchid dipping toward the table. "Esther and I have been friends since grade school, you know. How is she holding up with this dreadful murder?"

If they'd really been friends since school, shouldn't Bethany have called Esther by now to ask how she was feeling?

"As well as can be expected," I said.

"For Esther, that's not drowning in a puddle of tears every five minutes. She reminds me of how tulips droop when you don't water them. Don't know how that woman plans to run an entire spa on her own."

Maybe Bethany not calling Esther was a good thing. Might depress her dear childhood friend.

A rustling behind me drew my attention away from Bethany. I turned to see a man with a gray crew cut enter the room, dressed in a brown suit you could only find in a retro store nowadays and carrying a battered briefcase.

The man stuck his hand out. "George Sturgeon. I've got the Spinning Your Wheels tire shop at the edge of town."

Those names just sounded sillier and sillier. I shook his hand. "Pleased to meet you. I'm Dana, Esther's sub for today."

"Esther must be all tore up with this murder on opening weekend. The whole town was counting on her to bring in tourists," George said. "'Course we'll have to review her membership here."

"But Esther didn't kill the man," I said. "In fact, Maxwell's death has increased the number of tourists and newspeople spending money around town."

"That won't last. Once the news crews go home, people will only remember a man died at that spa. Can't have the bad energy run over into the committee."

He sat next to Bethany, who had pulled the daisy chain out of her hair and was ripping off petals one by one.

I sat down across from them, wincing as the seat's torn vinyl poked my thigh. "I'm sure people won't blame the committee for what happened."

Bethany dropped the petals on the tabletop. "Don't bet on it. George is right. We may need to cut her loose."

With friends like these . . .

George set his briefcase on the floor by his chair and extracted a sheaf of papers and a pen. "Dana, tell me what other committees you've been on."

"When I was ten, my best friend and I formed the Kids against Green Vegetables committee." We'd managed to raise fifty cents but then Mom grounded me when I refused to eat my broccoli, and we'd disbanded the committee shortly thereafter. "Does that count?" I asked.

Bethany tugged a petal so hard, the daisy head popped off the stem. "Not really."

"Nothing else?" George asked.

"Um, no. But remember, I'm only attending this one meeting."

"God," he muttered. "First this murder, now Esther sends you in her place."

No wonder Esther hadn't wanted to face the committee. What a couple of twerps.

"I'm here for this one meeting. I won't embarrass your committee." I checked the wall clock and saw it was a few minutes past four. Perhaps the rest of the members would arrive any moment and take the attention off me.

"How many others are you expecting?" I asked.

"Oh, we're it," Bethany said. "Roses in a town of weeds. No one else cares enough about this place to dedicate the time and energy we do."

I looked from Bethany to George and back. "The entire Blossom Valley Rejuvenation Committee is three people? And you're hassling me about my lack of experience? You should be thrilled I even volunteered to fill in for Esther."

George glowered. "Sending an extra body doesn't help much."

I could be nice up to a point, but I had limits, and George had reached them. I stood. "Fine. Then I'll leave."

Bethany thrust her arm across the table in an attempt to stop me. "Wait." She turned to George. "She's like the trellis for a bougainvillea. We'll need her support at the contest."

George rubbed the stubble on his head. "Didn't mean to get you all riled up. Go on and stay."

I sat back down, though I wasn't exactly ecstatic. But Esther had made it clear that this committee was dear to her heart.

"Let's try this again," I said.

Bethany leaned forward. "Thank you. We do need your

help. Imagine poor George and me putting on the cricket-chirping contest alone. It'd be like repotting a hundred petunias with a baby spoon."

Good Lord, make this woman stop with the flower metaphors.

"Esther mentioned the cricket contest," I said. "Something about twenty contestants already lined up."

"That's actually less people than last year," Bethany said. "'Course, we did have that little mishap."

"Mishap?" Couldn't be worse than birds eating the contestants in the worm races.

Bethany lowered her eyes. "The winner accidentally set the trophy down on his pet cricket. Squashed the poor little thing."

"What a mess," George said.

An awkward silence filled the room. I could have heard a cricket chirp, had one been hiding in the corner.

"Tell me what needs to be done for the festival," I said.

George uncapped his pen. "The contest is on Tuesday, down at the fairgrounds. I'll need you there by one to set up the tables and chairs."

Wait, what was happening here? I'd only volunteered to attend the meeting. "I'll tell Esther. I'm sure she'll want to help herself."

"Either way, make sure someone is there at one," George said. "I'll be judging the event. Bethany, you're in charge of manning the door and showing contestants where to set up at the tables." He turned to Bethany. "Did you want to say anything?"

Bethany swept her daisy petals into a pile. "You covered it all."

George stood up and stuffed his papers back in his briefcase. "Great. Meeting adjourned. I'll type up the notes."

He hadn't taken any notes, but considering the actual

meeting was about three minutes long, I guess he could remember the details.

"That's it?" I asked.

"We pride ourselves on getting in and getting out," George said.

Bethany rose from the table as well, so I stood up.

"Nice meeting you both," I said. *Nice* wasn't the correct word. *Mildly unpleasant* was more accurate, but Mom had raised me to be polite, even if I had to lie.

George snapped the clasp on his case. "I hope the police clear up the murder, for Esther's sake. I don't want to boot her off the committee."

"I'm sure the cops will make an arrest soon." I stepped away from the table, ahead of George and Bethany.

"In my book, that guy's assistant did it," George added.

I was almost out the door but stopped and turned back. "What did you say?"

"His assistant, that skinny kid."

"Logan?"

George shrugged. "Dunno. But he needs a haircut."

That was Logan. "What makes you think he's responsible for Maxwell's death?"

"You know how kids are these days. That sense of entitlement, the idea they can do no wrong. And Maxwell was sure insulting him down at the Daily Grind, right in front of the other customers. I bet the kid got so mad that he killed his boss."

Words failed me for a moment. When I had spoken with Logan at lunch, he hadn't mentioned any fight with Maxwell. Was that because he was worried about being implicated in the murder or because he wasn't nearly as upset as George believed him to be?

"Did you hear what Maxwell said?" I asked.

"Guess the kid wrote a screenplay that he'd asked his boss to read. There's that sense of entitlement I was talking about, thinking you should be first in line just because you work for the guy." George poked himself in the chest. "Back in my day, you got somewhere through grit and determination."

If George got sidetracked with the downfall of today's youth, we'd be here until dinnertime. "Maxwell didn't like the screenplay?"

"Said it was terrible. I believe his exact words were that he'd be saving the pages to housetrain his next puppy."

Ouch.

"And what did Logan say?" I asked, suddenly feeling like I could give Detective Caffrey some competition in the interrogation department.

"He didn't say nothing, wimpy little kid. Stood there like a statue and got all pale. Then he grabbed the pages from Maxwell and ran out. Not that he ran far. When I picked up my coffee and left, he was sitting out in that Mercedes, waiting to drive his boss somewhere. No spine in that one."

Bethany's fingers twitched as she stroked the orchid behind her ear, no doubt imagining the phone in her hand as she dialed her friends with this info.

Between what Heather had told me about the necklace and now George's description of Logan and Maxwell arguing at the coffee shop, a call to Detective Caffrey might be in order. I'd promised Esther to pass along any info that might help the police. Anything to speed up their investigation and remove this stain from the spa's reputation. If only I hadn't left his business card under the keyboard back in the office.

"Do you think the police know about the fight?" I asked.

George glanced at the clock and walked toward the door. "One of the deputies and his wife were sitting at a table when all this happened."

If a deputy had been at the coffee shop, he'd no doubt

passed the information on to Detective Caffrey. I didn't feel like driving back to the farm tonight. And I wanted to give Heather a chance to tell the police about the necklace before I did.

"Like I said, I'm sure the kid's the one who stabbed him." George squeezed past me and out the door, Bethany trailing behind.

Logan didn't seem like the killer type, but then neither did anyone else at the farm, including Sheila. And unless a stranger had snuck onto the property in the middle of the day with no one noticing, someone at that farm had stabbed Maxwell. And I needed to help the police figure out who.

12

Even with George's retelling of the argument between Logan and Maxwell, I was back in my car by half past four. A bit early to call it a day, but by the time I drove to the farm, it'd be time to turn around and go home. No sense wasting the gas. And if a deputy was in the coffee shop during the argument, then the info about the necklace could wait until tomorrow.

I nosed out of the parking lot and drove the few blocks home. The street was empty of cars, the yards devoid of late-afternoon gardeners. In San Jose, the traffic never stopped, people milled about the sidewalks at all hours. Here, a pedestrian was a novelty.

At home, Mom dusted photos on the mantel. I recognized her red blouse with the tiny white flowers as one she had sewn herself years ago. When she saw me, she carefully set the photo of Dad back and checked the clock.

"Dana, you're home early. Don't tell me Esther had to let you go?"

I dropped my purse on the couch. "No, my role has been redefined. I now maintain the Web site and do odd jobs around the farm, help everyone else when they need me."

Mom squeezed the dust rag. "That sounds iffy. She's not keeping you on as a favor to me, is she?"

That better not be the case. Talk about humiliating. "No. She likes my work. And Esther will let me go if she runs out of chores. But I'll pay rent as long as I can."

At the mention of money, Mom diverted her eyes to Dad's picture. "Oh, heavens, I'm not worried about that."

Mom couldn't downplay her money problems forever. I'd noticed she'd replaced all her favorite brand-name soups and yogurts with generic store brands. This from the woman who'd once declared Campbell's was the only can worth opening. But she believed the parent's job was to care for the child, not the other way around. We'd argued for an hour over whether or not I'd pay rent when I moved home. Mom backed down only after I insisted I needed to pay my way as a sign of my independence.

"If you're helping with meals and cleaning rooms, at least you'll be around the guests more," Mom said. "You can find out who knew Maxwell."

"Right. I just need to be careful I don't ask too many questions, or they'll get suspicious."

"Do your best. Esther needs us. With her husband gone and no children, she has no one else." She folded the dust rag into a square and stowed it in the hall closet. "Now, I'm going to gather some flowers from the yard, make a nice bouquet for the dinner table."

"I'll help," I said.

I followed Mom into the backyard and donned a pair of gloves, while she grabbed two pairs of gardening shears. I squinted in the sunlight, surprised at the brightness so late in the day.

Mom handed me a set of shears. "How is Esther's business? Did everyone pack up and go home?"

"The film crew did, everyone except Maxwell's assistant. And a few of the other guests went home as well."

"Too bad the film people left. I'm sure they all knew Maxwell to some extent."

"Like I said, Logan's staying."

Mom snipped a rose off the bush. "If most of the guests left, how will Esther's spa survive?"

I moved to the flowerbed. "We've already rented out the vacated rooms."

"I'll be darned. People want to stay where a man was murdered?"

"It helps that Maxwell was a famous Hollywood producer, though I'm not sure he's as big as his assistant claims."

"I heard that he made those terrible horror movies. Why anyone would want to watch someone get hacked to death is beyond me."

I loved the suspense and silliness of a good horror film, but it wasn't everyone's cup of tomato juice. I cut a large purple flower, watching the blade slice through the green flesh, and handed it to Mom.

"Here's a pretty one."

Mom accepted the flower. "An allium."

I readjusted the gloves, my fingers suffocating in the heat from the late afternoon sun. "Where did you hear about Maxwell's horror films?"

"I ran into Daphne at the grocery store." She plucked a snail from under a leaf and chucked it over the fence. Bet the neighbors loved that. "She was telling me how Maxwell's ex was staying at the spa, too. Talk about a coincidence."

"Right, Sheila Davenport. I don't know much about her." Except that she might have stolen an expensive necklace from Maxwell after she killed him. Maybe those two staying at the spa opening weekend wasn't such a coincidence. But I'd wait to share that accusation with Mom until after I'd spoken with Detective Caffrey or at least had more information.

Mom set the flowers on the patio table, then moved to her lilac bush. "Sheila Davenport? Well, doesn't that beat all. I never made the connection."

"You know her?"

"She rented from my friend Wilma over in Mendocino for a while after her divorce. My goodness, but she was mad when Maxwell abandoned her. She was his starter wife, you know."

"His what?"

"Starter wife. The woman a guy marries when he's up and coming then dumps for some young floozy the minute he turns into a success. Oprah did a whole show on the topic."

Ugh. I hated when my mom was hipper than me. "So you've met Sheila?"

Mom pulled a few brown petals from the clump. "Oh, sure, though I haven't seen her in ages. But every time I visited Wilma, Sheila would be moping in the sitting room. No matter what topic you brought up, she'd launch into a tirade about her ex. Got so Wilma and I started meeting at a cafe in Fort Bragg to avoid her."

"How long ago was this?"

Mom thought for a minute. "Let's see, Wilma took in boarders right around the time her son needed money for his vehicular manslaughter trial. I'm sure you remember me telling you about that. Wasn't it five or six years ago?"

Wilma's son had gotten into trouble as long as I could remember. I couldn't possibly keep track of all his arrests. But if Mom's time frame was correct, would Sheila have held a grudge that long? Sounded like Sheila was plenty upset about the failure of her marriage. Had she discovered Maxwell would be staying at the spa and saw it as her chance for revenge? She'd told Kimmie that she was ultimately happy about the divorce, but she could be hiding her pain.

"How's her jewelry business?" I asked.

"Fine, far as I know. I could ask Wilma if you'd like."

"No, that's okay." Whether or not her business was a success wasn't really related to how she felt about Maxwell, especially with the millions she'd inherited from her grandfather. And having a successful business or a truckload of money didn't necessarily lessen the sting of being dumped.

Mom set the pruning shears on the table and laid out the flowers, trimming each stem. I hadn't helped much with the flower cutting, but at least I'd gotten some dirt from Mom.

The screen door opened and Ashlee stuck her head out, her blond hair pulled back in a ponytail. "I'm starved. When's dinner?"

"I'll get going right now," Mom said.

"Good. I might faint if I don't eat soon."

She bounced up and down on the balls of her feet, not exactly the picture of someone suffering from starvation.

"How was work?" I asked, gathering up the loose stems. I tossed them onto the lilac bush, where they disappeared among the tiny branches.

Ashlee plopped into a patio chair and flapped her shirt hem to fan herself. "The usual. Except all the talk about the murder. I got to tell everyone how my own sister found the body. Britney was so jealous. All her sister's ever done was be a guest on *Jerry Springer*."

Maybe next week I could discover who really killed Anna Nicole Smith. That'd give her something to talk about.

I tossed the pruning shears into the plastic gardening bucket and the shears clanked against the bottom. "You make it sound like finding a dead guy is as fun as winning a trip to Disneyland."

Ashlee studied her hands. "I'm sorry. You must have been horrified."

An apology from Ashlee was so rare that I actually felt guilty for making her feel bad enough to offer one. How silly was that?

"What else did you guys talk about?" I asked.

"Everyone who works at the farm. How Gordon yells at his gardener when the guy doesn't trim the grass close enough."

Sounded like Gordon all right.

"What a ladies' man Christian is with his slick yoga moves. He especially likes the rich, older ladies," Ashlee said, wiggling her eyebrows.

I'd only seen Christian eye Tiffany, who I'd classify more as a girl than a woman, and definitely not a rich girl. But Christian might ogle all available eye candy, not just the geriatric crowd.

Ashlee removed a tube of lip gloss from her vet frock and applied a coat while she talked. "How bad we all feel that Heather has to leave her kids with her drunk mom all day so she can scrub other people's toilets. The troubles of a single mother."

This observation was so profound for Ashlee that I was momentarily speechless.

"And how loopy Zennia is. What a nutbar."

Ah, there was the Ashlee I loved and sometimes wanted to strangle.

We followed Mom into the house, where she deposited the flowers on the kitchen counter and pulled down a vase from the cupboard.

"Zennia's not crazy," I said as Ashlee and I sat down at the table. "She likes to eat healthy, which is a good thing."

"I'm so glad you agree," Mom called from the kitchen.

"I know you girls are going to love this buckwheat-coated salmon with spaghetti squash."

Ashlee and I wrinkled our noses at each other as we both reached for the fruit bowl. I selected an apple while she took a banana.

Mom leaned over the counter that divided the kitchen from the dining area. "Dinner in twenty. Don't even think about a snack."

I put the apple back while Ashlee slipped the banana under the table. I could see her arm move as she presumably peeled it. She glanced into the kitchen to make sure Mom was facing the stove, then popped a banana piece into her mouth. The story of my life: Ashlee does what she wants without getting caught while I obey the rules and go hungry.

I should be more of a rebel. I picked up the apple again from the bowl, then sensed danger. Mom frowned at me from the kitchen. She pointed a spatula at me and I put the apple back.

Guess I'd be a rebel tomorrow. Maybe I'd get to try out my new attitude at the spa.

13

The next morning, I parked in the lot and ran the gauntlet of reporters lobbing questions at me. The crowd was noticeably smaller today. Guess Maxwell's death was old news, even if he'd only been killed two days ago.

I hurried down the back path, glancing over my shoulder to make sure Jason wasn't following me this morning, and entered through the kitchen.

Esther stood near the door with a plunger in one hand and the phone receiver in the other, wet spots obvious on her denim shirt. She hung the receiver back on the wall.

"Dana, thank goodness."

A plunger, of all things. Not a good time for someone to be so happy to see me.

"A guest's toilet backed up this morning. I tried to fix it myself, and now water's coming up in the bathtub. And that handyman I usually call isn't home. Why that man doesn't get a cell phone is beyond me. Makes me madder than a momma cat when you take her kittens away."

I looked at the plunger, wondering where I fit in. "How can I help?" I felt obligated to ask.

"I've been so busy with the plumbing that I haven't had a chance to collect the eggs from the coop. Berta gets mighty cranky when I don't gather her offering first thing in the morning."

Visions of clucking and pecking hens filled my mind. Unclogging the toilet might be the better choice. If only I had plumbing skills.

"Um, any tips on the best way to retrieve the eggs?" Like how not to lose an eye.

"Oh, most of the hens won't bother you."

Most was not the same as all. "What about the hens that will?"

Esther switched the plunger to her other hand and glanced at the rooster clock. "I usually scatter some feed out in the yard to keep them busy. The basket's by the door to the coop," she called out as she walked away.

Well, great. Now I could add pig catcher, towel folder, and egg collector to my résumé. Everything but marketing maven. At least I had the daily blog and web updates. My skills wouldn't completely rust.

I left my purse in the office and headed back out the door and down the path. The sound of clucking chickens greeted me as I approached the coop, the volume increasing with each step. Two chickens pecked at the dirt outside the coop. One stopped to cluck at me as I made my way to the side of the building. I unlatched the wooden slatted door and opened it, wrinkling my nose at the stench of chicken poop in the dim quarters. As soon as I stepped inside, the chickens ran around the coop, flapping their wings and squawking.

I threw myself back out the door and slammed it shut, breathing hard. Not a good start. Looking around, I spotted the burlap bag full of feed, a scoop resting on top. I shoveled a pile out. Careful not to spill too much food, I carried the full scoop around to the front and flung the contents into the yard. Several hens emerged from their nests among a flurry of feathers and clucks. I returned to the coop and let myself back in, careful to shut the door behind me. No sense spending the day trying to catch a chicken. Unlike a pig, chickens could fly.

Two chickens waited on their nests, eyeing me and opening and closing their beaks. Their sharp, pointed beaks.

I removed the basket from the hook and stuck my hand in the first empty nest, connecting with a slimy substance. I yanked my hand back, my fingers now covered with yolk. Ick. I moved to the next nest, standing on tiptoe to peek inside. A single egg lay among the straw and loose feathers. I gently laid it in the basket, then moved down the line, listening for the clucks of any chickens returning from the yard.

After I collected a dozen eggs from the empty nests, I studied the two chickens still watching me. Did I need to gather every last egg? I had a lovely basketful. Why not let these poor chickens keep their eggs for one day?

But Esther had mentioned a cranky chicken if her egg didn't get picked up. I wasn't sure how you could tell whether a chicken was cranky or happy, but Esther had definitely seemed worried about it.

I approached the first chicken. "Hi, little hen. I've come for your egg."

She clucked. It was fairly dark in the coop, but I swear I saw a mean glint in her eye.

I tried to slip a hand under her breast. She jerked her head forward and pecked my wrist.

"Ow!" A red dot swelled on my arm.

The chicken blinked at me. Was that a smile?

I stretched my arm out and reached around to slide my hand under the back of the chicken, trying not to acknowledge that my new job involved touching chicken butt. How degrading.

This time, the chicken stood and flapped down from her perch. I would, too, if a stranger was touching my nether regions. I retrieved the egg and faced the last chicken. She stared back, not flinching. The back approach had worked so well, I decided to try again. As I touched her tail feathers, the bird craned her head around and pecked my hand. I gave her my best "don't mess with me" glare, but the chicken didn't even blink.

I reached for the egg once more, but she nailed me again. I stepped back, holding my brimming basket. If this was Berta, she could be cranky for one day. I let myself out of the coop, sure I heard Berta cackling, and vowed to eat at KFC next chance I got. I'd show that chicken.

As I turned to go, sunlight glinted off an object in the dirt, partially covered by leaves. A piece of metal? A fragment of glass? Neither one belonged near animals. I stepped away from the coop to retrieve it and the door swung open. Berta must be plotting to come after me. I relatched the door, checking to verify it was secure, then focused my attention on the patch of dirt again. With my free hand, I bent over and picked up the shiny object. A money clip.

I started to turn it over when hands shoved me from behind and I fell toward the fencing. I dropped the basket as the clip was snatched from my other hand. I caught myself on the chicken wire but couldn't stop my momentum. One knee thudded onto the hard-packed dirt.

I heard footsteps running away and craned my neck around. Branches waved back and forth where my attacker had barreled through, but no one was in sight. I pulled myself to my feet and ran along the still visible path for a few moments, then stopped. The footsteps had ceased. Everything was quiet. Whoever had pushed me was gone.

I returned to the chicken coop and picked up the basket of eggs. Two had fallen out and broken. Three more in the basket showed cracks. But the eggs weren't too important right now, considering what had happened.

Who had shoved me? And why? To retrieve the money clip was the obvious answer. Someone felt the clip was important enough to knock me down. Was it related to the murder? Did the clip belong to Maxwell?

Now might be the time to notify Detective Caffrey. But what would I tell him? I'd found a money clip on the ground but had no idea who it belonged to. I'd been pushed down by an unknown assailant and gotten nary a glimpse of him or her. Not exactly a breakthrough in the case. And who was to say any of this was connected to Maxwell's death?

I'd drop off the eggs and decide what to do after that. As I followed the path to the pool area, voices drifted toward me. I came around the redwood tree and spotted Christian and Sheila talking. Christian saw me, patted Sheila on the shoulder, and walked over. Sheila glanced at me, her normally styled hair uncombed, tears evident in her eyes. Was she crying about Maxwell? Or feeling guilty that she killed him? She turned and hurried toward her cabin, casting a backward glance at me.

Christian approached me, his tank top stopping just above the groin area of his biker shorts, providing no modesty. I tried not to stare. "My dear, how are you feeling?"

Was he talking to me? I glanced over my shoulder but no one was behind me.

He leaned in and gave me a hug. Startled, I automatically hugged him back, almost tipping the basket and spilling the eggs. I could feel his well-defined bicep against my back.

He released me, but kept one hand on my shoulder. "I've been hoping to speak with you."

"Why?" Did that sound as rude as I thought it did?

"Because of your traumatic experience. As someone

who has studied with a swami, I can help you move past your grief."

Was he talking about what had happened by the chicken coop? But of course not. He must be referring to Maxwell's death. "Um, actually, I'm fine. Quite a shock to find a dead man, but since I didn't know Maxwell, I'm not that upset." And if I were, I wouldn't confide in some silver-tongued yoga-meister that I barely knew.

Christian put his other hand on my free shoulder and gazed into my eyes. I remembered what Ashlee had said about his smooth yoga moves and tried not to giggle. I wedged the egg basket between us.

"You may think you're fine, but the human spirit often tamps down fear and trouble, only to have it resurface disguised as something else. Are you having trouble sleeping? Are you unusually tense?"

Only when being hit on at my workplace. "Loose as a goose," I said.

Christian squeezed one shoulder. "I suspect you'll discover that you're not over this tragedy. When you do, I can help you through the dark patches. Yoga was founded on the belief that we all are but servants who report to a higher being. He has a master plan for all of us."

Did he use this trick down at the Watering Hole? I could imagine some drunk and lonely barfly agreeing to go home with Christian as he sweet-talked her with this higher power bit.

"Thanks for asking," I said, "but I'm okay."

He dropped his arms, then scratched his chest through his T-shirt, harder and harder with each passing second. Not used to being rebuffed by the ladies? Perhaps my attitude was making him break out in hives. He was definitely handsome enough for me to swoon, but his intensity gave me the creeps.

"Hey, you there." A woman in her early twenties trotted toward us, one hand raised in salutation, her ample bust practically leaping out the top of her low-cut tank. I didn't know her name but I recognized her as one of the guests who had snagged a room after Maxwell's death.

"You're the yoga guy, right?" she asked Christian.

"Yes, miss. How may I be of service?"

She smoothed her long red hair. "I wanted to know about these things called chakras that a cute guy at my gym was talking about. I think he might ask me out and I don't want to look like an idiot."

Christian took her arm and led her to a nearby mat. "Chakras are too complex to explain to one who has not yet embraced the yoga lifestyle. Let me tell you about the classes I offer here at the spa. We can then map out your spiritual journey."

Classes were included in the price of a guest's stay, so I didn't know why Christian was pushing the classes instead of answering her question. Job security? I left them by the mats and carried the eggs toward the house, the incident from the coop already fading. Really, I wasn't hurt when I got pushed. No need to blow everything out of proportion.

In the kitchen, Esther sat with Jason at the table. Esther had changed from her denim shirt into a calico print blouse. At the sight of Jason in his navy blue button-up shirt, my heart did a little pitter-patter.

"Esther, sorry to interrupt. Didn't know you had company. My apologies. Here are the eggs," I rambled, setting the basket on the counter. What the hell was wrong with me?

"Dana, you've met Jason, right?" Esther said.

"Briefly." Then I'd run away. Twice. But newspapermen are notoriously untrustworthy.

"With Maxwell's death being such big news in town,

Jason is dedicating most of next week's *Blossom Valley Herald* issue to Maxwell and our little farm and spa here."

Jason stood. "Esther and I are done, and I'd like to interview you next, if you have the time. She mentioned you recently moved back to town after growing up here originally. I'd like to know what brought you back, and if you're planning to stay."

If Jason had a good relationship with the cops, now might be my chance to find out what they'd uncovered about Maxwell's death. But would I be able to trick Jason into answering my questions without being too obvious?

Jason was watching me, waiting for my response.

"Don't worry," he said. "I won't ask you about the murder. I'm strictly interested in you as a person."

Why did the way he phrased that give me such a thrill?

"Esther, did you have any more work for me first?" I asked.

"I'd much rather you speak to Jason for his article. Free publicity is better than that basket of eggs you got there."

"I guess you can interview me," I said to Jason, careful not to appear too eager, but my insides were as scrambled as these eggs would be at tomorrow's breakfast. Jason might be able to help me with the murder. I took a moment to wash up and steady my nerves. As I dried my hands on a dish towel, I caught a wisp of chicken odor. Great.

Jason picked up his notebook and stuffed it into his shirt pocket with his pen. "How about I buy you lunch? Then it won't seem as formal as an interview."

I glanced at the wall clock. Ten-thirty. "Bit early for lunch."

"Coffee then. I know where to get the best coffee in town, without the usual locals hanging around."

A secret coffee shop? Where I wouldn't run into my dentist, the mailman, or my high school teacher?

"Sign me up." I didn't know where he was taking me, or what questions he'd ask, but I'd use the drive to think up a few questions of my own.

And I wouldn't be telling him about getting shoved at the chicken coop either. At least until I knew I could trust him.

14

The moment Jason and I stepped out the front door, the six media people straightened up, cameras and microphones at the ready.

Jason held up a hand. "I'm interviewing her for local interest stuff. No break in the murder case."

Everyone lowered their equipment and resumed their conversations. As we passed by, I heard one blond reporter mumble, "What a waste. I can't wait to get out of this Podunk town."

I fought the urge to stop and yell at the reporter for dissing Blossom Valley. Sure, I felt the way she did most of the time, but I was born and raised here, so I was allowed to insult my hometown.

I pointed to where my Honda sat nearby. "We can take my car."

"I asked; I'll drive." Jason led the way across the lot. In the modest parking area, he'd managed to find a space with no surrounding cars, his silver Volvo gleaming in solitude.

With a flourish, Jason swung open the passenger side door. "After you."

I couldn't remember the last time a guy opened the door

for me. "Thanks." I slid into the seat, nestling into the leather like a mother hen, and clicked my seat belt in place.

"Nice car," I said, noting the immaculate interior. Not even a straw wrapper on the floor.

"Thanks. Volvo is consistently rated one of the safest cars out there."

Oh, my, a guy who bought cars based on safety ratings. Not exactly sexy.

Jason got in the driver's side, a whiff of lavender and spice tickling my nose. I inhaled the intoxicating aroma as he backed out of the lot and onto the freeway. We motored down the highway in silence and he took the exit for the older part of town.

The now-vacant lumber mill loomed over the surrounding auto shops and storage facility, the smokestack casting a cylinder-shaped shadow over the immediate area. Beyond the used-car lot, Jason pulled into the parking lot of a run-down diner, the battered sign out front announcing the Eat Your Heart Out cafe. The windows were smeared with dirt, the awning sagged, and the asphalt in the lot had long since turned to chunks.

"Best coffee in town," Jason commented.

"Didn't this used to be a biker hangout?" I recalled my parents talking about more than one bar fight, not that Mom would ever let us eat here ourselves.

"New owners," Jason said.

I stepped over the missing plank in the wood walkway and followed Jason inside. The interior was the exact opposite of its outer shell. Bright bulbs inside Tiffany-style lamps illuminated wood tables with cloth-covered booth seats. Light jazz played in the background from a jukebox in the corner.

At the counter, a heavy-set older man sipped a cup of coffee, a half-eaten Danish on the plate in front of him.

"Writing about the murder?" he asked Jason.

"Side story."

The man squinted at me, one rheumatic eye half-closed. "Say, aren't you Dorothy and Roger's oldest?"

"Yes, I'm Dana."

"Heard you was back in town working at that spa. I had high hopes that place would bring in more people, but don't know what's gonna happen after that murder."

Jason tilted his head toward the man. "Bill here carves animals out of old telephone poles. Sells them from his yard."

An image of his house on the edge of town, lawn filled with wooden bears, owls, and meerkats, popped into my head. "I remember you."

"Your daddy used to bring you around years ago. Weren't much bigger than those penguins I carve."

"Sorry to cut this short," Jason said. "But I have a lot of people to talk to today."

"Give your momma my best," Bill said to me.

As we walked away from Bill, a woman at a nearby table waved to Jason.

Her companion wiped his mouth. "Hey, Jason. Working on the big story?"

"You bet," Jason said as we continued to a booth in the back.

We passed another occupied table where two women ate breakfast. They watched us go by, then I heard rapid whisperings.

I slid into one side of the booth, facing the two women at their table.

Jason leaned forward. "We'll need to keep our voices down. Those two ladies we just passed will tell the whole town your background before I get a chance to print it, only half their information will be wrong."

As he said this, they picked up their plates and moved

to the booth next to ours, avoiding eye contact with me. Subtle.

"Don't look now," I whispered, "but we have company."

Jason glanced over his shoulder. "We'll have to move this interview outside as soon as we get our order."

I smirked. "Looks like the locals have discovered your super-secret restaurant."

"This place used to only attract out-of-towners and truck drivers. I don't know what happened."

"Guess everyone wants to see Blossom Valley's biggest reporter interview people."

Jason blushed.

A teenager strolled over, clearly in no hurry, her low-waisted jeans sagging atop her hips, her too-short T-shirt exposing a muffin top. She pulled an ear bud out, the faint strains of Lady Gaga reaching me through the tiny speakers.

"You ready to order?"

"Just coffee," I said.

She looked at Jason.

"Make that two. In to-go cups."

The waitress walked off. We sat in silence while we waited for our drinks. I twiddled with the saltshaker and glanced occasionally at the two women in the adjoining booth. They were also silent, obviously waiting for Jason to dish out a tasty gossip morsel to go with their eggs.

I glanced at the clock on the wall. Had the waitress flown to Colombia to harvest the coffee beans herself? I offered Jason a small smile and pulled a handful of napkins from the dispenser.

"You could probably go ahead and ask me those questions in here. No one could possibly care what I have to say about my personal life."

Jason glanced over his shoulder. "You're still a newcomer to town. And you found a body to boot. People will devour any information they can get." He crossed his arms over his chest. "We wait."

Touchy, touchy. "Fine. Working on any other stories right now? Or are you not going to talk about those either?"

As Jason opened his mouth to speak, the waitress returned with two Styrofoam cups and the tab. Jason paid at the register by the door and we walked over to his car.

He set his coffee on the roof and pulled his notebook and pen from his shirt pocket. "Guess this will be a parking lot interview."

I eyed the notebook. How was I going to transition Jason's interview of me into talking about the murder?

"Why'd you move back to Blossom Valley?" he asked.

I thought for a moment, figuring I'd have to answer his question first if I wanted him to return the favor. "I've been worried about my mom ever since my dad passed away. She'd completely withdrawn from her clubs and friends. When I called home, all she'd talk about was visiting my dad's grave and sitting at home staring at his picture. I decided she needed someone to push her back into her activities. Or at least get her to leave the house once in a while. Since I was unemployed, the timing to move was perfect." A little voice whispered in my ear about my teeny tiny lie—the timing had been far from perfect—but I shushed it up.

"Sorry about your dad." Jason jotted in his notebook. "How do you like being back in your hometown?"

I studied the concrete at my feet, noting the ants crawling in and out of the cracks on an endless quest. For food? For happiness? "I'm adjusting. Of course, finding Maxwell's body hasn't helped. Are the police making any progress on his murder?" Gee, that little change of subject wasn't too obvious.

Jason squinted at me, clearly confused by my question.

"Barely. Whoever killed Maxwell took the murder weapon and didn't leave much evidence behind. The cops have interviewed every guest and no one saw anything."

"Well, the entrances to the cabins face away from the pool area, so anyone could have hidden in those bushes and waited until Maxwell was alone." Oh, didn't I sound like a detective.

"Right, but let's not get off track here. What exactly are you adjusting to here? Life in a small town?"

I'd gotten some information from Jason. His turn again. "Partly. One nice thing about San Jose is the anonymity. I could trip over a dead body once a week and none of the neighbors would be any wiser. Blossom Valley is like living in a fish bowl. You can't even drink a cup of coffee without people whispering and pointing."

As if proving my point, a blue Saturn turned into the lot. The driver stared at us for so long, she almost hit a parked car. She braked within an inch of its bumper, then twisted the wheel and pulled into a vacant spot. Cell phone already to her ear, she got out of the car and watched us as she spoke. She appeared vaguely familiar but I couldn't place her name. That was the trouble with this town. Even the people I didn't know looked familiar.

I sipped the coffee. Scalding but weak.

When I didn't resume my answer, Jason stopped jotting notes.

"You said, 'partly.' What's the other part?" he asked.

"Being back home." I watched an ant that had strayed from the rest of the line and now wandered aimlessly. "I mean, I know I'm helping my mom, but I feel like I've taken a step back in life. I was making decent money at a job I was good at. Then I got laid off and wound up back here. And what do I have to show for it? Nothing."

That internal voice, the one that usually woke me at three AM, piped up again, reminding me I'd almost had something to show for it. I drowned out the voice with a slurp of coffee.

"Um, do you need to put that in your article?" I asked. "I sound like a bit of a loser."

"No, you sound like a lot of people around here in a tough economy. And I find it admirable that you want to help your mom."

"Thanks. But I'm worried that Maxwell's death will be a reminder of my dad's death and she'll slip back into a depression." Bit of a stretch on that one, but it was for a good cause. "How is it that no one saw anything suspicious near Maxwell's cabin?"

"Apparently the yoga class had broken up a few minutes before, and people were already in their cabins resting before lunch or visiting in the lobby, that sort of thing."

"So how will the police find the guy?"

He transferred his pen to the hand with the notebook, sipped from his cup, then put the coffee back on top of his car. "I'm sure they'll try to figure out exactly where everyone was when Maxwell was killed, see if they can catch someone in a lie. But unless the killer announces his guilt, the cops will have a hard time nailing this guy."

"Or gal," I said. "You don't need much strength to stab someone."

I stared at the ants on the sidewalk. The police might not find the killer. I'd seen Maxwell dead, clutching his stomach. He at least deserved to have his killer caught. And Mom was counting on me to help Esther.

I looked up to find Jason frowning at me. "What?" I asked.

"Last time I tried to question you about the murder, you practically ran screaming from me. Now that's all you want to talk about. What gives?"

I waved my hand at him, like he was creating a whole

beach from a handful of sand. "Idle curiosity, nothing more. So, uh, let's get back to that interview."

He studied me for a moment, then glanced at his notebook. "Why did you agree to work at the farm and spa?"

"Marketing positions are few and far between in this town. The farm was the first place that offered me a job." Boy, didn't that sound pathetic. I'd leave out the part where my mom actually arranged the job for me.

The two whispering ladies from the diner exited the restaurant and walked over to a red car parked near where we stood. One woman clutched a set of keys in her hand but made no move to open her door and drive away. Instead, they stood in silence.

After an unbearable pause, the other woman said, "Excellent eggs this morning."

More silence, while the woman with the keys cast sideways glances at Jason and me.

Jason opened the passenger door of his Volvo. "Let's sit in my car."

I smiled at the ladies, who pretended not to see me, and turned to step in. My foot caught in the asphalt crack and I fell toward Jason. I tossed my coffee cup to the left so as not to burn him and my hands landed on his chest. Even in my frantic state, I noticed the hard, muscular surface. I clutched his shirt and our faces came close together, our lips a mere inch apart.

For a moment, our gaze connected. I noticed little gold specks in his green, green eyes. I felt his breath on my lips.

"My car!" Jason yelled.

Behind me, a snort erupted. Guess those two women witnessed my little accident.

I straightened up, my face hot. I grabbed the napkins that had floated to the ground and wiped the top of his car, the flimsy paper causing the coffee to spread and drip off the edges.

Jason dropped his notebook, ran to his trunk, and popped it open with his remote. He returned with two towels. He tossed one to me and pressed his towel onto the coffee, trying to stop the flow down the side. I mopped up the spill on my end and crumpled up the empty cup.

"I'm sorry. I can't believe I dumped coffee all over your car."

"Everything's fine. We got all the coffee off."

I wasn't sure if Jason was talking to me or the car. Pulling a plastic bag from the trunk, he shook it open and dropped in the wet towel. I handed him my soaked cloth and he added it to the bag.

I slipped into the passenger seat, my face hotter than my coffee had been. Out the window, I could see the two ladies still watching us, now laughing. Losers.

Jason got in the other side, the notebook once more in his hand, and settled back in his seat, still breathing fast. He flipped to a new page. "Tell me what you do at the farm?"

Stumble over dead bodies, get pecked by chickens, act as a taste-test dummy for Zennia's abominations. Probably not the answer he was looking for.

"I was hired to create a series of brochures for the spa, plus finish the ones the original guy didn't get done. I also conducted market research here in town to discover what people expect at an organic spa and created a handful of press releases. Now I'm updating the Web site, plus helping out other employees as needed."

"Doing what?"

I was afraid he was going to ask me that. "You know, this and that."

"You had a basket of eggs in your hand this morning. What was that about?"

"I had to help collect them from the chicken coop, that's all." I moved my left hand to cover the fading red gouges on my right hand, my gift from Berta and her feathered friend.

"Quite the skill set you've got there," Jason said.

"It's a job. Something I'm grateful for." Even if I had no idea what I was doing half the time.

Jason wrote in his notebook.

"How about you? Did you grow up around here?" I asked, steering the questions around to Jason and away from my life as a fumbling farmer. "I don't remember you from school."

"No. I'm not from around here."

I waited for him to add more, but he didn't. "Then where are you from?"

After a moment's hesitation, he said, "Atherton."

"That rich little Bay Area town near Stanford? Why move to Blossom Valley?"

"These things happen."

Not exactly a specific answer, but Jason wasn't the one being interviewed.

He put the key in the ignition, clearly finished talking about himself. "That's all I need for the article. I'll get you back to work."

"I'm sure Zennia needs my help with lunch prep." Or the pigs needed a massage.

Jason started the car, the engine humming.

"You interviewing the rest of the staff now?" I asked.

"Soon as we get back. I noticed Esther is running a bit of a skeleton crew."

I waited until he merged onto the freeway, slipping in behind a semi hauling lumber. "She doesn't have the money to hire more staff until we see if the farm is a success."

"Looks like business is taking off, based on the number of cars in the parking lot."

"We're doing everything we can." I looked out the

window at the pear trees and nearby hills. With the continued heat wave, the green spring grass was turning brown, a contrast to the pear tree blossoms. "Once the thrill of Maxwell's death wears off, I'm not sure how much business we'll have. That's why the police have to solve this murder." Or else I did.

"Give 'em time."

We pulled into the farm lot, the cluster of reporters still hanging around the front door. Unless the police had a major breakthrough, the media couldn't possibly stay much longer.

"Thanks for the coffee," I said as Jason and I walked into the lobby.

Gordon stood at the front desk. When we entered, he stopped typing at the reservation computer and clasped his hands together. He steepled his index fingers and tapped them together, showing off a set of gold pinkie rings.

"Enjoying a late breakfast, Dana? Perhaps Esther would like to know about her absent employee."

A burst of anger shot from my gut to my face, blotting out my vision for a moment. The haze passed and I stared at Gordon in his three-piece suit and stupid polka dot tie.

Maybe I needed to talk to Esther myself.

15

I stepped up to the reservation counter and slapped my palms on the surface, keeping my voice steady. "Jason was interviewing me for the *Herald*, per Esther's request. You of all people know how important publicity is."

"In fact," Jason said, "if you have a moment, I'd like to ask you a few questions."

Gordon straightened his tie. "I am the manager of the farm. My job is critical to its success."

I managed not to roll my eyes and slipped down the hall. Gordon would talk Jason into a coma but at least that would keep him off my back for a while.

In the office, I typed up the day's blog, having composed it in my head the night before. I posted the blog to the Web site and checked the day's headlines before heading to the kitchen to help Zennia with lunch.

A row of shot glasses sat on the table next to a square of grass. Odd place to keep part of the lawn.

At the counter, Zennia, wearing a tie-dyed dress and Birkenstocks, sliced okra. My stomach did a little rumble of complaint as I eyed the green vegetable. Should have grabbed a Danish to go with my coffee.

"Dana, perfect timing. You can prepare the wheatgrass."

My hearing must be going. "Wheatgrass?"

"One shot a day provides all your amino acid needs. The guests will appreciate the health benefits."

I opened the fridge and studied the contents. Yogurt, milk, and chicken breasts occupied the shelves, but nothing that looked like wheatgrass. I shut the door and walked over to the table.

"Is this piece of lawn the wheatgrass?" I asked.

"Right. Stick a little patch in the juicer and fill each shot glass."

Not convinced I understood Zennia correctly, I cut off a piece of grass, loaded it in the juicer, positioned a shot glass below the spout, and pushed the button. Three seconds later, a thick green liquid jiggled at the bottom of the glass.

I sniffed the contents and got a whiff of freshly mowed lawn. Somehow I didn't see the guests lining up after lunch to thank the chef.

"How are you doing, Zennia? Since the murder, I mean."

"My entire digestive tract is definitely off," she said. "Must be the lack of sleep. I seem to lie awake a lot, wondering whose soul is so black that they would take another life."

I deposited more grass in the juicer. "I'd like to know that myself." I bumped the shot glass just as I hit the button. The wheatgrass plopped onto the table. I wiped up the mess. "You should take a yoga class with Christian. Help yourself relax."

Zennia lifted the cutting board and dropped the sliced okra into a skillet on the stove. The okra hissed in the pan. "I've never been particularly flexible. I prefer meditation each morning, although my focus has been less directed than usual."

I finished juicing the wheatgrass, then poked my head

into the dining room. Guests were filtering in the side door, many sitting at tables. I went back to the kitchen for the first four glasses, ready for lunch service.

After an hour of steady work, everyone had managed to swallow the wheatgrass with minimal groaning and the dining hall emptied out. I carried the dirty dishes to the kitchen, helped Zennia clean up, then wandered out to the herb garden, admiring the dill and chervil. I knew it was chervil because Zennia had stuck a sign next to each plant following a guest request.

In the corner, a figure crouched over the cilantro, fingers scratching at the soil around the plant. I recognized the hair as belonging to Logan. Was he digging something up or burying something? As if sensing my gaze, he stood up and turned around.

"Hi, Logan," I said. "Lose a contact lens?"

Logan blushed, as if caught smoking the greens instead of fondling them. "Checking to see how deep the roots are. I'm trying to relax, but doing nothing is harder than I thought."

I gestured to the BlackBerry clipped to his belt. "I bet if you turned that off, you'd relax more."

The mere mention of his gadget made Logan check the screen. "Let's not get crazy." He brushed hair out of his eyes, but the strands immediately flopped back into place. "Besides, I need to be available. Looks like Wilcox over at Tiger Shark Studios is hiring me. I start next week."

"Congratulations. That was fast." He'd found a job in two days and I'd taken almost a year? Next time I needed employment, I'd call Logan for tips.

Logan tapped his chest with his index finger. His nails were manicured, his skin smooth.

"I know people," he said.

He must know important people to land a new position that fast, especially in Hollywood, where every breathing body wanted a job in the movies.

"I remember you mentioned that Maxwell was your gateway to new projects. Think his death will hurt your plans?"

A blue jay squawked from its perch on a nearby oak tree branch.

"Wilcox knows the right people. And I've heard he's not as difficult to work for as Maxwell."

"I can't believe you toted his silverware around and ironed his clothes on Sundays."

"Those chores were only part of his absurd demands. Try running to Wal-Mart at midnight to buy his jock-itch cream. Or hustling his latest bimbo out to a taxi so he wouldn't have to wake up next to her in the morning." He gestured to his clothes. "And these khaki pants and white shirt? Maxwell insisted I wear the same outfit every day."

I was wondering why a hip, young Hollywood up-and-comer always dressed like an electronics store employee. "And you tolerated all his demands for a screenplay?"

"Working for Maxwell was my first major studio job. But looking back, I should have refused his requests. One of life's lessons, I guess."

"Did Maxwell ever read your screenplay?" I asked, thinking of the argument George had overheard in the coffee shop.

Logan's face darkened so much I actually glanced at the sun to see if a cloud was passing over. Nope.

"Maxwell's vision was more limited than I realized when I signed on. He'd accept any plot if the movie contained enough special effects or nudity. But he couldn't appreciate the finer films."

"So he hated the screenplay." Heaven knows why I was

poking a hornet's nest, risking a sting, but I couldn't help myself.

Logan bent down and yanked a cluster of leaves off the cilantro. I swear I heard the plant scream.

"The man was an idiot. He wouldn't know a good movie if Steven Spielberg screened it himself. When he told me my screenplay was undeveloped and boring, I lost all respect for him."

I eyed the squawking blue jay, seeming to mock Logan. "But you think this new boss is smarter?"

"Wilcox is a man of integrity. He'll recognize the value of my work."

Logan had probably said the same thing about Maxwell at one time.

"Now excuse me," he said. "I need to make a phone call." He stomped away, trampling the chervil. Guess he needed a few more days of relaxation to start respecting the vegetation.

I thought about our conversation. Logan must have been furious when Maxwell insulted his screenplay, especially after all the humiliating chores he'd performed. But had Logan been angry enough to kill him? He'd been in the dining room for the entire lunch period. Had Maxwell been killed prior to lunch or during the meal? Would the police be able to narrow down the time of death to such a small window?

I glanced over my shoulder to make sure Logan was out of sight, then bent down and dug around the cilantro plant. My fingers only found damp soil and pebbles. Maybe Logan really was checking the roots. Or I'd interrupted his attempt to hide something.

I stood and brushed off my hands. Two days ago, my biggest problem had been how to swallow Zennia's meals without gagging. Now, I spent my time wondering which person at the spa had committed murder. Life had certainly taken an interesting detour.

Esther came out the back door, clad in brown slacks and a denim shirt embroidered with corn stalks and scarecrows, an oversized purse slung over one shoulder. Her gray hair sported fresh curls and a touch of rouge brightened her already ruddy cheeks. She was certainly gussied up.

"Dana, any trouble with the clog today?"

Uh-oh, had another guest clogged a toilet? "Weren't you taking care of that problem?"

"Remember how we talked yesterday about you updating the Web site?"

My mind went blank. What did a clogged toilet have to do with the computer?

"You're supposed to write something every day," Esther prompted.

"Oh, the *blog*," I said. "I posted the blog today with no problems."

Esther reached into her purse and extracted a compact. She popped it open and studied her reflection in the mirror, rubbing at the rouge. She snapped the compact closed. "Oh! Where is my mind today? I meant to ask this morning how the committee meeting went?"

"The group was smaller than I expected, but the meeting went fine. A bit short."

"That George hates long meetings. Sometimes I don't even get a chance to speak."

The blue jay was back to shrieking, his voice almost drowning out Esther. I tried to tune the bird out.

"But with only three members, wouldn't everyone be able to speak?" I asked.

"Not with George in charge. He used to be a sergeant in the army. Doesn't have time for chitchat. I just wish we could get more people to attend."

"Have you tried recruiting other business owners?"

"People do join for a while, but eventually they all drop out. I'm afraid our festivals and contests haven't drawn the numbers we wanted and people get frustrated."

I patted her shoulder. "I bet this cricket-chirping contest is a huge success." *Please don't let God strike me down for lying.*

"I sure hope so. With all these new reservations helping the farm, a huge crowd for the cricket chirpers would be the cream on the peaches."

"Speaking of the contest, George wants you at the fair-grounds at one tomorrow afternoon to help set up."

Esther frowned and I noticed that she'd applied her lip-stick unevenly, adding a good half inch to her left side. "Goodness me, I'm not ready for that."

Uh-oh. Visions of unfolding chairs and dragging tables around filled my head. "Nonsense. You said the farm is prospering. Get out there and hold your head high." *Please, oh, please, don't make me do it.*

Esther plucked at a button on her shirt. "No, it's too soon. George and Bethany will hound me for all the details of the murder. I'm afraid I'm not up to it yet. But I know you'll do a great job, Dana."

Ugh. So much for escaping the drudgeries of cricket chirping. *But it's a job*, I reminded myself. One to which I had agreed.

"I'll protect this year's winner from the giant trophy."

Esther frowned. "I'd almost forgotten about that. But if you run into Jason, make sure he mentions in his news coverage how the farm is helping the community with our involvement."

"Jason?" A little spark jolted my chest.

"He covers all the Rejuvenation Committee projects. Isn't that boy just as cute as a june bug?"

I'd never seen a june bug, but I'd definitely agree that Jason was good looking. "I'll be sure to talk to him." No problem there. But would I look too silly popping open metal chairs and directing contestants to tables while wearing high heels and my silk blouse with the plunging neckline?

"Good. I know Gordon likes to handle the press for the farm, but he'll never help with a committee project."

"Why do you tolerate that man?" The question had slipped out before I could stop myself, and I pressed my lips together before I could say more.

Esther fiddled with her purse clasp. "I know he can be like a burr in your backside, but he's good at his job. He's still upset from when his bed and breakfast went under."

"He had a B and B?"

She nodded. "That's why he knows all the ins and outs of the business. He jumped right in, filed all the permits and paperwork for the spa, and saved me a mess of headaches. Without him, I'm not sure I would have had the confidence to open the spa." Esther glanced at her watch. "My goodness, so late? I have a meeting at the bank."

She turned and hurried back inside the main house. I wandered through the herb garden and down the path, trying to think up more blog ideas. I was already planning to blog about Zennia's wheatgrass, but I wanted to make a list of go-to topics for those days when I was stumped. As I rounded the bend near the redwood tree, I saw Sheila step onto the path up ahead, dressed in white pants and a silk tunic. She had a spa bath towel tucked under her arm. I expected her to turn toward the cabins at the juncture, but instead, she headed toward the Chicken Run Trail.

Interesting. Why would someone carry a towel into the woods? No creeks ran along the trail. Esther certainly wasn't hiding a swimming pool back there. And if Sheila expected to get sweaty on her walk, why wouldn't she carry a handkerchief or hand towel?

Unless she was trying to hide something. Like the murder weapon. What better way to dispose of the knife that killed Maxwell than to roll it up in a towel and hide it among all the trees and bushes?

As Sheila disappeared around a corner, I picked up my pace, eager to see where she was going. She walked steadily ahead, as if she had a destination in mind. I stayed close enough to keep her in sight, but far enough away that I could dart back around a corner if she stopped.

After several minutes of following her, the sweat began to form along my hairline and I brushed at the liquid with the back of my hand. Maybe Sheila would lend me her towel to dry my forehead. We had to be approaching the back of the property by now, the trees becoming denser, the terrain more sloped as it neared the mountains.

Sheila stopped on a straight part of the path, next to a birch tree. She jerked her head to the right. Instinctively, I jumped back behind the nearest pine tree, hoping the trunk's girth would protect me from detection.

Did she know I was following her? Was she staring at the tree this very instant?

The sound of snapping branches reached my ears. Was Sheila trying to trick me into poking my head out? Or was she hiding the knife? The desire to find out was so strong that I clenched my teeth, my hands pressed firmly against the trunk.

I silently began counting in my head, trying to calm my breathing at the same time. When I reached ten, I decided to take a peek.

Keeping my back to the trunk, I stepped to the side and eased my head around the corner.

An empty stretch of path waited for me. Nothing more.

Holy crap.

Sheila was gone.

16

I blinked several times, wondering if all this walking was causing me to hallucinate, but the path remained empty. No sign of Sheila.

Had I hidden behind the tree that long? At her pace, she couldn't have possibly rounded the next bend before I checked. Had she spotted me and run?

I came out from behind the tree and hurried down the path, trying to keep my steps quiet while catching up to wherever she'd gone. I practically jogged around the next corner, body tense, ready to hide behind another tree if Sheila was just ahead. But the trail was still empty, another straight section of dirt.

I returned to where Sheila had stopped. Maybe the snapping branches hadn't been from Sheila hiding something, but rather the sound of her moving off the trail. As I got closer, I could see a faint path through the thick undergrowth.

Better arm myself before I wandered into uncharted territory. I scanned the ground and grabbed a fist-sized rock, hefting it up to test the weight. Not the best weapon, but I probably wouldn't find a better one under the circumstance. Taking a deep breath, I plunged into the opening, breaking more branches, the loud cracks making me wince. If Sheila was really disposing of a weapon, maybe I should be quieter.

I slowed down and inched my way through the brush, trying to move the twigs and leaves ahead of me, the rock heavy in my hand. A fly buzzed by my eye and I swatted it away. By now, I could feel a layer of sweat sitting on my face, mingling with my foundation. Gross.

Up ahead, movement caught my eye. I could see where the foliage ended and an open space began. Sheila stood near the base of the hill, staring at something. Then she bent down and dropped from sight.

I pushed my way through the last few feet of bushes, cringing at every sound. If Sheila hadn't disposed of the knife yet, I didn't want her using it on me when she heard me coming. The rock I carried could only do so much.

Just as I stepped past the last tree, Sheila sprang into my field of vision. I raised the hand with the rock at the sudden movement, ready to strike. Sheila threw up her hands and shrieked.

I slowly lowered my arm and stepped out into the open space. For a killer, Sheila certainly didn't look dangerous. Had I scared the bejeezus out of one of the guests because of my overactive imagination?

"Sheila, you okay?"

She backed up a foot, hands at her chest, partially blocking the butterfly pattern on the front of her silk tunic.

"Look, I know I probably shouldn't be back here. I just . . ." her voice trailed away, her eyes focused on the rock in my hand.

I dropped the rock, suddenly aware of how threatening I must appear. "When you jumped in front of me, I freaked out. Sorry I scared you." I skipped the part where I'd followed her from the spa with the hope of catching her getting rid of a murder weapon.

I glanced past Sheila to where the towel lay on the ground, still rolled up. Nearby, a pool of water shimmered in the sun.

She smoothed her tunic, drawing my attention back to her. "I heard you coming through the bushes and was worried that you were a wild animal or, worse yet, the killer."

I brushed past her to look into the pool, where little bubbles rose to the surface. Dropping the murder weapon into the water would be the perfect plan. "What are you doing out here?"

Sheila joined me and gestured to the water, a bracelet with large colored beads encircling her tanned wrist. "I was walking through the woods yesterday, looking for inspiration for my next line of jewelry pieces, and stumbled across the springs. The water is so warm and the area so peaceful that I came back today to soak my feet."

"That explains the towel," I said more to myself than to Sheila, suddenly feeling like the world's biggest jackass, chasing guests through the woods, threatening them with rocks.

Sheila grabbed the towel from the ground and it unrolled, revealing more white terry cloth fabric and no knife. Big surprise.

She shook out the towel. "I almost didn't bring it. Esther hasn't said we have to stay on the path, but I wasn't sure if we were supposed to be back here, what with no trail or markers. I knew I might attract attention if I strolled away from the cabins with a towel tucked under my arm, heading in the opposite direction from the pool."

Well, she'd certainly attracted my attention.

Sheila spread the towel out. "Do you mind if I dip my feet for a moment?"

Would Esther mind? Did she even know about the springs, tucked way back here at the base of the hill, nowhere near the path? Being alone with Sheila might be my one opportunity to ask about the necklace or where she was when I was collecting eggs. Just because she wasn't the one who'd killed Maxwell, didn't mean she didn't push me. I hadn't caught a glimpse of my assailant. The attacker could have been a man or woman.

"You did walk all the way out here," I said.

Slipping off her sandals, she plopped on the ground, making me cringe on behalf of her flared white pants. Not like Sheila to get so dirty.

She rolled the fabric up a few inches and swung her feet into the water. "Love it," she said, but her voice lacked enthusiasm.

"Everything all right?" I asked.

In the sunlight, I could see gray roots peeking out from her hair part.

Sheila swirled her leg in the water, ripples gliding across the surface. "Thinking about poor Maxwell."

I walked over to where she sat and crouched down. "I heard you two were married. I'm sure his death was a shock." Especially if she caused it in a moment of fury.

"Not just a shock but a waste. I know most of Maxwell's movies were those silly horror flicks, but every now and again, he'd produce a beautiful film, one that resonated with people and could open their eyes to others' plights."

Guess she wasn't referring to *The Dead Man Always Rings Thrice*, one of Maxwell's early works.

"At least you can take comfort that his memory will live forever through his movies." I scooped up a handful of leaves and tossed one into the water, watching it float lazily on the surface. I tossed in another leaf.

Tears tumbled down Sheila's cheek, rolling into the crease around her mouth. "It certainly will."

I touched her shoulder, almost tipping over from my crouched position. "I didn't mean to upset you."

"You didn't. I've been missing Maxwell since he was

murdered." She raised her head and looked at the trees on the hill. "He wanted us to get back together, you know."

"Get out." I slapped a hand over my mouth and waited for a tongue-lashing at my inadvertent rudeness, but Sheila let out a chuckle.

"I know I'm not young. My beauty has begun to fade."

I started to correct her, but she talked over my attempt at interruption.

"And Maxwell could have any starlet he wanted. But he realized that what he wanted was a woman who would stand behind him, not one who would climb over him to advance her career."

I sat down in the dirt, rubbing the ache in my knee caused by crouching. "He told you this?"

Sheila twisted her bracelet, admiring the leaf pattern etched in the large gold clasp. "On Friday. He came to my cabin after dinner. Said he wanted to see how I've been doing the last few years. We hadn't spoken since the divorce, you see."

"How long since you two split up?" Sheila's leg movement had sent the errant leaf back to the edge and I scooped it out of the water.

"Five years. We parted on fairly rotten terms. At the time, I was consumed with anger, but I'd forgiven him." She plucked a pine needle off her pants and snapped it in half.

"And now he wanted you back?" If her story was true, she didn't have much of a reason to kill Maxwell over a bad divorce. Having your ex-husband want you back was the best revenge.

Sheila rotated the bracelet again, fingering the beads. "Something happens to men after their midlife crisis ends. They wake up one day and realize that flashy cars and flashier girls don't guarantee happiness. Maxwell was tired of questioning everyone's motives, and being used for his connections in the industry. That Tiffany hounded him day and night for a role in his next movie."

I thought back to what Tiffany had said, about how she hadn't had to sleep with Maxwell, although she'd sounded ready if the need arose. "She does seem ambitious," I commented.

Sheila twisted her mouth. "Ambitious is one word. Predatory is another. But Maxwell was done playing those games."

"And you're sure he was sincere?" I asked. The man did create a world of fiction for a living, after all. And Sheila's fairy tale story of the egotistical man trying to woo back the only woman who was ever good to him sounded a bit clichéd, like a late-night Lifetime movie.

"Yes, he bought me a necklace as a reconciliation gift. Quite generous for Maxwell. Gave it to me on Saturday after yoga. Must have been right before he was killed."

So Maxwell had actually given her the necklace between the time he caught Heather trying it on and when I'd seen it in Sheila's room.

Sheila choked back a sob. "He must have spent a fortune. All those gems."

"You don't need to tell me. Man, that baby sparkled."

She turned toward me. "How do you know? Did Maxwell show you the necklace?"

Oops. Couldn't exactly admit I was snooping in her room while changing towels. "Um, I don't remember where I saw it."

Her face settled into an expression of neutrality, like a shop that's closed for the night.

"You must be right," I lied. "Maxwell showed it to me."

Her expression remained elusive.

"Were you interested in his offer?"

Sheila wiped a tear away. "Not a chance. I mean, sure, his advances were flattering. And one thing I definitely missed about Maxwell was the sex. That man was hung like a horse."

Oh, ick, yuck. First Queenie talked about a temptress in the woods, now Sheila just had to brag about her well-endowed ex-husband. What was it about me that compelled people to share these details?

Sheila didn't seem to notice my discomfort as she kept talking. "But I've moved on, created a wonderful life for myself. I didn't want to go back to being somebody's wife." Another sob escaped her.

I patted her back, all knots and hard spots. "Don't beat yourself up. You made the right decision."

"It's not that," she said. "I can't help but think that if I'd been more gracious when Maxwell presented me with that necklace, he'd still be alive. Instead, I laughed at him for buying me such flashy jewelry." She gestured to her bracelet. "Really not my style, but Maxwell never worried about that sort of thing. If he liked something, he figured everyone must like it."

Sounded like most of the guys I'd dated, unable to see outside their own little world of beer kegs and *God of War* marathons. "Did Maxwell get mad when you laughed?"

"Stormed out. Always did have a lightning temper. That silly man." Sheila started crying again.

I continued to pat her back, while watching a water strider bug skate across the surface of the springs. While we'd been talking, the sun had moved lower in the sky and now appeared to rest atop the hill. I'd wanted to help Zennia with dinner service, but Sheila was in no shape to stay here alone.

I gave her shoulder a squeeze. "Let's go back to the cabins where you can rest before dinner."

Sheila pulled her feet out of the water. "Good idea." She shook her feet off and dabbed at them with the towel before standing up. She wiped her eyes with the hem of her tunic. "Thanks for listening." She stuck her feet back in her sandals and picked up the towel.

"Glad to lend an ear," I said. Especially when I learned new information. While she hadn't confessed to killing Maxwell, at least she'd cleared up the mystery of the necklace.

I walked toward the bushes that would take me back to the farm, Sheila following a few steps behind.

One question still gnawed at me. After we emerged from the underbrush and stepped back on the trail, I turned to Sheila as we walked. The sun, low at our backs, bathed the ground in golden rays.

"Did you leave a note on Maxwell's nightstand that asked him to meet you behind the chicken coop for a little fun?"

Sheila's eyes widened. "Of course not. That's absurd."

"Well, you mentioned how good the sex with Maxwell was." Talking about her sex life, my face suddenly felt warm. Must be from the sun.

Sheila fiddled with her earring. "I'm a little old for a secret rendezvous."

I tended to agree with her. A more likely choice was Tiffany, if she was throwing herself at Maxwell as he had told Sheila. I'd ask Tiffany next time I saw her.

A loud ringing erupted from my pocket and I pulled out my cell phone. "Hello?"

"Dana, where are you?" I recognized Zennia's voice.

"On Chicken Run Trail. Is something wrong?"

Static crackled in my ear, almost obliterating Zennia's words. "People are due for dinner any minute and I need an extra set of hands."

Dinner was starting? "I had no idea it was so late. I'll be right there."

I pressed the END CALL button. We had reached the cabins, and I turned to Sheila.

Before I could speak, she waved her hand. "Go on. I need to change for dinner."

I jogged around the cabins and past the pool. Sure enough, people were wandering in the side door leading to the dining room. I hurried in the kitchen door.

Zennia had both hands in a glass bowl full of clams, her apron with a cow embroidered on the front covered in bits of slimy stuff. She gestured with her head toward the plates on the counter.

"The Brussels sprouts are ready to go out."

I rinsed my hands, then grabbed two plates. The smell of my least favorite vegetable hit me in the face and I tried not to gag. Mustn't let the guests know what they were in for. They'd find out soon enough.

I carted the plates out to the dining room and set them before the first two diners. Both crinkled their noses and looked at me.

"Tonight, we're starting our meal with a delicious serving of sautéed Brussels sprouts," I said brightly, pasting a smile on my face. Then I turned and hurried out before they could ask any questions.

Once I'd finished serving everyone, I stepped back and surveyed the room. Neither Tiffany nor Logan was at dinner. Perhaps they were dining out together. A Hollywood starlet and a producer's assistant, plotting to storm the movie industry.

I noticed an odd silence in the room. Where was the clinking of silverware on china? Several sets of hungry eyes gazed upon me with displeasure. I hastily removed the salad plates, trying not to make eye contact. Someone might stab me with their fork.

I took the dishes back to the kitchen where Zennia stirred a giant pot on the stove.

She glanced at the full plates. "No, Dana, you serve those to the guests."

"I did. Apparently, Brussels sprouts aren't a spa favorite."

"Everyone here wants to see where Maxwell was murdered. These guests don't care about their health and the role vitamins and minerals play in their diets." She gestured to the counter. "Oh, well, serve the stew. You can eat the sprouts when you're finished."

I eyed the giant green orbs. "Um, thanks, Zennia, but I promised my mom I'd eat dinner with her when I got home."

"Fine." She took two plates, stepped on the pedal to open the garbage can, and dumped the contents of both plates into the trash. "But when your colon is suffering, don't complain to me."

"I promise, not a word." I picked up two bowls of stew, wincing as I touched the hot ceramic, and hurried out to the dining room. I thumped the bowls on the table, sloshing broth over the side of each.

"Sorry," I told the diners, dabbing at the tablecloth with an extra napkin. "Hot bowls."

If working at the farm didn't pan out, waitressing should clearly be avoided.

With the diners busily slurping their stew, I returned to the kitchen. Zennia was wiping down the counters.

"Thanks for your help, Dana. I can handle the rest of the dishes if you'd like to go home."

My stomach growled and I clapped a hand over it. "Thanks, I bet Mom's waiting right now with that dinner." If not, I'd make a run through a drive-through somewhere.

I stopped by the office for my purse and found Esther at the desk, a notepad before her.

"Dana, I didn't realize you were still here," she said.

I slid the desk drawer open to the left of Esther and

retrieved my purse. "On my way home right now. I just finished serving dinner."

"Aren't you a dear. I know you weren't expecting to do all this extra work, but I can't possibly afford to hire anyone else, even part time."

"I like the variety." And the paycheck. If it weren't for Esther keeping me on to do these odd jobs, I'd be standing in the unemployment line right now.

Esther shook her head. "With all this trouble we've been having, poor Arnold would turn over in his grave—if I hadn't had him cremated."

"The place just needs a boost, something new to distract everyone from the murder." I snapped my fingers. "Say, Esther, did you know about the hot springs off Chicken Run Trail?"

Esther pursed her lips and tapped them with a finger. "The hot springs? Haven't thought about that area in a coon's age. It's so far back on the property."

I could hear the excitement in my voice as I proposed the idea. "But you could open it to the guests. Offer a nice soak in a natural spring. People would love it."

Esther's eyebrows came together as she frowned. "But it's not that close to the trail. How would people even reach it?"

"You'd have to clear out all that brush, make a new trail, maybe add some benches and a shower area. But think of the payoff. That place up the highway, the one that boasts about Jack London being a regular guest, has been open for years."

"Gee, sounds awful expensive. I don't have that kind of money right now."

I swung my arm as I spoke, almost hitting Esther with my purse. "You'd make the money back in new reservations for sure."

Esther offered a half smile. "I'll sleep on it. Thanks for trying to help."

"I know we can make this place a success. We just have to try."

I left Esther and walked to my car, purse slung over my shoulder. Daylight had all but vanished, emphasizing how fast darkness descended in the country, compared to San Jose and all its lights. I slipped behind the wheel of my Honda and drove home, traffic almost nonexistent on the highway. The few minutes of driving gave me quiet time to reflect on Maxwell's death.

What did I know so far? Mostly that no one had a very strong motive for killing him. Logan only worked for Maxwell to get his screenplay produced, and after all those silly and sometimes humiliating errands, Maxwell had ridiculed his work. But that seemed like a weak reason to murder someone, especially if Logan was already thinking about finding another job. Had Logan applied to Tiger Shark Studios before Maxwell was killed or after?

What about Heather? Maxwell had caught her trying on the necklace intended for Sheila, but even if Maxwell had reported the incident to Esther, surely Heather would have known that Esther wouldn't fire her over one guest complaint.

Which brought me to Sheila and the necklace. How odd that those two would just happen to stay at the spa at the same time and that Maxwell would suddenly decide to reconcile in such a short time. Sheila's story was a little too pat. I'd have to keep my eye on her.

At home, Mom had turned on the porch light and a warm glow embraced the front door. I pulled in the driveway, surprised to see Ashlee's car missing. The sound of my engine's fan accompanied me as I exited the car and walked up the path.

I opened the front door, stepped inside, and stopped. Mom stood in the entryway, arms crossed over her chest.

"Dana Marie Lewis, how could you betray me like this?"

Uh-oh. My mind flipped through my actions of the last few days, trying to locate the source of her anger. I wasn't sure what I'd done, but whenever I heard my full name, I was in deep doo-doo.

17

Before I could speak, Mom took hold of my wrist and dragged me inside, glancing around, probably wondering if the neighbors had seen her in her pink sweat suit with the rhinestone-studded collar, a Christmas gift from Ashlee.

She slammed the door shut. "To think I had to find out from Sue Ellen, of all people."

Uh-oh. Sue Ellen was Mom's archenemy in all things gossip-related. Whatever I'd done, Sue Ellen finding out first would only add to Mom's ire.

"Please, Mom, calm down."

She stared at me, tapping her slippered foot at warp speed. "Calm down? Calm down? My daughter is dating an absolute hunk and she can't even tell her own mother?"

"Wait, are you talking about me or Ashlee?" After all, Ashlee was the serial dater in the family.

"Stop playing games, young lady. Sue Ellen saw you on your little date at the Eat Your Heart Out café with that reporter, Jason."

The fog in my brain cleared. Now the sun shone down with brilliant clarity on those little gray cells. Sue Ellen was the driver of the blue Saturn, the one who had almost hit another car because she was so busy staring at us.

"Jason was interviewing me for the *Herald*."

"Over coffee?"

"He suggested moving off site to make the interview more casual. When he was done asking questions, he took me straight back to the farm where he talked to the rest of the staff."

"Haven't I told you to stay away from that café? All the bikers hang out there. You'll get a reputation."

"New owners. Not a biker in sight."

Mom continued to tap her foot but had slowed to Greyhound Bus speed. "And you weren't kissing outside the restaurant?"

"Of course not."

"Sue Ellen swears she saw you give Jason a quick smooch while standing by his car."

What on earth was wrong with Sue Ellen? Then the scene from the parking lot came to mind, and I laughed.

Mom eyed me with clear suspicion, ready to disbelieve whatever I said.

"I tripped. On that crappy pavement. I was getting into his car when I stumbled into him."

"A likely story."

I shrugged. "It's the truth. Besides, I'm twenty-eight. I could marry Jason if I wanted to and wouldn't have to tell you or anyone else." I pointed down the hall. "I'm going to make my dinner now."

"No need. I waited for you. The butcher had a big sale on calf liver today."

Geez, I should have eaten Zennia's Brussels sprouts. "Where's Ashlee?" Wouldn't want her to miss out on liver.

"On a date. At least Ashlee tells me when she's dating someone."

"I'm not dating Jason!"

Mom walked into the kitchen, calling over her shoulder, "If you say so."

I rolled my eyes and followed behind, watching as she lifted a platter out of the oven. I pulled forks and knives from the silverware drawer.

"Who's Ashlee seeing now?"

"Some fellow named Rockford."

I set the glasses on the table with a clunk. "Where did she meet a guy named Rockford?"

Mom placed a hot pad in the middle of the table, then went back for the platter. "Through her friend, Karen. He's one of her clients."

"Isn't Karen a parole officer?"

Mom speared a giant piece of liver and slapped it on my plate. "You know how kindhearted Ashlee is. She believes everyone deserves a second chance."

I stared at the dark slab of meat. Would she say the same about Maxwell's killer?

The next morning, I mucked out the sty, while Wilbur and the other pigs snorted at my inexperience. Next time Esther requested I perform this particular chore, I was going to suggest she include it as a possible guest activity. I could already visualize the brochure: EXPERIENCE REAL LIFE ON A FARM! PLAY WITH THE LITTLE PIGGIES! Someone was bound to fall for it.

I spread fresh straw in their bedding area, my cell phone flopping from my pocket onto the ground. One pig tried to sniff it, possibly looking for a snack, but I grabbed the phone and stuffed it back in my pocket. I hosed down the outside ground and dumped a bucket of feed into the trough.

Suddenly Wilbur and the gang weren't smirking at the new girl.

I stepped out of the sty, checking over my shoulder for any pig followers, but their noses were buried in the trough. The slurping noises turned my stomach a bit. Holding the fence rail for support, I slipped off one rubber boot and stuck my foot in my sandal, then repeated the process with my other foot. Time to wash up.

At the kitchen sink, I squirted extra liquid soap on my hands, scrubbing the skin under hot water until my hands burned. Zennia sat at the table, her black hair up in its usual braid, arranging late-season daffodils in a shallow bowl. The yellow of the flowers was almost an exact match to the color of her scoop-necked blouse. Several cuttings and a matching empty bowl sat on the counter.

"Beautiful flowers, Zennia."

She moved several daffodils over and added fern sprigs. "Flowers are vital to one's health, you know. Their beauty and fragrance relax one's body and free the mind." She stepped back and eyed the bowl. "I'm setting a bowl on each picnic table."

"Let me." I inhaled the scent of the yellow flowers as I carried the bowl out the back door and around to the patio.

Tiffany and Logan sat at the end of one table, playing cards.

As I set the bowl in the center, Logan laid down his hand. "Gin."

Tiffany giggled. "You are so good at this game. You need to teach me your secrets." She touched Logan's hand and he blushed.

Well, weren't these two kids cozy? Perhaps Tiffany had heard about Logan's new job and she had her eye on Tiger Shark Studios' latest movie project.

On the edge of the patio, Sheila sat in a chaise longue, writing in a journal. She wore a beige strapless mesh cover-up over her black one-piece swimsuit.

She glanced up. "Morning, Dana."

I walked over to where she sat. "How are you feeling today?"

"Much better, thanks. I'm sorry I burdened you with my problems yesterday."

"I know you guys weren't married anymore, but I'm sure you still loved Maxwell. My dad died last year and I miss him all the time." I felt tears form in my eyes as I said the words. I was still surprised at how emotional I got talking about him. And those unexpected reminders were the worst. He'd sometimes buy us cupcakes on Saturdays as a surprise, and even now, walking into a bakery made me cry.

Sheila gripped her journal. "Maxwell will always hold a special place in my heart. That's why I'm writing in my journal today. To deal with all these emotions. I learned that in my anger management class."

"Anger management?" I asked sharply.

Sheila waved her hand. "A minor transgression after too much wine. Nothing worth talking about."

Unless she hadn't gotten a handle on that anger. Then it was definitely worth talking about. I glanced around, noting the empty pool and vacant lounge chairs. "Awful quiet this morning."

"Most of the guests decided to caravan over to Mendocino for some early morning whale watching, followed by boutique shopping and wine tasting. They invited me along, but considering I live in Mendocino year round, I've sampled enough wine to start a second career as a sommelier."

Oh, to have such problems. Instead, I needed to retrieve the second bowl of flowers. As I turned toward the house, Christian and Gordon emerged from the back door and walked to the edge of the pool.

"If I move the mats to the patio," Christian said, "we'll have the necessary space."

"Unacceptable," Gordon said. "Guests like to socialize by the picnic tables. We can't cover the area with your silly yoga mats."

Christian gestured toward the smaller patio. "With the increase in class attendance, we can't all fit on that side of the pool. We need to move to a larger area where our energy can flow freely."

Gordon stepped closer to Christian, the muscles in his jaw tightening. "Then find a place out of the way. Those mats are a tripping hazard."

I wedged myself between the two men. "Christian could set the mats out immediately before the classes and remove them as soon as a class is over."

"Dana, stay out of this," Gordon said.

A wave of anger rose up in me, and my jaw seized up. "I'm trying to help, Gordon."

"I'll handle Christian and his mat issues. You need to focus on your little blog."

Before I could snap back with a witty retort that I was sure to think of any second, I heard "Yoo-hoo, Dana!"

Esther hustled out of the house, carrying the second bowl of daffodils.

I removed myself from between the Gordon and Christian bookends and met her by the edge of the large patio.

"Morning, Esther. What can I help you with?"

"I wanted to thank you for helping out this morning with the pigs. You really saved my bacon." Esther chuckled at her own joke. Maybe I'd suggest she perform a stand-up routine for the guests if nothing else panned out.

I straightened a chaise longue that sat at an angle from the others. "It was fun once I got the hang of it." And the pigs stopped laughing at me.

"Oh, good. So what are your plans for today?"

"I was about to write my blog and then the cricket-chirping contest is this afternoon."

Esther slapped a hand to the side of her face. "How could I forget the contest? Too bad you'll miss Zennia's famous French honey walnut dessert. I'll see if she can save you some." I could almost see her writing a mental note as she pressed her lips together. "I never asked how Queenie was when you bought that honey. She wasn't too much trouble, was she?"

Let's see. She'd threatened me with a shotgun, ranted about sinners, and scared an extra five years off my life. "Nothing I couldn't handle."

Esther leaned toward me. "I don't mind telling you, she turned more than one hair gray the first few times I saw her. But she's a kindhearted woman. And quite the Bible lover."

"She did quote a lot of scripture when I was there. In fact, I think she mentioned Maxwell, though I couldn't quite figure out what she was babbling about."

Esther's hand fluttered to her heart. "Maxwell? Did she know him?"

"Probably not. But she might have seen him with a woman on that bench near her trailer."

"A woman?"

I leaned in. "Queenie mentioned a golden-haired hussy."

A faint blush crept up Esther's throat and into her cheeks. She fanned herself with her hand. "Oh, my goodness me."

Gordon cleared his throat at my elbow, and I jumped.

"Do you ladies mind if we don't entertain the guests with this salacious tale?"

I glanced over at the patio. While I'd been regaling Esther with the details, Sheila had lowered her journal and Tiffany and Logan had set their cards on the table, all eyes on me. My bad.

When my gaze settled on Tiffany, she bent her head and stared at her hands. Wish I hadn't mentioned that part about the golden-haired hussy. "Esther, I'd better write that blog now."

The steam from Gordon's anger practically formed a cocoon around him. I turned away from everyone, and slinked into the house, feeling the pressure of everybody staring at my back.

In the office, I drummed my fingers on the desk. Writing a blog every day was proving harder than I had imagined. Well, the writing part was easy. Thinking of a topic was the hard part.

I hadn't come up with my list of extra topics yet, so I Googled other overnight spas to see if they had their own blogs and whether I could glean some ideas from those. The first hit was a spa in Oregon that catered to the nudist crowd. The next spa, in Arizona, offered rattlesnake taming as an option. The third hit was actually a newspaper article about a spa back east where a woman had been scammed out of her life savings by a gigolo. Guess we weren't the only spa with a scandal on our hands. But none of these sites was helping me find a blog topic.

I pictured Sheila writing in her journal, remembered her comment yesterday about looking for jewelry inspiration. Living among nature here at the spa clearly helped her tap into her creative side. And that's what I'd recommend to readers. I typed up the blog, touting the benefits of fresh air and healthy food, and finished by suggesting the spa as an artists' retreat.

As I hit the POST button, I saw Heather walk past the door. I hadn't talked to her since I'd confronted her about the towels. She might have seen something in Maxwell's cabin the morning he was killed that would give me a clue as to why he was angry before yoga.

I jumped up from the desk chair and hurried into the hall. Heather was at the kitchen doorway.

"Heather," I called.

She stopped just as I heard voices at the other end of the hall. I turned toward the sound and saw Esther and Detective Caffrey enter from the lobby. The detective wore that neutral expression all cops seemed to master, offering no clue as to whether he suspected me of killing Maxwell or was trying to remember if he had enough clean underwear until laundry day.

"Dana," Esther said, "Detective Caffrey needs to talk to the staff again about Maxwell's murder."

I looked back toward Heather to ask her to wait for me, but the doorway was empty. I'd have to catch her another time. Right now, I'd rather try to gather information from Detective Caffrey, if he was willing to share.

"Any progress?" I asked him as he and Esther stopped before me.

"I don't comment on open investigations. But we need to go over your statement." He pointed a thumb over his shoulder. "Let's go sit in the dining room."

Now was my opportunity to pass along all the information I'd gathered, from Queenie witnessing Maxwell's little tryst and talking about blood spilling, to someone pushing me, to Sheila having possession of the necklace. Even if she claimed Maxwell gave her the jewelry as a gift, the police would want to verify her story.

I followed the detective across the hall. The tables were set, ready for the lunch crowd, the silverware and maroon napkins laid out atop the cream tablecloth. Out the glass doors, I could see Sheila still sitting by the pool. Tiffany and Logan were no longer at the table.

Detective Caffrey pulled a chair out, then sat down on the opposite side of the table. Guess this was my interrogation seat.

I sat down and clasped my hands in front of me on the table. "I'm so glad you're here. I've found out quite a bit that I want to share."

As he yanked his notebook from his dress shirt pocket, the springs hooked on his tie and he struggled to extract the cloth. "Let's start with what you saw the day of the murder. Oftentimes witnesses will remember details on the second or third telling, once the emotions have calmed down."

I leaned forward. "First, let me tell you what Queenie said."

"Ms. Lewis, again, we're talking about you."

My hands bumped a fork and I lined it back up with the knife. "But her information might be important."

The muscle below his eye began to twitch. "Is there a reason you're being difficult, Ms. Lewis?"

I leaned back in my chair. Why wasn't he listening to me? "That's not my intention. But I told you everything last time."

"So tell me again. From the last time you saw Maxwell Mendelsohn on Sunday. Alive, that is."

I drummed my fingers on my knee and studied the daffodil in the bud vase on the table. "Well, I was helping Esther catch a loose pig when I saw Maxwell in Christian's yoga class."

"Who else was there?"

"Tiffany, Sheila, and a woman I hadn't met. I believe she checked out the next day, and I never saw her after that yoga class."

Detective Caffrey scribbled in his notebook, the pen's scratching noises clearly audible in the quiet room. "How did Mr. Mendelsohn appear?"

"Fine. I noticed he was eyeing Sheila, his ex-wife, although I didn't know she was his ex-wife at that point."

Detective Caffrey wrote in his book. The eye spasm had ceased.

When he didn't say anything, I continued. "Maxwell

couldn't complete the tree pose and got mad. Stormed off before class ended."

"Then what did you see?"

I thought back to that day, Maxwell walking off, everyone returning to yoga. "Nothing. But when I talked to Logan later, he mentioned that his boss was angry before yoga, though he didn't know why."

Detective Caffrey stopped writing. "Let's focus on what you personally saw."

"But whoever Maxwell was upset with might have killed him. And did you know Maxwell wanted to reunite with Sheila? Even bought her a fancy necklace."

At this, Detective Caffrey closed his notebook with a snap. "Ms. Lewis, I was afraid of this."

My heart stilled. "What do you mean?"

"This is a criminal investigation."

"I know, that's why I'm passing along all this information."

Detective Caffrey frowned. "What you're doing is looking at a charge of obstructing justice."

Criminy, what did I do?

18

"Obstructing justice? I'm helping you." The nerve of that man!

The tic started below Detective Caffrey's eye again. He should really see his doctor about that. "We don't call it *helping* when a citizen gathers information from suspects in a murder investigation."

"You make it sound like I'm interviewing people." I put my hands on my hips to show him how offended I was by his accusation, though the table partially obscured his view and probably ruined the effect. "I mean, if I run into someone, I might talk about the murder—everyone is—but I'm certainly not trying to do your job. People tell me things. It's a curse." Especially when they tell me about their ex-husband's package size.

Based on the speed of his eye twitch, I could only assume my answer didn't please him. Maybe the curse remark was a stretch.

"Let me be clear," he said. "I cannot have regular citizens interfering. I'm warning you to stay out."

"I'm no ordinary citizen. I found the body, remember?"

Detective Caffrey glowered at me. I felt my skin heat up, little beads of perspiration forming at my hairline.

"I mean, yes sir."

With a sigh, Detective Caffrey opened his notebook again. "Let's jump ahead to when you found the body."

"Right. I was taking clean towels to each room. Maxwell's door was unlocked, so I stood outside for a minute . . ."

The detective held up his hand. "Hold on. His door wasn't locked?"

"Didn't I tell you that before?"

"No. See what I mean about remembering extra details? But go on."

"I poked my head in, saw his feet, and debated whether to come back. But then I figured I'd try to sneak in and not wake him. That's when his phone rang. When he didn't wake up, I stepped up to the bed and saw that he was dead."

I tried to ignore the fact that I'd made a rhyme, but the phrase *I'm a poet and didn't know it* popped into my head. Good grief, we were talking about a dead guy and all I could do was act like a ten-year-old.

Detective Caffrey and I sat in silence while he jotted my information down.

"Say," I finally said, "did you guys figure out who that note was from? The one that asked Maxwell to meet them behind the chicken coop?"

Detective Caffrey stilled, all but his tic, which increased in pace. Uh-oh.

"Did you tell anyone else about the note?" His voice was calm, his words carefully spaced.

"I don't think so." Had I?

"Ms. Lewis, that note may be critical to finding the killer. Letting that information slip would be worse than your habit of talking to suspects."

I felt like creeping beneath the tablecloth under his cop stare. "I won't mention it. But speaking of the chickens, now might be a good time to tell you how someone shoved me when I found a money clip by the coop. Snatched it right out of my hand."

He flipped to a new page in his notebook. "You were physically assaulted? When?"

"Yesterday morning."

Detective Caffrey sighed again. Did I tire him out that much?

"Why didn't you contact me?"

"I wasn't hurt. And I didn't see the person. And who knows if the clip is connected to the murder." The reasons had sounded plausible yesterday, but sitting before the detective, I wondered if keeping quiet had been the best decision.

"Tell me what the money clip looked like."

I picked at a speck of lint on the tablecloth. "I only saw it for a second. It was silver."

Detective Caffrey clicked his pen, repeatedly. His expression held a hint of exasperation. "That's all for now. I may have additional questions. And will you contact me immediately if anyone assaults you again?"

"You bet." Just call me Miss Cooperation.

He rose, stuffed his notebook in his shirt pocket, and walked out of the dining room.

I stayed in my chair, studying the silverware and thinking about our conversation. That detective was one tight-lipped fellow. I'd learned nothing about the investigation.

Maybe I needed to stay out of the way, like the detective said. Of course, if people volunteered information, I couldn't help that. What was I supposed to do, plug my ears?

I stood and stretched, feeling the muscles in my back loosen a bit. I should listen to my advice to Zennia and try Christian's yoga class. Improve my flexibility. Or I could stop by the Watering Hole for a margarita instead. That'd relax *all* my muscles.

As I stepped from the dining room, Esther exited the

office across the hall, pulling the edge of her green blouse down to cover her belly.

"Dana, are you done with the detective?"

"Just finished. Now I need to see if Zennia needs help with lunch."

Esther waved her hand. "I'll help her. You need to leave for the cricket-chirping contest."

I glanced at my watch. "Setup isn't for over an hour. I could help here."

"Nonsense. You skedaddle now. You're a sweetheart for filling in at the contest for me."

Or a gutless wonder for not refusing her request.

The interior of my Honda was too warm for comfort and I pulled away from the seat, trying to keep my shirt from sticking. Though summer was a few weeks away, the temperature continued to rise. I hit the air-conditioning switch and pulled out of the lot.

With an hour to kill, I exited at State Street, zipped through the Taco Bell drive-thru, and drove my gordita and chalupa treasures home.

Ashlee's Camaro sat in the driveway. *She must be on her lunch break.* I flipped a U, pulled up to the curb, and got out, waving to Mr. McGowen, our thirty-year neighbor working in his yard next door.

The inside of the house was dark and cool. I headed straight for the kitchen, the aroma from my Mexican food making my mouth water.

At the table, Ashlee ate the last quarter of a tuna sandwich.

When she saw my plastic bag, her eyes lit up.

"If I'd known you were stopping at Taco Bell, I'd have put in my order."

I nodded toward her plate. "Tuna not doing it for you?"

"With low-fat mayo, tuna packed in water, and whole-wheat bread, that chalupa wrapper would taste better. But gotta keep those pounds off."

I sat down across from her and emptied my bag, more interested in eating tasty food than losing weight. "You on your lunch break?"

"Nope, off for the rest of the day. Fleas took over the office, so the vet had to close this afternoon."

Cheese spilled out of my chalupa as I unwrapped it and I stuffed every last shred back in. "Where's Mom?"

"The store. Buying more food we're not going to like."

I bowed my head and pretended to weep. "Thank goodness for fast food."

With her last bite of sandwich gone, Ashlee pushed her plate away, then sipped her bottled water. She studied me a moment, clearly wanting to say something.

"Yes?" I asked, sinking my teeth into the gordita shell.

"I'm wondering what you're doing home."

"Eating lunch."

"I mean, why did you move back?"

I wiped my mouth with a napkin. "To spend more time with you."

"I'm serious, Dana. You had a killer job at that computer company. I'm sure you could've landed a new spot at another company. Why are you here?"

I gazed at Ashlee with her too bright lipstick and overload of eye shadow, not sure how much to say. But even though she was my little sister, now would be a good time to treat her as an adult.

"Because I don't think Mom is coping very well with Dad's death."

Ashlee crossed her arms over her chest. "She's fine. I'm here all the time."

"But I know Dad's life insurance barely covered the

funeral and he had such a small pension. Money is tight, and I want to help out."

"Go get another high paying job in San Jose and mail a check every month."

I resisted the urge to tell Ashlee how I'd turned down a generous offer from a large Bay Area firm. She wouldn't understand.

"Mom barely accepts my rent check. She wouldn't allow me to mail money home just to help. Living here, I can buy groceries, gas up her car, and lighten the burden."

Ashlee tugged at the label on her bottle. "I do what I can, but the vet cut my hours and he was a cheapskate to start with."

"But together, we can help Mom pay her bills and more importantly, heal from Dad's death."

Before I could say more, I heard the familiar hum of the garage door. A moment later, Mom stepped into the house, carrying a paper sack with a celery stalk poking out the top.

I crumpled up my gordita wrapper and took the bag from Mom. She sat down in my vacant chair as I unpacked the groceries.

"Boy, eating more fruits and vegetables is certainly increasing my trips to the store," she said.

"Then we should definitely go back to the way we used to eat," I said. "You'd save money and time."

Mom laughed. "Nice try, but our new diet is here to stay." She glanced at the clock, a hint of worry around her eyes. "What are you doing home so early?"

I shoved the vegetable crisper closed and folded up the paper bag. "Eating lunch before I set up for the cricket-chirping contest at the fairgrounds."

"Is it that time of year already?" Mom asked.

I stuffed the bag in the thin space between the fridge and the counter. "You mean you've heard of this contest?"

"Well, sure, Fester Cartemberg from up the street came in second place last year."

So the contest really existed. For some reason, I'd secretly believed that when I arrived at the fairgrounds, no one would be there. That the cricket-chirping contest was a mass delusion of the committee.

"There's a contest where people chirp like crickets?" Ashlee asked.

"Your idea's better," I said. "Instead, people bring their pet crickets, and whichever is the best chirper wins."

Ashlee drained her water and plunked the bottle on the table. "This I've got to see. Mind if I tag along?"

If the cricket contest was a bust, maybe Ashlee and I could entertain the contestants with our little "Me and My Shadow" dance routine from grade school.

Then again, maybe not.

"The contest's open to the public, but if you want to go early with me, you'll need to help set up."

"You bet."

I knew Ashlee's idea of helping would be to keep a chair seat warm, but I've been wrong before.

"We'd better go if we don't want to be late."

She tugged her T-shirt at the waist. "One sec, I have to change."

Was there a cricket-chirping dress code I hadn't heard of? "You look fine. Besides, we don't have time for you to pick out a new outfit."

Mom checked the clock again. "You have a few minutes, Dana, and you know Ashlee takes pride in her appearance."

Ashlee stuck her tongue out at me and strolled into her room.

With Mom watching, I tried to stifle my impatience. Instead, I threw my lunch wrappers in the trash, washed Ashlee's sandwich plate, and wiped down the counters.

Still no Ashlee.

I opened the fridge door and shuffled the yogurt and milk cartons around on the shelves, lining the yogurts up like soldiers in a dairy parade. I shut the door with a snap and paced around the kitchen.

"Dana, for heaven's sake. Sit down and relax," Mom said.

While I'd been puttering, she'd opened an issue of *Star* magazine. I stood over her shoulder and read about the starlets hitting the clubs and the latest romances. Mom occasionally glanced over her shoulder at me but didn't say anything. I made sure to breathe extra loud until she flipped the magazine closed.

"Ashlee! Hurry up!" Mom hollered.

I heard the door to Ashlee's room open and she entered the kitchen.

"I'm ready."

I studied her outfit. She'd changed into a black short-sleeved blouse and black miniskirt with black stockings and black boots.

"How is that getup better than what you were wearing before?"

Ashlee gave me a look like she questioned my sanity. "Hello? I'm dressed like a cricket. They're black, right?"

I squeezed my eyes shut. "Oh, God, make the pain stop."

"What pain?" Ashlee asked.

Mom smacked my arm.

"Nothing," I said. "Let's go." Time to enter the exciting world of cricket chirping. Jason had better show up or this was going to be one long afternoon.

19

Ashlee plopped herself in the passenger seat of my car. I slid into the driver's seat, started the motor, and pulled away from the curb.

"How'd you get roped into this cricket stuff anyway?" Ashlee asked, popping a piece of gum in her mouth.

"Esther belongs to a committee devoted to improving Blossom Valley commerce. The murder left her too embarrassed to attend the meetings and she asked me to fill in."

Ashlee adjusted the air vent on her side. "What's she embarrassed about? She didn't kill the guy."

I checked for traffic at the intersection and hung a left. "I know. But Maxwell was killed on her farm during opening weekend for this fantastic spa that was supposed to help Blossom Valley draw in a tourist crowd. Instead, it's attracted a bunch of negative press and some crackpots who want to see where the guy was murdered."

"Word on the street is that Maxwell was the victim of a mafia vendetta. He tried to swindle Freddie Three Fingers and got whacked."

I swung around to look at Ashlee, jerking my arm in the process and almost swerving the car into a tree. "Freddie Three Fingers? Whacked? Seriously?"

Ashlee blew a bubble, then sucked the gum back into her mouth. "I got the lowdown from my friend Katie who heard it from her mom's dry cleaner at Pressed for Time."

The same business where Gordon got all his suits cleaned. Guess he'd spread the mob rumor after all. And now my sister was talking like an extra from *The Sopranos*.

I pulled into the fairgrounds parking lot, noting that only one other car occupied the lot. George apparently wasn't kidding when he said I was in charge of setup. Across the lot, two large buildings squatted like sumo wrestlers waiting to battle. Off to the side, a third, smaller building sat alone.

I parked in the space closest to the buildings and turned off the air conditioning; the car instantly heated up. I got out, grateful for the tiny breeze that ruffled my hair.

Ashlee followed me to the first building, past a row of vending machines, and I tried the door. Locked. I jiggled the metal bar to be sure, then walked past the row of liquid amber trees and pushed the bar on the door to the second building.

The door swung open, revealing one large room with high windows. Huge lamps hung from the ceiling, casting circles of light on the hardwood floors. When the fair was in town, jars of jams, jellies, and pickled asparagus shared space with quilts and 4-H projects. Now, the room was bare, a blank canvas to be filled by chirping crickets, their owners, and their fans.

I spotted the rack of folding tables in the far corner. My shoes squeaked on the floor as I walked. Ashlee clacked behind me. With the size of the tables, I was glad she'd decided to tag along.

"You grab this end and I'll hold the other, then we'll walk it back over by the door."

Ashlee glanced at her hands. "I got a manicure yesterday."

"No nails will be harmed in the making of this cricket

event," I cracked. "But if you break one, I'll spring for another manicure."

She pointed a polished nail at me. "I'll hold you to that, Miss Funnypants."

Together, we heaved the table off the rack and carried it across the room. We each popped a leg out and tilted the table up and level.

The main door opened, a shaft of sunlight forming a rectangle on the floor. George Sturgeon walked in. Today, he'd skipped the retro suit in favor of Dockers, a polo shirt, and boat shoes.

He clapped his hands twice. "All right, ladies. Let's get these tables up. The contest starts soon."

"George, this is my sister, Ashlee."

"No time for introductions. These tables won't stand up by themselves."

If I had to work at this ex-army sergeant's tire store, I'd go AWOL.

He joined us at the rack and dragged the next table down. I held the top vertical while he unfolded the legs. Ashlee stood to one side.

"How about you set up the chairs while we handle the tables?" I asked her.

Ashlee eyed the metal folding chairs leaning against the wall. "By myself?"

"We need two per table, one at each end," George said.

She moved to the rows of chairs and unfolded the first one, while I turned my attention back to the tables. George and I set up the remaining eight.

By that time, Ashlee had unfolded all the chairs, set them in the middle of the room, and now sat in a chair by the door.

She caught me watching her. "I couldn't put the chairs in place until you finished the tables, so I decided to man the door. Or woman the door." She laughed at her own joke. "Anyway, you'd better hurry. I see cars pulling in."

I grabbed the chairs from the middle and stationed them by the tables, Ashlee peering out the door from her seated position.

With everything ready, I stepped back and surveyed the room. The tables and chairs lined the walls, leaving an enormous amount of floor space in the middle, presumably for all those cricket-chirping fans that would be mingling with the contestants. If no one showed up, this would be a sad, sad day for the Blossom Valley Rejuvenation Committee.

I could hear doors slam in the parking lot. While I'd been arranging chairs, Bethany had arrived and now stood by the propped-open door, a bouquet of daisies in her hands. As each person entered, she handed out a flower. Ashlee had moved her chair back to make room for Bethany and now typed on her iPhone.

"I'm getting a soda out front. You interested?" I asked her.

She stood without answering, gaze fixed on her gadget. She followed me toward the door. When I stopped to let two people enter, Ashlee bumped into me.

"Watch where you're going!"

"Sorry." She shuffled out the door ahead of me, eyes focused firmly on the screen. Maybe she'd run into a parked car.

We walked back to the first building to where the vending machine sat to one side of the door. The machine sucked the dollar bill from my hand and I hit the button for Pepsi. I waited for the clunk and scooped the can out of the trough.

Ashlee looked at me expectantly, eyebrows raised, so I dug out another dollar and repeated the process. We stood in the shade of the building and drank our sodas as several people parked their cars. Perhaps the contest would have a decent turnout after all.

Beside me, Ashlee released a hearty sigh. "So boring."

"The contest hasn't started yet."

"But you know it's going to suck wind. I can't believe the junk you have to do for your job."

I took a sip of soda to swallow my annoyance. "You're one to talk. You shovel cat poop and help spay animals all day. Jobs aren't exactly growing on trees, you know."

"But you should have waited it out down in San Jose. Gotten a good job."

I blew out a rush of air. "For your information, I did get offered a good job."

Ashlee tilted her head in disbelief. "Yeah, right, that's why we're at a cricket-chirping contest."

"I'm serious. It was a fantastic position with great benefits and good pay and smart people. Working there would have been almost as good as working at Google."

Ashlee tapped one manicured nail on the side of her soda can, the taps increasing in speed as she spoke. "You're making this up. Why on earth would you turn down something so awesome?"

I fiddled with my necklace chain. Good question. "I'd already promised Mom I'd move back home. The offer came three days before I was scheduled to leave."

Ashlee still looked unconvinced, so I plowed ahead. Might as well tell her everything now that I'd gotten started. "Have you looked at Mom lately? I mean really *looked* at her? She'd aged so much when I came up to visit for her birthday in February." I pictured her once ramrod-straight back hunched as we sang birthday wishes to her. "Part of that was my fault."

Ashlee crossed her arms, a few drops of caramel-colored soda spraying out the can opening as her arm swung around.

"I thought we settled this at lunch, Dana. She's just taking Dad's death a little hard."

"I know, and I wasn't here when she needed me most. Instead, I fled back to San Jose as soon as Dad's funeral was over. I never once thought about Mom needing me here."

"I'm here. I've been supporting her."

I squeezed my soda can and heard the aluminum crinkle. "And I'm glad for that. But when I saw Mom on her birthday, I couldn't believe how bad she looked. No way could I call her at the last minute and tell her I'd changed my mind about moving back." I'd summed it up in a simple explanation, but the move had been so much more complex. Had I missed my one shot at guaranteed success in the Bay Area? Would I be stuck in Blossom Valley forever?

"So you came home. To take over like you always do, the big sister and all that," Ashlee said, the resentment clear in her voice. She turned away from me and brushed imaginary lint off her black top.

I dropped the empty can into the recycling bin and ran my hands down my jeans, worried I'd hurt Ashlee's feelings. "Hey, nothing against you. I just think Mom needs both of us here right now. A double support team, like I mentioned earlier."

"I guess." Ashlee turned back toward me, her lips still in a slight pout. "She has been pretty down."

"Right. But she seems to be getting better. She's even started wearing lipstick again."

"Yeah, I saw that. Of course, that shade she always wears doesn't match her skin tone at all. Too much orange undertone."

I rolled my eyes. "Whatever. Anyway, it's progress. Now we need to focus on getting her out more."

Ashlee checked her iPhone, then glanced at me. "She goes to the grocery store all the time."

"I mean social outings. Buying low-fat milk and flaxseed doesn't count." I glanced at the handful of people moving through the parking lot. "Maybe we should have asked her to the contest today. I didn't even think of that."

Ashlee smirked. "Please, it's gonna be so lame. Mom'd never leave the house again if we made her suffer through this."

"Come on, it won't be that bad." But if it was, Ashlee would be sure to tell me all about it. For the next twenty years.

Ashlee put her hand on her hip. "We've set up the tables like they asked. Let's leave now."

I considered Ashlee's request. How exciting could a cricket-chirping contest possibly be? Didn't those little insects all sound the same? And George had only requested that I set up the tables, not stay for the competition.

"All right, let's go."

"Thank God. I don't even know why I asked to come along."

As I turned toward the parking lot, movement near the other building caught my attention. George, his crew cut unmistakable, gestured for me to join him.

Drat.

I nodded toward him as I spoke to Ashlee. "Let me see what George needs first, then we'll go."

Ashlee grabbed my arm. "Pretend you don't see him."

Pointing with my free hand, I shifted away from her. "He's looking right at me. Now let go of my arm."

She dropped her hand, her lower lip already jutting out.

I ignored her and joined George near the entrance to the other building, Ashlee right behind me.

"Glad you're still here," he said. "We need you inside, in case people have questions."

"I thought I was only in charge of setup."

George scrubbed at his crew cut with the palm of one

hand. "With me judging and Bethany at the door, we need someone inside. That's you."

I could feel Ashlee hovering by my shoulder, willing me to say no. But as a stand-in for Esther, I had to help.

"No problem." I could almost feel the gust of air riffle my hair as Ashlee let out a huge sigh.

"Great, follow me," George said, leading the way through the door.

Back inside, a crowd of roughly ten people milled about the middle of the room, looking tiny in the open space. The folding tables each held one or two small cages, the owners standing to the side.

I walked around the outside of the room, trying to catch a glimpse of these gifted crickets, Ashlee still trailing behind me.

"Come on, baby," one woman cooed to her cricket, lifting the cover on the cage to coax the insect. "Eat the tomato. You need to keep up your strength."

I stopped next to a man slouched in his chair, his head resting on the metal back. He surveyed the room, never once looking at the cage next to him. His face sported a scraggly beard and his hair hung over the top of his collar, reminding me of Johnny Depp in *Pirates of the Caribbean*, though this guy was more like Johnny Depp's slightly shady cousin.

"How's it going?" I said. "I'm helping the committee that organized the contest. Think your cricket's up to today's challenge?"

The man's gaze lingered on Ashlee before shifting to me. "You betcha."

"Is this your first cricket-chirping contest?"

"Yeah, first one."

With no one needing my help, I might as well see why people were here. "What made you enter the contest?"

The man scratched his chin, his fingertips disappearing in the clump of hair. "The five-hundred-dollar prize."

"Five hundred dollars for a cricket?" Ashlee said. "How dumb."

I whirled on my sister. "Ashlee, shush. Don't be rude." I turned back to the man. "Have you had your pet cricket long?"

"He's not a pet. I caught him in my backyard last night. Used the little cage I had a frog in once. I'd never have a stupid bug for a pet."

At the next table, a woman with a pageboy haircut and wearing a red corduroy jumper over a beige turtleneck with sheep on it glared. "Some people," she mumbled under her breath.

"Think I'll go talk to that nice lady," I said. We certainly didn't need any disgruntled cricketeers ruining the festivities.

The man winked at me. "Knock yourself out."

"I'll stay here," Ashlee said.

Hmm . . . surely Ashlee wasn't attracted to this guy, though he was sexy in a rocker kind of way. Maybe her ex-con date had been a disappointment.

Moving to the woman at the next table, I sat down in an empty chair. She cast angry glances at the guy.

"Would you like to tell me about your cricket?"

"You mean King Arthur?"

Oh, lord, her cricket was named King Arthur.

"My name's Agatha, by the way, Agatha Parson."

She pulled the cover off the cage, revealing a lone black cricket, much like other crickets I'd seen in my mom's yard. His cage was carpeted and held a miniature bed and chair.

"You gave him furniture," I said.

Agatha ran a hand over the top of the container. "King

Arthur is a member of the family. I couldn't have him sitting in an empty cage."

Of course not. Cricket furniture made perfect sense.

"How long have you had King Arthur? You two seem cozy."

"Two months." Agatha blew a kiss toward the cage. "We've been inseparable."

"I read somewhere that a cricket's average life span is two months."

Agatha set the cover on the table. "It's true King Arthur is in his twilight years. But crickets lead such rich lives, they don't require a lot of time on this earth, unlike humans."

I studied King Arthur in his cage. "I didn't realize crickets were so calm," I said. "He hasn't moved a muscle. I guess he's priming himself for the big contest."

Leaping from her seat, Agatha shoved me out of the way and bent down to peer into the cage, her glasses bumping the wire mesh.

"King Arthur? King Arthur?" She shook the cage. The cricket skittered back and forth across the carpeted bottom. He landed feet up. "Arthur!" she wailed.

I saw others rising from their chairs, staring at the sobbing woman.

"Her cricket, um, King Arthur, died," I said.

A simultaneous gasp rose from the crowd, and everyone rushed to Agatha, touching her arms and shoulders, plucking at the material of her turtleneck.

"It's okay."

"Such a tragedy."

"Can we help?"

I inched my way backwards and extricated myself from the mass, bumping into someone. I turned around to apologize and found myself staring at a T-shirt. My gaze traveled upward and I stared into Jason's green eyes.

"You're causing a commotion," he said.

Was he flirting with me? Was I creating a little excitement for him?

Jason nodded toward Agatha's table. "What did you do to that poor woman?"

Oh, that commotion. Wasn't I full of myself? "Nothing, but her prize cricket has gone to that big field in the sky."

"Guess she won't win the contest."

"Odds are slim," I agreed. "What brings you here?"

I noticed he'd dressed down for the event, swapping his usual button-up shirts for a Pearl Jam T-shirt.

Jason held up his notepad. "Covering the event for the *Herald.*"

"Must be big news around here." Well, great, with that one statement, I'd managed to not only belittle the town, but his job, too.

"I can't write exclusively about the murder. Those little old ladies get upset when I don't talk about their bridge clubs or local contests."

"I thought they just read the obituaries, like my mom."

Jason laughed. "That, too."

We stood together for a moment, the hum of background voices only emphasizing our silence. I glanced around the room, frantic for anything to talk about, but the harder I tried, the blanker my mind got.

Jason cleared his throat. "Guess I'd better interview some contestants."

"Right, see you around." Not my best parting line.

As Jason walked toward George, I watched his fine-fitting jeans move back and forth. That man should be in a Levi's commercial.

Then I mentally slapped myself. While I'd been ogling his butt, I'd totally missed my chance to ask him about the murder. If I wanted to help Esther, I really needed to focus, not get distracted every time a cute guy talked to me.

Shoulders slumped, I returned to where Ashlee sat with the same guy, the only two people not comforting Agatha. Judging by Ashlee's smile, she wasn't too upset about having to stay for the contest anymore.

"Bobby Joe was telling me all about his army adventures," Ashlee said.

"You were in the army, huh?" I said.

The murmurings from the crowd continued as Agatha let out an occasional wail.

"You bet. Got to ride in the tanks and load the cannons, slide down the ropes out of the helicopters. Man, I miss those days."

I eyed his slouched posture and greasy hair. "Now that you're out of the service, what do you do?"

Bobby Joe took a can of chew from his back pocket and stuck a wad in his lip. "I pump gas at Running on Fumes, the station over off the highway."

"I know the place."

Turning to Ashlee, Bobby Joe said, "It's more important than it sounds. I deal with all kinds of rich clientele."

Ashlee smiled, flashing her dimples. "I'm sure. You're probably the man in charge over there."

"You got it, baby. Why, just this past Friday, I helped some rich guy change the oil in his Mercedes."

"A rich guy, huh?"

Bobby Joe spit into an empty soda can, a brown blob puddling on the tab. "The car cost eighty thousand if it cost a dime, and he'd almost let it run dry. Tried to blame it on his assistant. Dumb ass."

"He from around here?" This conversation could put an insomniac to sleep, but no way was I talking to anyone else. Another cricket might die, a senseless tragedy.

"Nah. Out-of-towner. Said he was staying at that new spa."

Forget what I said about a boring conversation. "Was his name Maxwell?"

Bobby Joe licked his thumb and rubbed at a spot on his jeans. "Yeah, that sounds right. At least that's what the hot chick called him. Of course, she wasn't as hot as Ashlee here." He winked at her.

Ashlee giggled in return.

Good grief.

"What hot chick?" I asked, inching away from Ashlee so Bobby Joe would focus on my questions.

Bobby Joe adjusted the band on his watch, a tarnished gold Rolex with three links missing. "Some blonde in a real tight, real short dress. Said she was the star he was looking for."

Tiffany certainly fit the description of a blonde in skin-tight minidress. "What did he say in response?"

"Come on, Dana, who cares?" Ashlee asked. "Bobby Joe and I are trying to talk about us."

I made a shooing motion at Ashlee. "This could be important."

Bobby Joe scraped at the dirt crusted on his thumbnail. "He laughed at her, said so many girls had told him they were his next star that he could form his own galaxy. Boy, did she get pissed at that. Surprised she didn't scratch his eyes out with those fake nails of hers."

Out of the corner of my eye, I saw Ashlee curl her fingers into her palms to hide her nails.

"Then what happened?" I asked, shifting from foot to foot.

"God, Dana," Ashlee said. "You're totally ruining the mood here."

"What mood? It's a cricket contest," I said. "Now let Bobby Joe answer."

Bobby Joe patted Ashlee's knee. "I'll answer her questions, then we'll have all the time in the world." He turned to me. "She was blathering about how she'd got a copy of some script and had been practicing for weeks. He told her to stop bothering him, paid for his gas, and hightailed it out of there."

"And that was all?" I stopped fidgeting as my hope for a big story faded.

"Nah, I didn't tell you about the big finish. That dame chased after him and tried to grab his arm to stop him. He turned around and gave her a shove, knocked her clean on her ass. Hopped in his car and roared off. 'Course, I don't abide hitting no woman." This last bit was directed at Ashlee. "But she wouldn't have fallen if she hadn't been wearing those silly shoes."

Maxwell had pushed Tiffany, if indeed the girl had been Tiffany. Not only pushed her, but laughed at her claims about her acting skills.

Would she have taken that as his final word? Or did she go to his room to confront him?

Had she ended up killing him?

20

A microphone-amplified voice interrupted my thoughts as I mulled over Bobby Joe's comments about Tiffany and Maxwell at the gas station.

"Everyone, listen up," George said. I spotted his crew cut among the other heads in the center of the room. "The chirping contest is about to begin. All contestants, return to your tables and wait for us judges. Unless we're at your table, keep your cricket uncovered so it doesn't interfere with the judging. Now scoot."

At the table next to Bobby Joe's, Agatha packed her things, sobbing.

The other people hurried back to their stations and pulled off the covers to peer at their crickets, probably to assure themselves that their crickets hadn't joined the one Agatha would be burying. Once the place had quieted, George and Bethany emerged from the handful of spectators still standing in the middle and stopped at the closest table.

I couldn't hear what George and Bethany said, but the cricket owner looked jumpy. Crickets. Jumpy. Ha! I cracked myself up.

Next to me, Bobby Joe and Ashlee had their heads

bowed together, Ashlee giggling at whatever Bobby Joe was saying. I stood to the side, marveling at my sister's ability to pick up any man, in any place.

Across the room, George and Bethany moved to the next table. I glanced at my watch. At this rate, the contest wouldn't be over for at least an hour.

My cell phone rang, and I pulled it from my pocket, happy for a moment's distraction. I glanced at the caller ID as I hit the green button, but I didn't recognize the number.

"Hello?" I said.

A recording greeted me. "Do you own your own home? Are you sick of paying too much for insurance?"

Ugh. I hit the OFF button. That better not count against my monthly minutes.

I looked across the room and saw Jason trailing behind the judges as he jotted notes and watched the proceedings. He glanced over to where I stood, smiled, and waved.

I placed my phone on the table behind me and waved back, wiggling my fingers like a five-year-old. God, I was such a dork. I turned away and studied my sandals, wishing I'd taken the time to paint my toenails.

After an eternity—during which I walked around the building a few times, kept an eye on Jason while pretending not to check him out, and listened to Ashlee flirt—George and Bethany reached Bobby Joe's table. He slowly rose from his chair, brushed off his jeans, and threw the cover onto his cage. His cricket chirped so loud that a woman three tables down grabbed her cricket cage and walked out the door.

George and Bethany wrote on their respective clipboards, then moved to one side and murmured to each other while consulting their notes. After a few minutes, George returned to the middle and removed the microphone from its stand.

"Tough competition this year, folks, but one cricket

stood out from the orchestra. We're pleased to announce the winner of the sixth annual cricket-chirping contest is Bobby Joe Jones," George said. The small group of fans and the other contestants burst into applause as Bobby Joe stepped forward and accepted his money and the trophy, which was definitely big enough to squash a cricket. Jason snapped a picture of Bobby Joe.

"How long you been raising crickets, Bobby Joe?" George asked. The hair on the back of my neck perked up. This wouldn't be good, considering what Bobby Joe had already told me.

Bobby Joe held his five-hundred-dollar check at arm's length to read the amount, licking his lips. "What? Oh, right, the cricket. Yeah, I don't raise 'em. I found this one last night when I let my dog out."

"You mean, you don't know anything about crickets?" George asked.

"Nah, they're stupid bugs. I'll probably feed this one to my lizard when I get home."

An angry buzz filled the room as the crowd muttered to one another. "Cricket killer!" someone near the back shouted.

Eyes wide, Bobby Joe jumped. As one, the crowd chanted, "Cricket killer! Cricket killer!" People moved toward the center of the room. Jason snapped a picture of the winning cricket, no doubt wondering if he'd get another chance. Then he took pictures of the crowd as they edged toward the winner.

Bobby Joe glanced again at his money. "Yeah, thanks for the dough. See ya." He ran past two women heading his way and blew through a side exit, leaving his cricket on the table. The crowd followed him out, shouting.

I stepped over to Ashlee, who had picked up the cage and clutched it to her chest.

"Where is he going?" she whined. "We're supposed to have coffee after the contest."

"I think Bobby Joe might be busy avoiding the mob. But I'm sure you'll see him again." I indicated the cage. "If nothing else, you need to return his prized possession."

Ashlee brightened. "True." She cast a look around. "Now, let's get out of here. These bugs are creeping me out."

We left the building, Ashlee carrying the cage. The sound of peeling rubber filled the parking lot and I spotted a beat-up pickup truck roaring onto the street, a cloud of dust hovering where he'd been.

Ashlee held up the cage in her hands, clearly annoyed Bobby Joe hadn't stopped long enough to reclaim his cricket.

I pulled my car keys out of the pocket of my khaki shorts. "Too bad you didn't have a chance to give him your number."

Ashlee snorted, reminding me of Wilbur. "Of course I gave him my digits. You always do that early on, in case you get interrupted. Usually, it's some drunk girl claiming to be the guy's date, but you need to be ready for any situation, even an angry cricket crowd."

As if on cue, I heard Katy Perry singing. Ashlee set the cage on the pavement and checked her iPhone. She was almost as bad as Logan when it came to electronics.

Ashlee smirked at me while she answered. "Hi, Bobby Joe. I knew you'd call."

I rolled my eyes and tried to think of a snarky comment, but none popped into my head. Wasn't that the way it always worked?

As I listened to Ashlee gush to Bobby Joe, giggling and flirting, I couldn't decide if I was disgusted or insanely jealous at how easily she attracted men. Probably a bit of both.

Ashlee snapped her phone shut. "Let's get home. Bobby Joe's picking me up in an hour. I barely have enough time to get ready."

"You look fine. He already thinks you're hot enough to ask out."

She fluffed her hair with one hand while she opened the car door with the other. "Well, sure, but now I have to look even better. It's expected."

I slid into the driver's seat. "Gonna doll yourself up for a man. How 1950s of you." I said, but I automatically tucked a lock of hair behind my ear. I could mock Ashlee all I wanted, but her methods obviously worked.

"Whatever," she said as she buckled herself into the seat, balancing the cricket cage on her knees.

I roared out of the lot.

At home, Ashlee vanished into her room for all her primping and prepping while I sat with Mom in the living room for the tail end of *Ellen*. Unable to focus on the guests, I went to my room, popped open my laptop, and caught up on the day's news while sitting on my bed.

After a quick dinner of chicken and brown rice, I changed into my favorite pair of ratty sweats, loose strings and holes included, and settled in for a night of mediocre TV.

Mom joined me in the living room and perched on the couch.

"I keep meaning to ask you if you've found anything to help the police yet?" she asked.

I muted the TV and set the remote on the end table. "Hard to say. I tried to tell the detective on the case everything that I've uncovered, but he told me to butt out."

Mom put a hand to her mouth. "You didn't get in trouble, did you?"

I remembered the detective glaring at me, his eye twitch

at full speed. Did the threat of an obstructing justice charge count as trouble? I'd keep that to myself until I needed to call Mom for bail money.

"No, but I can't believe he blew me off like he did."

"I'm sure the police want to solve this on their own." She crossed her legs and settled into the cushion. "But I'd love to hear what you've found out, if you suspect anyone."

I picked at a loose string on my sweats. "I keep changing my mind. I really had my eye on Sheila—she is the ex-wife after all—but then I found out that Tiffany and Maxwell had a big fight, and I have to wonder if she did it."

"What was the fight about?"

"Tiffany wanted to star in Maxwell's movie and he let her know that her chances were nil. Plus he pushed her to the ground, but that could have been an accident. Maybe her pride was so wounded that she killed him."

Mom tapped her bottom lip. "What about that assistant who is still at the farm? Have you found out anything about him?"

I straightened up in the chair, glad I could use Mom for a sounding board. "He has a motive, but it's pretty weak, so he's my last choice at the moment."

"Do you think the killer is still even at the farm? They could have been one of the guests who checked out the next day."

The thought had crossed my mind, but I'd shoved it to the side. "Let's hope not, or the police might never catch them. But if it's not one of those three guests, then that really only leaves the staff and I'd hate for Esther to have a killer working at the farm."

Mom shivered. "Don't even think that."

"Can't help it. But other than Heather, I don't know of any motive. I'm not even sure Zennia and Christian met

Maxwell. And while Gordon has a quick temper, I think that's just because he's so dedicated to the spa after his own bed and breakfast went under."

"Well, keep digging. I have faith in you."

I smiled at Mom. "Thanks."

"Now, if you'll excuse me, I'm off to take a shower." Mom rose and retreated to her room.

I stayed in the recliner and poked at a hole in the sweats material covering my knee, feeling a bit restless. Nothing wrong with a night in. So what if Ashlee was off on a date? My job was demanding. I was tired.

The doorbell rang. I could hear Mom's shower running, so I jumped up and went to the door, hitting the porch light switch as I leaned forward to peer through the peephole.

In the dim light, I recognized Jason standing on the porch.

What was he doing here? He couldn't possibly have more questions about my finding Maxwell's body. Did he have a follow-up question for the other article? But he could have asked at the cricket-chirping contest today.

I put my hand on the knob, then glanced down. My stained, holey sweats looked back at me.

Crap. I couldn't answer the door like this.

Maybe if I didn't open the door, he'd go away.

But I'd already turned on the porch light.

"Um, just a minute, I need a sec, I'll be right there," I called through the door.

I ran down the hall toward my bedroom, almost tripping as I slid my sweats off before I'd stopped moving. I tossed the sweats on the bed, snatched up the jeans I'd folded on the chair, and slid them on, snagging my foot in one of the legs until I jammed it through.

A knock sounded on the door.

"Coming," I hollered. I made a quick detour to the

bathroom to run a brush through my hair and frown at my lack of makeup. Oh, well, at least I didn't look like a slob anymore.

I heard the shower water turn off as I charged to the front door and yanked it open.

Jason took a step back from the sudden movement. He'd changed from the Pearl Jam T-shirt he'd worn at the contest into a striped dress shirt and dark blue jeans. "Everything all right?"

"Yes, fine. Why do you ask?" Sure it'd taken me five minutes to open the door, but he hadn't called first, so it was his own fault.

"I thought . . . you just . . . never mind."

"Can I help you with something?" I asked, studying his defined jaw in the porch light. Mouth-to-mouth resuscitation? A date for a cousin's wedding?

He held an object out, and I stepped onto the porch, pulling the door closed behind me.

I put out my hand and he dropped the item into my palm. My cell phone. I stared at the phone like it was a five-legged pig.

"You left it at the contest this afternoon," Jason said.

I recovered my wits and stuffed the phone in my back pocket. "Thanks for dropping it by. You didn't have to."

Jason dug the toe of his Oxford shoe into the welcome mat. "I can't live without my phone. Figured you'd want it back."

How pathetic. My phone had been missing for hours, and I hadn't even noticed. What did that say about my social life?

A thought struck me. "How did you know where I lived?"

He gestured toward my rear end, which totally threw

me for a second. What did my butt have to do with my address?

"Ashlee's in your list of contacts."

Oh, he was talking about the phone in my pocket.

He continued. "Gave her a call and she was more than happy to tell me the address. Even provided directions."

I could picture Ashlee grinning as she clutched her phone and gave Jason the information. If she'd seen him in person, she would have drawn him a map. Or driven him home herself. She was hell-bent on getting me a boyfriend.

But I had more important things on my mind.

"Any new leads on Maxwell's murder?" I asked, not bothering to think up a ruse to get the information. "Last time we talked, you said the police didn't have much to go on."

Jason glanced around at the neighboring houses, all shuttered for the night, and stepped closer. "Still not a lot of clues, but they have managed to uncover a few motives."

I held my breath. Finally, some progress. "Like what?"

"One of the deputies overheard Logan and Maxwell arguing in the Daily Grind."

The same fight George had mentioned.

"And Maxwell caught the maid looking at an expensive necklace in his room right before his death."

So Heather had told the cops about the necklace. Good for her. "Heather would never kill Maxwell over a misunderstanding like that."

Jason swatted at a moth that fluttered in his face on the way to the porch light. "She's in the middle of a custody dispute with her ex and she was worried that a theft accusation would tilt the judge in his favor."

Heather hadn't mentioned the custody battle when I'd spoken to her. Women had been known to go to extremes to protect their children. Even murder.

Jason stuffed his hands in his jeans pockets and leaned his back against the wall. I couldn't help but admire the curve of his lean body.

"The cops are working those two angles right now while they dig for additional motives," he said.

Not exactly the breakthrough I was hoping for. I already knew that stuff.

I pulled my phone out and opened it while I thought about possible suspects, slightly annoyed that I'd had no new calls all afternoon. "I talked to Maxwell's ex-wife, but I don't see a motive for her. She told me that he wanted to reconcile. He was tired of the phony Hollywood women."

"Really. A couple of guests mentioned seeing Sheila and Christian in a lovers' embrace the night before the murder," Jason said.

"Sheila and Christian? I thought he was interested in Tiffany." Had I misread that look he'd given her during yoga? Was he merely a guy admiring a pretty girl?

Jason rubbed his chin with the back of his hand. "Maybe they're wrong. Or Christian's a busy fellow." Under the porch light, the red in his hair gleamed, tinged with gold.

The moth flew away from the light and settled in his hair. I brushed it gently away with my fingertips. "I hope not. I'd like to think there are some decent men left in this world. Or at least this town."

Jason studied his fingernails. "Me, I like to date one woman at a time." He glanced up and smiled.

My breath caught in my throat. Was he talking about me? "I couldn't agree more. Why play the field? Get to know one person first, see if it's a good match."

He took a step forward, until our shoes were almost touching. Being so close, my face grew warm and my heartbeat picked up.

"Absolutely," he said. "You have to find out if you share chemistry." His breath smelled minty.

I definitely wouldn't mind doing a chemistry experiment with him, mix together a few fluids, see if they combusted.

Without another word, Jason cupped my face in both his hands and leaned in.

My lips tingled in anticipation.

The front door opened.

Son of a birch tree.

21

Jason dropped his hands as we both turned toward the door, but I could feel the imprint of his fingers on my cheeks.

"Dana, I thought I heard voices," Mom said. She was dressed in her favorite housecoat, the pocket torn, the collar threaded. Her face had been scrubbed of makeup and her hair stuck out in all directions from when she'd toweled it off. "When I got out of the shower and didn't see you, I thought you'd gone somewhere without telling me. If I'd known I was interrupting a little romance, I wouldn't have opened the door."

Someone kill me now.

"I left my phone at the cricket-chirping contest and Jason was kind enough to drive it over," I said.

"And they say chivalry is dead. Pretend you never saw me," Mom said. "I'll go back to watching my shows." She started to close the door, then swung it back open. "By the way, you write wonderful articles for the paper."

"Thank you, Mrs. Lewis."

She turned to go.

I felt my shoulders relax.

She turned back. "I especially loved that piece on the history of the lumber mill."

"Thank you."

I silently willed Mom away but she didn't move.

"My uncle used to work at the mill," she added.

"You don't say," Jason said, shifting his feet and sticking his hands in his pockets, obviously not interested in talking about my uncle.

"That's great, Mom. Good night." Maybe that'd give her the hint to go back inside. Not that it mattered now. Jason was probably already thinking that any time he spent with me would also involve Mom and her memory trips back to the golden days of Blossom Valley. Living at home wasn't exactly a selling point where men were concerned.

"See you in a minute, Dana." She closed the door with a click. Through the window, I watched her figure retreat, then hang a left toward the living room.

I looked at Jason, fully illuminated in the glow of the porch light, his lips red and inviting.

"I should let you go in," he said. He stuck out his hand. "A real pleasure."

A handshake? Nothing more? But the moment was gone, replaced by a hint of doubt. What had possessed me to almost kiss Jason in the first place? I barely knew the guy.

I extended my hand and we shook. He held onto my hand for an extra moment, then released it and walked down the path. At the sidewalk, he turned and waved. I waved back, then went into the house, listening to the sound of his engine fade away as I shut the door.

Mom was waiting in Dad's recliner, pretending to watch television. As soon as I stepped into the living room, she hit the MUTE button.

"Jason seems nice," she said.

I sank onto the couch. "Yep." I picked up the latest *People* off the end table and flipped through the pages.

"You could do a lot worse, you know."

"I know." He was definitely hot, and smart to boot, but did I want to get involved with anyone right now, when my job and future were so uncertain?

Mom stopped looking my way and focused on Dad's picture on the mantel. I snuck peeks at her as her expression softened and her eyes grew misty.

I closed the magazine. "Say, Mom, don't you take salsa classes on Tuesday nights?"

"I quit when your father died."

"Have you thought about joining again?"

Mom pulled a tissue from the box on the table and blotted her nose. "A woman in mourning should not be gallivanting around town, laughing and dancing."

I rolled the magazine into a tube. "Dad passed away almost a year ago. He certainly wouldn't expect you to be sitting at home after all this time, letting your own life come to a standstill."

Mom gripped the arm of the recliner. "I just miss him so much."

I swallowed, trying to remove the lump that had magically appeared in my throat. Just seeing Mom in that recliner brought back all the nights Dad was sitting there, the two of us watching *Jeopardy!*, shouting out the answers together. I touched the St. Christopher medal around my neck. "I miss him, too. But when I keep busy and don't have time to dwell, the pain doesn't hurt as much."

She offered a half smile. "When did my daughter get smarter than me?"

As Mom said this, I heard the roar of an engine outside. Was a plane landing on the lawn? A moment later, the front door opened and Ashlee burst into the room. At first I thought she had a handkerchief tied around her waist, but then I realized she was wearing a miniskirt. I hadn't seen so much leg since Tiffany's getup at the spa.

"How was your date?" I asked. With all that leg showing, I could guarantee Bobby Joe had been happy.

"Awesome, of course. Bobby Joe took me four-wheeling in his pickup." Ashlee clasped her hands to her chest. "Oh, my God, I have a great idea. I met Bobby Joe's cousin tonight and he's a real cutie. We should totally double-date. Wouldn't that be the best?"

I pictured Ashlee and Bobby Joe playing tonsil hockey while his cousin and I tried to focus on whatever movie was playing at the drive-in. Not a pretty sight. "Let me just think about that one," I said.

"Don't think too long or some other girl will snatch him up."

I snapped my fingers. "And I'll just kick myself if that happens." I rose from the couch. "I'm off to bed."

Ashlee winked at me. "Next time I talk to Bobby Joe, I'll ask if his cousin is single. We'll get you a man yet."

I stuck my tongue out at her and stalked down the hall. I didn't need Ashlee to set me up with random cousins of her latest conquests. I could get my own man. Couldn't I?

After a quick tooth brushing, I stripped off my clothes, threw on my pajamas, and flopped into bed, still picturing Jason's lips, remembering his hands on my cheeks, as I drifted off to sleep.

The next morning, I wolfed down scrambled Egg Beaters and soy bacon, checking the wall clock as I choked on the salty cardboard. I'd failed to set the alarm and was running behind schedule. To top it all off, I'd found a patch of poison oak on my arm, another hazard of working at the spa. I'd dug up a bottle of calamine lotion that had been under the bathroom sink since before I went away to college, but the medicine wasn't helping the itching.

Mom walked into the kitchen. "Slow down, you'll get indigestion."

"Running late. No time to chew." I swallowed a lump of egg substitute and gulped my orange juice.

"What's the rush?"

"I wanted to swing by Queenie's place this morning on my way to work." It had suddenly occurred to me that I needed to pry more info from the honey lady. I didn't know whether the two people on the bench had anything to do with Maxwell's death or what those references to blood meant, but if I could convince Queenie to speak in plain English, I might learn something.

Mom retrieved a bowl from the cupboard and poured in a pile of bran cereal. "I bought honey from Queenie once. Frankly, she freaked me out with all her doomsday yelling."

"That's Queenie all right. Her place is off the Pine Cone exit, right?"

"Yes, hang a left onto Pear Tree Lane. Her driveway is the one with all the TRESPASSERS WILL BE SHOT signs."

And judging by how comfortable Queenie had been with her shotgun, those signs weren't just threats. I wiped my mouth and carried my empty plate to the sink. I glanced back at Mom, dressed in a silk blouse and knee-length skirt. She was wearing lipstick, her hair styled and set. "You're sure dressed up. Going anywhere special?"

Mom fiddled with her spoon. "After our little talk last night, I realized you were right. I've been using your father's death as an excuse to avoid people."

"You have so many wonderful friends. I'm sure they miss you."

"I was worried about those pity stares and awkward comments. But I've decided to join the bunco group again."

I gave Mom's shoulders a quick squeeze. "Fantastic. You'll be happy you did." For the first time, I felt like my moving back home was having a positive effect, helping to pull Mom out of her slump.

I grabbed my purse and car keys. "Wish me luck with the honey lady."

"Walk slow and call out before you get too close."

In the car, I jetted down the highway, risking a ticket in my effort to make up for all the time I'd lost while oversleeping. After taking the Pine Cone exit, I hung a left onto Pear Tree Lane. My coffee cup jiggled in its holder as I maneuvered around the ruts and potholes that littered the road. After a mile, I spotted the hint of a driveway among a clump of shrubs and oak trees. Every tree sported at least two signs, each one warning trespassers to stay away. How did Queenie expect to sell any honey with this attitude? Tourists wouldn't dare stop here, even if they could find the place.

I turned onto the tiny dirt road and eased along, waiting for the ping of buckshot on my car hood. The trees thinned out, then vanished, as I emerged at the edge of the field. Queenie's trailer sat in the middle, all quiet. I stopped the car where the lane ended and parked.

As I stepped out of the car, a steady buzzing filled the air. To one side, a stack of frames towered out of the grass, dozens of bees hovering around the hive, landing for a moment, then regaining flight. A bee flew by my head and I waited while he investigated my car hood and windshield. When he wandered away, I took a tentative step forward, keeping one eye on the hive. The other bees ignored me.

The dry field grass scratched my calves as I walked toward the trailer, making me regret my choice of shorts when dressing this morning. I sidestepped a gopher hole, then stopped when I was still a good distance from the trailer.

"Queenie?" I called. "I'm here from Esther's farm again. To buy some honey." A total lie, but if I announced that I was here to gossip about the lovers on the bench, Queenie might shoot me.

The only response to my shouting was the constant buzz of bees and occasional cricket chirp. Too bad I hadn't taken that cricket to the contest yesterday. That five-hundred-dollar prize would have been mine, no problem.

"Queenie?" I said again. I waited for the trailer door to fly open, for Queenie to stomp down the metal steps.

But the door remained closed. If she was sleeping, I'd have to wake her. I needed to get to the spa. I was already late.

I approached the trailer, whistling "Michael, Row Your Boat Ashore" the whole time, in case Queenie woke up and thought an intruder was breaking in. When I reached the bottom step, I leaned forward and knocked on the trailer door.

No response.

This time, I pounded on the door, the sound echoing in the metal frame. The door creaked open, revealing a sink and stove, cabinets overtop, a skillet hanging off the side at one end.

"Queenie?" I walked up the steps and poked my head in.

As my eyes adjusted to the light, a waft of enclosed trailer air hit me, bringing with it an odor I'd smelled once before. Oh no.

I spotted an arm sticking into the aisle between the sink and the small table across the way. My heart raced and sweat oozed onto my palms. I sprang back, lost my footing, and fell to the ground on my rump.

Someone was dead in there.

22

I sat frozen in the dirt, staring at the trailer. The fake eggs and bacon roiled in my stomach as I recalled the scene inside. Whose arm was that? It must belong to Queenie. Could she be alive?

Not a chance. I recognized the smell of death. And the odor was three times as strong here as when I'd found Maxwell's body. I needed help. Now.

With a last look at the open trailer door, I jumped up and ran to my Honda. Twice I stumbled on the uneven dirt but kept running. When I reached my car, I wrenched the door open and pawed through the contents of my purse until I found my phone. Reception bars lit up the screen and I almost sobbed in relief.

After a quick call to the 911 operator, who instructed me to wait for emergency crews, I stood by the hood, trying to regain a bit of control. How could I have found another dead body so soon after the last? What were the odds?

Across the field, the trailer door swayed slightly in the light wind, emitting a squeak. Bees buzzed to the side of me, a steady reminder that life still existed.

A breeze tickled the nape of my neck and I whirled around. The copse of trees and shrubs loomed behind me, blotting out the road that led to freedom. A rustling in the grass reached my ears and I swung back around. Probably a feral cat. I sensed the shadows behind me again and my skin prickled.

I clutched my cell phone and climbed back into the car. I yanked the power lock button three times, listening to the click each time, and then checked my rearview mirror. Only the trees reflected back.

How had Queenie died, if her body was the one lying in the trailer? I'd only met her once, but judging by her Medusa hair and filthy teeth, health care wasn't high on her list of concerns. She might have had cancer, or even malaria. But I'd had the same question about Maxwell, and look how that had turned out. Better wait for the authorities to determine the cause of her death.

Movement in the rearview mirror caught my eye, and I swung around in my seat. A fire truck rolled down the lane, oak tree branches snapping against the side, shrubs scratching the tires. I got out of the car and the truck pulled up next to me, engine rumbling, revealing an ambulance and an unmarked police car behind the massive vehicle.

Detective Caffrey stepped out of the car, dressed in a navy blue polo shirt and khaki-colored Dockers, his scalp gleaming between the hairs of his buzz cut. If he'd had a whistle around his neck, he'd have been the spitting image of a high school gym coach. He said something to the paramedics, and they trotted toward the trailer, slowing to a walk after one guy stepped in the gopher hole and almost fell. They disappeared inside, but one paramedic immediately reemerged.

He started back across the rough ground and Detective Caffrey met him halfway. They conferred for several moments, then the other paramedic stepped out of the trailer. Even in the quiet field, I could only hear the murmur of voices. But the fact that the paramedics weren't in a rush confirmed my certainty that Queenie, or whoever was in the trailer, was dead.

Of course, I'd know that for sure if I wandered over to the men. Surely Detective Caffrey would want to speak with me, and if I just happened to overhear what the paramedics were saying while fulfilling my civic duty, he couldn't get mad. Could he?

I made my way over the crumbly ground and reached the trio just as one paramedic said, "ligature marks." Then he spotted me over the detective's shoulder and stopped talking.

Ligature marks? Didn't they use that term when someone was strangled? Or was it when someone had been tied up?

Detective Caffrey glanced at me, his frown deepening, then turned back and nodded to the paramedics before facing me.

Without a word, he put a hand on my elbow and led me a few feet away. When he spoke, the smell of coffee reached my nose.

"Ms. Lewis, explain to me how you managed to stumble across yet another body."

I shook his hand off my elbow and crossed my arms. "I stopped by to chat with Queenie on my way to work this morning."

"I wasn't aware that you and Queenie were such good friends." The sarcasm oozed from his voice like a dollop of honey on a drizzle stick.

"We're not. But you blew me off when I mentioned how Queenie saw a couple of people near her property, and I wanted to find out what else she might know."

Detective Caffrey pulled his notebook from his pants pocket and flipped through the pages so fast a page ripped off. He stuffed it under another page and kept flipping until he reached a blank one. "You sure don't listen very well. I told you to back off and let us do our jobs."

"Look, if I can find out new information, you might solve the murder faster."

The detective wiped a hand across his mouth, probably brushing away all the dirty words he wanted to shout at me. "Never mind that now. Let's focus on the events of the morning. What did you do when you got here?" he said.

I pointed to my car. "I parked right there and called out to Queenie. When she didn't answer, I banged on her trailer door. It came open, I got a whiff of the interior, saw an arm, and called you guys."

"That's it?"

"Yes."

"Did you see any other cars on the road when you drove in?" he asked.

"No." Would it have been better if I'd seen a car? Someone to back up my claim for when I arrived? Or did he think the killer might still be nearby? Detective Caffrey's expression provided no answers and I waited for his next question.

"Did you touch anything? We may need to fingerprint you for comparison."

Fingerprint me? Like a criminal? "Are you saying Queenie was murdered?"

"How do you know the body is Queenie? You told the 911 operator that you didn't step inside the trailer."

My throat constricted as a ball of anger swelled. "Stop trying to trick me. Who else would be in that trailer?"

"You tell me. You're the one who keeps finding bodies."

My breathing quickened at his question. "I'm having a run of bad luck. Surely you don't think I had anything to do with either death?"

Detective Caffrey removed his sunglasses. "All I'm saying is that in my professional experience, no one discovers two bodies in one week unless they are somehow involved."

I blew out a gust of air, along with my exasperation. "Look, Detective Caffrey. I don't like your insinuations that I had anything to do with Queenie's death. I mean, that trailer stank. She's been dead a while."

"The medical examiner will determine time of death." Detective Caffrey flipped the notebook closed. "You can go, but make sure you're available for more questions." He stalked off toward the trailer.

I watched his back, not sure where to go, what to do. Work was the last thing on my mind, but I had an obligation to Esther.

Two bodies in four days. In Blossom Valley. Was Queenie's death tied to Maxwell's murder? Too early to jump to conclusions. Queenie could have tripped over a honey jar and broken her neck, for all I knew.

The sound of snapping twigs carried across the field and I looked in the direction of the farm. Gordon came thundering out of the underbrush like a charging rhino, if a rhino wore a pin-striped suit and too much hair gel. I saw Detective Caffrey momentarily rest his hand on the butt of his gun before relaxing.

Gordon marched across the terrain, impervious to the holes and ruts, and stopped before the trailer. He spoke with Detective Caffrey for a moment, the detective shaking his head repeatedly, then Gordon saw me.

Oh, joy.

He stomped over, burrs sticking to his slacks, twigs clinging to the gel in his hair. "What happened with the crazy lady?"

"Queenie?" Maybe mentioning her name would remind Gordon that yesterday she was a living, breathing person. "All I know is she's dead."

Gordon scowled. "Better not be another murder. Think what that'll do to the farm."

How about the poor dead people? Did he care about them at all?

I looked back at where he'd burst through the shrubbery. "How did you even know anything had happened?"

Gordon had been picking the burrs off his pant leg, and he now straightened up. "Why do you ask?"

"Wondering what brought you over here. The trailer isn't exactly in the middle of downtown, and you can't see it from most places on the farm."

"If you must know, Esther told me about the hot springs and I went to check out the area. I saw the emergency vehicles from there."

That didn't sound right. When I'd been at the springs with Sheila, I hadn't noticed a view to Queenie's trailer. In fact, I'd thought her property was much farther south. "You can see her trailer from there?"

"If you know where to look." He avoided my gaze and picked at his pants again.

Gordon wasn't normally one to act coy. I wondered what was really going on, not that he'd tell me.

"You working today?" he asked.

I ran down the options. Go home and mope. Go to the farm and mope. Go home and watch bad daytime TV. Go to the farm and suffer Zennia's cooking. At least her food would distract me from my late-morning discovery. And the aroma of Brussels sprouts might replace the smell of death that clung to my nostrils, barging into my awareness at unexpected moments. Then again, the sprouts might add to the stench.

"I'll give work a try. Did you want a lift to the farm?"

Gordon pointed over his shoulder with his thumb. "I don't mind the walk."

Good. Much as I wanted to know why he was lying about seeing the vehicles from the hot springs, being trapped in a tiny automobile with Gordon was not on my list of things to do today. Of course, neither was finding a body.

"I'll see you over there, then," I said.

As I walked to my car, I kept an eye on Detective Caffrey, half expecting him to wave me down and insist I stay for more questions, but he was talking to a fireman by the trailer and didn't notice me.

With a puff of dust and a spin of tires, I turned around and drove down the lane, squeezing past the emergency vehicles. A few right turns brought me to the farm and I parked in the lot. The news crews were completely absent today, thank goodness. Guess they hadn't heard about Queenie's death.

I walked in the front door to the lobby, grateful no one was waiting, eased down the hall, and slipped into the office, closing the door with barely a whisper. Explaining the situation to anyone sounded like too much work at the moment. Gordon could spread the word when he got back. Right now, I'd focus on my job and type up today's blog.

For the next hour, I sat before the keyboard, pounding out a piece describing the benefits of the sun and how even an overnight stay at the spa would expose you to hours of sunlight, whether while participating in Christian's yoga classes or walking on the trails. Every so often, I heard voices in the hall as people walked by the office but no one opened the door. After the first draft was complete, I saved the file and stood. Couldn't hide out forever.

The hall was empty when I opened the door, but I heard voices in the lobby, one of which sounded like Jason's. My heart hammered at the thought of seeing him, and my hand flew to my hair to brush down the errant strands before I made my way down the hall.

In the lobby, Tiffany and Jason chatted by the front door, Tiffany all giggles. When he saw me, Jason smiled, making my insides melt into a puddle.

"Dana, I'm glad to see you."

Tiffany glanced at Jason, then raised her eyebrows at me, grinning. "Looks like I'm in the way here."

"Don't be silly," I said.

Jason spoke up. "Actually, I need to talk to you in private. About Queenie."

My stomach sank. If Jason wanted to question me, Queenie most likely hadn't died of natural causes.

Tiffany waved her hand. "I'm hitting the beach over in Mendocino today, so don't let me interrupt you two cuties." She sashayed out the door, drawing attention to the snug fit of her sweatpants. According to the glittery letters on the back, her butt was "Hot Stuff."

To his credit, Jason didn't even notice. He sat in one of the wingback chairs and patted the cushion of the other one.

"Sit. Tell me about finding Queenie."

I sat in the indicated chair and glanced at my knees. Blond stubble poked out in all directions where I'd missed a few spots while shaving in a hurry this morning. I placed my hands over the offending area.

"What have you heard?" I asked.

"I spoke to the cops at the trailer. Detective Caffrey tried to keep the info from me, but one of my buddies from the department was out there. He said they're waiting for the autopsy but someone most likely strangled her."

God, how horrible. Putting your hands around someone's throat and squeezing the life out of them seemed so personal compared to a quick jab to the gut.

"This has to be related to Maxwell's death," I said.

Jason nodded. "Two murders so close together are absolutely connected. But how?"

I thought about the only time I'd spoken to Queenie, her vague ranting and raving. "When I talked to her, she mentioned how when someone spilled blood, their own blood would be spilled in return. Think she saw something related to Maxwell's murder?"

Jason leaned forward, completely absorbed with what I was saying. "It's entirely possible. Did she say anything else?"

"She mentioned Maxwell and a woman making out on a bench near her property," I said slowly. "But why would that make her such a threat?"

"No idea. Unless the woman needed to hide her identity, keep her husband from finding out."

"I found a pair of underwear near the tree. They didn't look like married lady's undies."

Jason raised his eyebrows at this announcement. "Do you inspect a lot of married women's undergarments?"

I screwed up my mouth. "Don't be gross. But I would guess the thong belonged to Tiffany. And I can't imagine why she'd need to keep a liaison with Maxwell secret. Plus, she's got those little stick arms. Could she possibly strangle a grown woman?"

Gordon walked into the room from the hall. "Who got strangled?" Then he noticed Jason had his notebook out, and his face turned a mottled purple. "So the cops are sure that honey lady was murdered?"

Jason stood. "Do you know anything about her death?"

"Nothing," Gordon choked out. "Except Dana here seems to find a dead body everywhere she goes. Makes you wonder."

"Hey!" I jumped to my feet. "What I'm wondering is how you knew the paramedics were at the trailer. You can't see the area from the hot springs."

Jason's grip on his pen tightened as he watched Gordon and me argue, no doubt adding fodder to his story about Queenie.

"Well, I—I," Gordon sputtered, "I won't tolerate these accusations." He stormed past me and down the hall.

Jason touched my arm. "I didn't hear you actually accuse him of anything."

"But he's definitely hiding something," I said.

"The question is what." Jason looked down the hall, as if Gordon would suddenly return and explain his anger.

With his temper, Gordon seemed like a likely candidate to have killed Queenie. But why? And if Queenie's death was tied to Maxwell's, what possible reason did Gordon have to kill him?

"I have to talk to the cops more," Jason said, "but I'll try to stop by later." Jason gave my shoulder a squeeze before walking out the door.

What was happening to my quiet little existence? I felt tears prick the corners of my eyes. Who could be killing people in Blossom Valley?

I returned to the office, needing a moment to myself to process the murder. I absentmindedly scratched the poison oak patch on my arm, my mind unable to settle, the image of Queenie's arm and the inside of her trailer popping up time and time again. Two murders. Impossible.

What did Queenie know about Maxwell's death that had gotten her killed? Was it related to the scripture she'd shouted at me? Man, I wish I'd pushed her more that day, found out what she was talking about. Now the chance was gone. Just like Queenie.

I rose from the chair. Lunch was fast approaching. Serving the guests and listening to them grumble about the food would take my mind off finding Queenie.

In the kitchen, Zennia was cutting a salmon into chunks, the loose sleeves of her blouse dragging through the raw fish at every slice. If the killer didn't get to the rest of the guests, the salmonella might.

"Need any help?" I asked.

Zennia spun around, her grip firm on the cutlery. "Dana, you gave me a heart attack." She set the knife on the cutting board. "I've been on edge since I heard about Queenie's death."

"You already heard about it?"

"My nephew works for the sheriff's department. He called to warn me to be careful."

Did her nephew think we were all in danger now? A shiver ran through me. "But what can we do?"

"Nothing, really. Focus on the guests and pray that detective solves the murders soon." Zennia pointed one scale-covered finger at the bowls on the counter. "You can deliver that gazpacho to the guests, if you'd like."

I grabbed two bowls, glad to have something to do, and swung around into the dining room. I stood in the doorway, gazpacho held aloft, staring at an empty room. Was I early?

I returned to the kitchen and glanced at the clock. Noon on the nose.

Zennia frowned at the bowls in my hand. "Aren't people hungry?"

"There are no people. No one showed up for lunch."

"What?" Zennia snatched the towel off the rack, wiped her hands, and dropped the cloth on the counter. She brushed past me and into the dining room, then reappeared a moment later.

"Still no one?" I asked. "Maybe people are running behind today."

"Everyone?"

Good point. A handful of people might lose track of the time, but not every single guest.

"Maybe they've all heard about Queenie's death already and are watching the police work at her trailer. It'd be just like these people," Zennia said. She gestured toward the counter. "What am I going to do with all this fish? I can't waste this beautiful wild salmon."

"I'll find out what's happening." I walked toward the

lobby. If Gordon was at his usual spot behind the counter, he might know where the guests were.

As I approached the front of the house, loud voices reached my ears.

"I want my money back. Now."

"We're not staying here. We might be killed."

Yikes, the guests had definitely heard the news.

I emerged into the lobby. Esther stood behind the counter, a barrier to the mob of guests who clustered around. Several had suitcases at their feet.

Esther's panicked gaze flitted to me. "Excuse me for a moment," she told the crowd.

One man leaned over the counter and tried to grab her sleeve as she hurried toward me. "I want out of here right this minute," he said.

"I'll help everyone in a second." Esther slipped down the hall in front of me and I followed her. She stopped near the office door.

"Oh, Dana, everyone knows about Queenie's death. They're all demanding refunds." She clutched the front of her blouse. "I'm ruined."

I hugged her, looking over her shoulder toward the empty dining room. Going out of business should be the least of her worries. The bigger question was whether or not the killer was finished.

23

Esther stepped back. "What are we going to do, Dana?" She brushed at her tears, smearing her rouge. "Help me save my farm."

"Can we rent the rooms at half rate?" I asked. "Offer a free night? Run a contest promotion?" Gordon was always spouting off about his genius at running the farm. Where was he with a clipboard of ideas? Off ironing his ties?

Esther twined her fingers together. "Everyone's so angry. I'm afraid to even suggest they stay."

"We have to try. If everyone leaves, can the farm remain open?"

"I don't see how, especially if we give people a full refund," Esther said.

"Then we won't. It's perfectly reasonable to charge guests for the days they've already stayed."

The murmuring from the lobby was increasing in volume. I glanced in that direction, envisioning a crowd of angry villagers marching down the hall, waving torches and pitchforks.

"We need to act right now," I said.

I gripped Esther's arm and practically dragged her back

to the lobby. At the sight of us, the mass of guests moved together and inched toward us.

Esther squirmed out of my grasp and darted behind the counter, as if the flimsy board would protect her.

I held up my hands, noting dirt under my nails from when I'd stumbled at Queenie's trailer. "Everyone, please listen. We'd be happy to accommodate those guests who would like to check out. But first, let me offer you a fantastic deal."

The man who'd tried to grab Esther earlier glared at me. He'd better not try to touch me or I'd poke him in the eye.

"Forget your deals. I want to leave. And I want my money back."

"You're welcome to leave, sir," I said. "But for the rest of you, we'd like to provide the remainder of your stay at half the usual price."

"You can't buy our lives," Mr. Big Mouth said.

"Yeah," a woman in the back yelled. "I'm outta here."

I waited for Esther to take charge as the owner, but she gripped the counter, her eyes open wide, her mouth closed tight.

Guess I'd have to deal with the guests myself. I squeezed past her to reach the computer. "All right, form a single line and we'll get you out of here as quick as possible. We'll charge for the nights you stayed, but anyone who prepaid will get a refund for any additional nights, no penalty for checking out early."

More murmuring ensued as people shuffled into place. After a moment, a ragged line snaked from the counter to the front door. First up was Mr. Big Mouth.

"I've never heard of such nonsense," he said, "having to pay after something so shocking."

"Did you enjoy your stay up until this morning?" I asked.

He scowled at me as he signed his credit card slip.

"I should get a full refund. Being chased off by a killer like this."

"I'm sorry your stay ended with an unexpected death. Of a stranger," I added. "Here's a copy of your receipt." I glanced over his shoulder and made eye contact with the petite blonde behind him. "Could I help the next guest please?"

Mr. Big Mouth picked up his suitcase and barged for the door, bumping into several guests on his way out. The door swung shut behind him and the tension in the room dropped a notch.

Considering most of the guests had checked in to be close to the site where the famous Maxwell Mendelsohn was murdered, they sure were in a hurry to leave now. Guess they hadn't bargained on a second death.

I made short work of the remaining clients until only one guest remained. After I'd completed the paperwork, I carried her duffel bag to her car while she wheeled her suitcase.

When I returned to the lobby, Esther still stood behind the counter, her eyes glazed, almost as if she were in a trance. I waved a hand in front of her. "Esther?"

She blinked several times. "Why did everyone leave?"

Because two people were dead? Because one murder was sensational but two were scary?

Gordon strode into the lobby from the hall, clipboard in hand, a few burrs still sticking to his pants cuffs. I hadn't seen him since our little exchange in front of Jason and my stomach tightened at the memory.

"Where are the lunch diners?" he asked Esther.

Esther opened her mouth to speak and burst into tears.

"Get a grip on yourself, woman." He turned to me. "What the hell's going on?"

Gee, this guy was all heart.

"Most guests checked out after hearing about Queenie's death," I said.

Gordon slapped a hand on the counter. "And you let them go?"

"I offered a discount, but no one was interested." Thanks to Mr. Big Mouth.

"You should have insisted. Kept them here until you convinced them."

I swept my arm around, indicating the lobby. "We're a spa, not a prison. If people want to leave, they can."

"You blew it this time, Lewis," Gordon snarled.

I felt my hands curl into fists, every muscle in my arms tense. "Me? Where were you? Your job is to man this desk and handle the guests."

A hand settled on my arm and I glanced at Esther. Tears still pooled along her lower lids.

"Please stop," she whispered. "I can't stand the fighting."

My anger immediately dissipated and I uncurled my fingers. "Sorry, I'm upset about the loss to the farm."

Esther sniffed. "Me, too."

"If you women can get hold of your emotions," Gordon said, his upper lip curled in disgust, "we can assess the damage. Everyone couldn't have checked out."

I bristled at his comments, but now wasn't the time to engage in a war on sexism. "A few are still here," I said.

"We'll focus on convincing them to stay."

"How? Gift certificates to local restaurants?" I ticked off the ideas on my fingers. "A guided tour of the trails? Or one of us could drive everyone to Mendocino for whale watching."

"Good ideas," Gordon said.

Did he just compliment me?

"I can rent a limo," he continued. "Really glam it up. Let me see who the remaining guests are and I'll make some calls."

Esther stood silent during our little exchange, in that trance-like state again. Sometimes I wished she'd stiffen up and take charge, considering her farm was at stake.

"Esther," I said, "we need to keep running the farm like it's a full house. Did Heather clean the rooms this morning? I don't remember seeing her."

"She has a custody hearing today." She blinked twice. "Dana, could you help me clean the rooms?"

The idea of scrubbing floors and laying out fresh sheets sounded soothing for some reason. But if I opened a door and found another body, I'd be leaving almost as fast as Mr. Big Mouth. "Let's get the equipment."

Gordon stepped over to the computer as Esther and I walked down the hall to the laundry room. The maid's cart sat waiting, the bottles full of cleaner. I pushed the cart out of the house and onto the path while Esther followed with the vacuum cleaner. The wheels on the vacuum rattled down the cement path, but Esther and I were the only people around to hear the sound.

We stopped at the row of cabins. Some guests had been in such a hurry to leave that they'd left their room doors open, adding to the air of desertion. I looked at the handful of doors still closed, wondering if the cabins were occupied.

Esther stepped on the vacuum base to release the handle. "I'll vacuum the first room while you clean the second, then we'll switch. How does that sound?"

"Fine." I grabbed a spray bottle and rag from the cart and stepped up to the closed door. I raised my hand to knock, then stopped, my pulse quickening. What if another dead body was waiting for me? How much more of this could I take? I stared at the wooden door, frozen.

"Dana?" Esther said.

I snapped my head in her direction.

"Everything all right?" she asked.

I nodded, feeling foolish. I knocked at the cabin, then entered the room while Esther knocked on the one next door. Sure enough, no dead body. I stripped the bed, remade it with clean sheets, and went to retrieve the dirty towels from the bathroom.

No towels. People actually stole hotel towels? Tacky, tacky, tacky.

Esther and I alternated cleaning the next few cabins. I knocked on the sixth cabin and called out, "Housekeeping." The door opened and I backed up a step in surprise.

"Sheila," I said. "I didn't realize you were in your room. I'll come back."

She seized my arm and yanked me inside, almost making me drop my bottle of cleaner.

"Dana, tell me what's going on. Was someone else really murdered?"

"Afraid so."

Sheila sank onto the couch. "My God, another guest?"

"No, a woman over on the next property. Her death probably isn't related to the farm. She'd spent time in prison, apparently."

"Did she just get out? Did someone finally get the chance to kill her?"

"Well, she was released a couple of years ago."

Sheila fiddled with the charm on her earring. "So her prison stay had nothing to do with her death."

I switched the cleaner bottle from one hand to the other, knowing my theory was a stretch. "Maybe whoever killed her just got paroled. They had to wait to get revenge."

Sheila looked about as convinced as I felt. She plucked at her sarong. "I want to stay, but I'm scared."

I sat down on the other end of the couch. "Go with your gut." As an employee of the spa, I should probably have given her a laundry list of why this was the best place ever, but what if something happened to her? What if the killer wasn't done?

"I'm not here strictly for the relaxation," she said.

What then? Zennia's food? A chance to catch poison oak? I scratched the rash on my arm at the thought.

A flush crept up Sheila's neck and I recalled Jason's comment from last night. "Are you talking about Christian?"

Sheila put a hand to her throat. "You won't tell, will you? I don't want to get him in trouble."

So Jason was right. I leaned toward her and rested my hand on the couch cushion. "Esther does have a no-dating policy between guests and employees, but you're both adults and I don't see the harm."

She reached over and squeezed my hand. "Thank you. He's such a wonderful man. I think we have a future together."

Her relationship with Christian might be the real reason she'd rejected Maxwell's advances. "Have you two been dating long?"

Sheila blushed a deeper shade of red. "We met at the opening night party. I'm sure I sound like a love-struck teenager, but we had an instant connection. At my age, you act on these impulses. They don't happen very often."

Age had nothing to do with it. I was half Sheila's age, and that sudden spark with a guy was just as rare.

"So you definitely weren't interested in Maxwell, then."

Sheila pressed her lips together, her eyes narrowing. Then she noticed me watching her and forced her face to relax.

"Absolutely not." She rotated her bracelet around her wrist, fingering the beads. "Like I said, he tried to bribe me with that necklace, but I recognized all of Maxwell's tricks. He couldn't manipulate me like he used to. I shut him down good."

Shut him down with a knife thrust to the belly?

A knock sounded on the door. "Housekeeping." I recognized Esther's voice and inwardly groaned at the interruption.

I rose from the couch. "Guess I'd better finish my rounds." I spritzed the mirror on the dresser as Esther entered.

"Goodness, Dana," she said. "We don't usually clean the rooms with the guests in them."

"I told her to come in," Sheila said. "I was on my way out."

"Of course," Esther said. "I should have known better."

Sheila slipped on her mules and walked out the door, giving me a little wave when Esther was busy with the vacuum.

I made quick work of the bed and moved into the bathroom to wipe down the counters. Esther switched off the vacuum and carried in a stack of clean towels.

"Did Sheila ask about the murder?" she asked.

I scrubbed a spot on the mirror. "She heard about Queenie. She's worried about her own safety now."

Esther lowered her voice, although we were alone. "I know Gordon wants us to press the guests into staying, but I can't. Queenie's death has me so nervous, I jump when the pigs snort too loud. I can't lie to the guests and tell them everything's right as rain."

"I hear ya." Sheila would probably stay, but no thanks to any effort on my part.

I wiped down the toilet and then loaded the cleaning supplies into the cart. As I dropped a bottle of cleaner into its slot, Esther wheeled the vacuum from the room. Without a word, we walked straight past Maxwell's cabin and on to the next one.

Esther finished cleaning while I was still pulling on fresh pillowcases.

"See you in the next cabin," she said and pushed the vacuum out the door.

I moved into the bathroom and stepped over the pile of dirty towels on the floor. I was pretty sure this was Logan's room, having seen a closet full of khakis and white dress shirts.

I shoved his bottles of hair spray, gel, and smoother to one side to spray cleaner on the counter. Logan's Black-Berry sat behind a can of Aquanet. My heart rate picked up. Now was my chance to find out who Logan was always texting.

Grabbing the BlackBerry before I lost my nerve, I pushed a button. The screen sprang to life, a cursor blinking in the password box. Uh-oh. I hadn't expected the phone to be locked. What would Logan's password be?

I typed *Hollywood*.

An error message appeared.

Production.

Nothing. Well, crap. My one chance to do a little spying in a guest's room was disappearing faster than the guests.

As I started to type *Money*, I heard a key in the lock and froze. The sound of bird chatter and the far-off hum of farm machinery increased in volume as someone opened the door, then decreased. I heard the latch of the closed door snap into place.

"Hello?"

No answer.

"Esther?" A little louder this time.

Silence.

Who was out there?

Had he come for me?

24

I silently set the BlackBerry on the counter and snatched up the spray bottle. Holding my breath, I tiptoed from the bathroom. I sensed movement to my left and swung around, finger convulsing on the bottle trigger.

"*Aaa!*" Logan threw his hands up, swiping at the mist on his face and dropping his iPod, the ear buds flying from his head.

"Oh, no!" I grabbed a cloth with my free hand and tried to wipe his face.

Logan seized the material and threw it on the floor. He squinted at me. "What the hell is wrong with you?"

"I'm so sorry. I didn't know who was walking in here."

"I used my key. This is my cabin. Who else would it be?"

I gestured uselessly with the arm holding the sprayer. "Guess I'm on edge."

Logan's eyes teared up, no doubt a residual effect from my spritz of cleaner.

"So what they were saying at the Daily Grind is true? Some lady was killed around here?"

I picked the cloth off the floor and crumpled it in my hand. "Afraid so."

Logan glanced at his Louis Vuitton suitcase in the

corner. It must have cost him a month's salary. I guess if Maxwell was going to insist he wear khakis and white shirts, Logan needed to spend his money on something.

"I'm out," he said.

"You sure? Gordon was going to drive a limo over to Mendocino for some whale watching." I felt lame telling him, like a used car salesman who knows he's lost the deal but throws pathetic offers out there anyway.

Logan grunted. "I'll pass, thanks. No offense, but this spa is boring. I only stayed because the room was prepaid."

"You and Maxwell didn't strike me as spa aficionados."

"Not even close." Logan walked to the closet and pulled a dress shirt off its hanger. He tossed it on the couch and reached for the next shirt. "This whole trip was Maxwell's grand scheme to woo his ex-wife."

"Wait. This was planned? He didn't decide to reconcile after accidentally bumping into her here?"

Logan stripped the shirt off the hanger. "Maxwell left nothing to fate. He always had a plan. A mutual friend mentioned that Sheila would be coming here, and next thing I knew, he had me call for reservations and buy some overpriced necklace to wrap up." He tossed the last shirt on the couch, opened his suitcase on the coffee table, and began stuffing in the clothes.

I resisted the urge to pull the shirts back out and fold them. "Did he think he could win her back so easily?"

"Like I said, once he spotted a goal, he went all out. If he hadn't been killed, I'm sure he and Sheila would be engaged by now." Logan moved to the dresser, pulled open the top drawer, and tossed a stack of underwear into the case.

Sounded like Maxwell liked to bully people into agreeing with him. But Sheila was dating Christian now. How would she have responded to Maxwell's pressure to get back together, especially if she had anger-management issues? "Somehow I doubt Sheila would have agreed to date him again."

Logan moved past me and into the bathroom. "We'll never know," he called back. He walked back out, Black-Berry in hand. He studied the screen, then frowned at me.

I pasted on my most innocent smile and crossed my fingers. He looked at the screen again, stuffed the phone into his shirt pocket, and went back into the bathroom. I let out a sigh.

He returned with a load of bottles and tubes in his hands, dumped them on top of the underwear, and zipped the suitcase shut. "All done."

"I'll walk you to the office," I said, trying to think of any last minute questions I could ask.

"Say, I never found out where you were when Maxwell was killed," I said. Maybe a direct question would shock him into answering.

"That's because it's none of your business," he said, not bothering to look at me.

So much for that plan.

"Do the police know you're leaving? They might need your help."

Logan didn't even break stride. "They have my contact info."

We made our way past the deserted pool area with its empty lounge chairs.

"Won't you be saying good-bye to Tiffany?" I asked as a last ditch effort to delay his departure. "I thought you two hit it off."

Logan shifted his suitcase to his other hand. "Tiffany's a sweet kid, but she's not for me."

I was pretty sure that was a guy's way of saying he'd struck out, but I didn't press the point.

We arrived at the front office where Gordon frowned at

the computer. When he saw Logan, he hit the charm switch to his personality, his face aglow with a smile.

He smoothed back his hair. "Logan, one of our faithful customers, how nice to see you." He eyed the suitcase. "Please don't tell me you're leaving us. I've got a wonderful whale-watching trip lined up. Why didn't you tell him, Dana?"

"She did. But I'm not much of a whale guy."

Gordon pressed his palms together as if praying Logan would fall for his pitch. "My good man, we'll be doing much more than whale watching. Lunch at Le Poelon, sweets from the Mendocino Chocolate Company, shopping at the Artists' Co-op."

Logan shook his head. "I've got a long drive back to L.A. and I need to get going."

"Did Dana tell you about our half-price room rate?"

"My room's already paid for." Logan set his suitcase on the floor. "I want to go home."

Gordon glared at me, like I'd convinced Logan to leave.

"He heard about Queenie," I said.

"I can assure you her death is not connected to this farm in any way," Gordon said, sounding a bit desperate.

"Doesn't matter," Logan said. "I'm ready to go."

Gordon banged his fingers on the keyboard for a few seconds and the printer spit out a page. He snatched it from the tray. "You'll need to sign out."

Logan grabbed the pen from its holder.

"Have a safe drive home," I told him. "Please come back and stay again." Unless, of course, he'd killed Maxwell. Then he could stay away forever.

"Don't keep a room vacant on my account," Logan said and walked out the front door.

Gordon folded up the paper, grumbling under his breath, and I walked down the hall. Esther and I had cleaned the rooms, no one waited for meals to be served, and I'd written my blog. Now what?

As I passed the open door of the office, I heard a quiet sobbing and poked my head in. Esther sat at the desk, elbows on the surface, handkerchief in hand, blotting her eyes. She saw me and tried to smile, her lips twisting into a grimace.

"Dana, sorry for the waterworks."

I placed a hand on her shoulder. "This whole thing will blow over."

"Two murders? In a pig's eye." She sniffed. "Do we have any guests left?"

"Sheila is here, and I don't believe Tiffany has checked out either."

Esther set the handkerchief down. "They will."

"Let's not give up yet," I said, though even I had to admit the future looked bleak. I glanced around the room, noting the cheery needlepoint landscape scene on the wall, the framed picture of her late husband. The farm couldn't close now, not so soon. "Anything I can help with?"

Esther gestured to an empty cardboard box at her feet. "Maxwell's production company, Galaxy Creations, called me a bit ago. Really, those company lawyers called. With Maxwell working on a movie when he died, the company is worried about someone stealing their ideas. What was that word? Proper? Popular?"

"Proprietary?" I offered. At least that was the word in all those confidentiality agreements I'd constantly had to sign at my last job. We'd had to take an entire class on guarding company secrets, how corporate spies were everywhere, especially at the local bars where office workers frequented.

Esther nodded. "That's the one. Now, they want Maxwell's things quicker than a jackrabbit. I'm trying to build up the courage to walk over to his cabin. I know the police took his body away days ago, but what if his spirit is waiting for me?"

I picked up the box. "I'll take care of his belongings. I'm not a big believer in ghosts."

"I don't know what I'd do without you, Dana." She glanced at her husband's picture, reminding me of Mom always looking at Dad's picture. Hopefully both women would find their way again soon.

I walked toward the door and turned. "You're sure the police have finished with Maxwell's room?" I wasn't exactly eager to pack up a dead guy's belongings, but at least I didn't have to wear hip boots or stick my hands under chickens to complete the task.

Esther nodded. "Yep, all done. Leave the box here in the office, and I'll label it when I get back."

"No problem."

Walking across the hall and out the dining room door, I couldn't help but note the silence on the back patio. With no people swimming or lounging by the pool, the place appeared deserted, ready to close down. I shook off the sense of desolation and let myself into Maxwell's room; the police tape no longer stretched across the door.

The mattress sat bare, stripped of linens. The dresser top and coffee table held traces of powder, probably from the police fingerprinting the area. They'd probably cleared out anything related to the murder, but at least I could snoop around while I packed.

Five Tommy Bahama shirts and three pairs of slacks hung in the closet. A pair of penny loafers sat on the floor. I placed the shoes in the box, then pulled the clothes from the hangers and folded them before placing them on top of the shoes. A check of the dresser revealed only a single stack of undergarments, not exactly earth shattering. Either the police had taken most items with them or Maxwell traveled light. Only his bathroom toiletries, his laptop, a small printer, and his yoga book remained to be packed.

Surely, Galaxy Creations didn't want Maxwell's disposable razor and half-filled tube of toothpaste returned. The laptop probably held the only items of interest for the company, and I was surprised the police hadn't confiscated it. Guess they didn't believe info on his hard drive was connected to his death. I swept everything from the bathroom counter into the trash and prepared to add his yoga book to the box but stopped.

Back when I'd been working in San Jose, I'd attended yoga classes at the gym. Once I'd lost my job, exercising in an air-conditioned room full of televisions felt decadent, and I'd cancelled my membership. I'd been tempted to join Christian and his students in their yoga poses and Pilates moves, but mingling with the guests was not exactly professional. Of course, with only Sheila left, I could now get semiprivate lessons.

I flipped through the book, glancing at the glossy shots of the yoga master in the Boat and Spider poses. I read snippets from the middle of the book as the author explained that yoga is not a religion but rather a discipline, how the goal is to unite a person's consciousness with the universal consciousness.

What was I doing? I should be focusing on Maxwell's killer, not yoga philosophy. I wasn't going to find any clues in a book. I started to swing it shut when folded papers at the back caught my eye.

What was this? A clue after all?

I unfolded the sheets, three in all. The top paper was a printout of an e-mail to Logan saying that Nathaniel Wilcox of Tiger Shark Studios had received Logan's résumé and would be considering his request for employment. Wilcox had entered Maxwell's name in the blind carbon copy field. The e-mail was dated the day of his death.

Apparently, Wilcox respected Maxwell enough to let him know about his less-than-loyal employee. Had this been the reason Maxwell was so angry before yoga? Not because he'd thought Heather was going to steal the necklace but because Logan was leaving him for a rival studio? That would explain why Maxwell hadn't told Logan why he was so upset.

I slipped that paper to the back and focused on the second page. It appeared to be a contract of some kind. I scanned that sheet and the next one, which ended with signatures from Maxwell and Logan, dated roughly six months earlier. Logan had mentioned he'd worked for Maxwell for about that long. I didn't understand all the legalese in the contract, but the gist appeared to be that while Logan was under Maxwell's employment, anything Logan produced relating to the movie industry was automatically the property of Galaxy Creations Studios.

Could that be right? I'd heard of similar stipulations at computer companies from a software engineering friend, but didn't realize it extended to the movie industry. But the e-mail and the contract stored together in the back of the book couldn't be a coincidence. After Maxwell had scorned Logan's screenplay, would he stop Logan from pitching it elsewhere once he found out Logan was quitting?

And what did it have to do with Maxwell's murder? Or Queenie's?

Logan had left as soon as Queenie's body had been discovered, ostensibly to drive back to L.A. But maybe he'd kept going, all the way to Mexico.

Had the police—had *I*—let the killer escape?

25

I read the e-mail about Logan applying to Tiger Shark Studios again, but the words told me nothing new.

Bet Detective Caffrey would like to see these papers. Of course, he'd told me not to meddle. And how embarrassing that the police had missed the papers when they'd searched the room. Would Detective Caffrey accuse me of suppressing evidence, suggest I'd found the notes earlier and hidden them? Maybe I'd keep this info quiet for a bit. At least until I had a chance to talk to Logan myself. Like, right now.

I stuck the notes in my pocket and the book in the box. I'd come back for the box later. First I needed to track down Logan, find out if Maxwell could really lay claim to his screenplay. Would Logan fight it in court? Could he even afford to on an assistant's salary? Murder might be a lot easier and cheaper to free himself from the contract. With a last look around the room, I pulled the door shut and made my way down the path.

Back in the main house, I went straight to the front desk, where Gordon jotted notes in the ledger, waiting behind the counter for all those guests who weren't showing up.

Without preamble, I asked, "Did Logan mention stopping anywhere on his way out of town? I don't recall him saying anything."

Gordon kept writing for a moment, never one to hurry when I was the one waiting. He finally raised his head. "Not that I know of. Why do you want to know?"

"I, uh." I stopped. I what? Wanted to accuse him of murder? Find out if he had a valid motive to kill his boss? "I just boxed up Maxwell's stuff and thought he could take it back with him, save Esther the shipping charges." I patted myself on the back for thinking up such a quick lie. Wait—was that a good thing?

"He must be well out of town by now."

Gordon was probably right. "Maybe he stopped for a bite first. If you could give me the contact number out of his reservation file, I'll give him a quick ring."

"Total waste of time, if you ask me."

I shrugged and gave Gordon my most disarming smile. "Can't hurt to try."

Grumbling under his breath, Gordon moved to the computer and punched a few keys. He squinted at the screen and jotted something on the tablet of paper in front of the keyboard. He tore off the sheet and handed it to me.

"I'm assuming this is his number, but the reservation was under Maxwell's name, so I can't be certain."

Great. Maxwell's phone had been next to him when I'd found his body. My luck, the phone was still in police evidence and when I called, Detective Caffrey would answer. How would I explain the call when I wasn't supposed to be meddling?

I took the paper. "Thanks." I rushed down the hall, certain that Logan was long gone but not ready to give up completely. I plunked down in the chair, snatched up the receiver, and punched in the number, crossing my fingers that Caffrey wouldn't be on the other end. After three rings, I recognized the click as I was transferred to voice mail and let out my pent-up breath as Logan's voice came over the line.

"Yo, it's Logan. Leave a message."

As the beep sounded, I mentally slapped myself for not preparing what I was going to say. I stumbled through the message. "Logan, hi, it's Dana, you know, from the spa. The O'Connell Farm and Spa, that is. Well, what other spa would it be?" I let out a weak laugh and felt my face flush. "Anyway, I had a question regarding your stay here and need you to give me a call." I rattled off my cell phone number and slammed the receiver down.

Lamest message ever. But maybe I'd been vague enough to pique Logan's curiosity. I'd try his number again later to cover all the bases.

As I turned in the chair, Esther walked down the hall past the open office door, then popped back. Her face was devoid of makeup, her eyes red like she'd been crying. "Dana, I'm calling a staff meeting. See if you can round up the others. We'll meet on the patio."

A staff meeting. A lead weight sat in my belly. Esther wasn't usually so official. Whatever she wanted to tell us couldn't bode well for my future employment. Or the fate of the farm.

I popped back into the lobby, where Gordon still stood at the computer. I'd love to know what he did all day, always looking so official with his ledgers and clipboards.

"Any luck with Logan?" he asked.

"No, guess I'll have to ship the box. But Esther wants everyone on the back patio for a staff meeting. Pronto."

"What the hell does Esther know about staff meetings?"

"She is the boss, you know. See you there." I hurried down the hall, looking for the others.

Zennia sat at the kitchen table, shelling peas, wearing

her cow apron. The bowl in front of her was half full of the green balls. A bowl beside it held the empty pods.

"Staff meeting, back patio," I said.

"Why is Gordon calling a staff meeting?"

"Not Gordon. Esther."

A crease formed on Zennia's forehead and she dropped the pod in the bowl. "Be right there."

I walked out the back door to find Christian. The pool and surrounding chaises were still empty. Not surprising with no guests. Esther sat on a bench at one of the wooden picnic tables, head bowed. As I made my way to the cabins, I glanced over my shoulder and saw Gordon step out of the dining room and join her.

I rounded the corner to the cabins and stopped outside Sheila's door. If Christian wasn't at the main house or the general pool area, perhaps he was with Sheila. I chanted a quick prayer that I wouldn't find them flagrante delicto, then knocked.

"Hello? Anyone there?"

Voices murmured behind the wood and the door opened. Christian stood shirtless before me, and I tried not to ogle his six-pack.

He froze in the doorway, like a ground squirrel that's seen a hawk and is too far from his burrow. "Dana, I was teaching Sheila some meditation techniques."

I didn't have time to deal with the little soap opera when Christian discovered I knew about his relationship with Sheila, so I got right to the point. "Esther's called a staff meeting. Everyone's waiting on the patio."

"Is the farm closing down?" he asked.

My question exactly. "I don't know, but we'd better hurry," I said, "or people will wonder what's taking so long."

"I'll be back later to finish those meditation studies,"

Christian told Sheila. He slipped a tank top over his head and followed me down the path.

"Sheila told me about that woman's death," Christian said. "We'll definitely need to offer our support to Esther. I'm not sure she can save this place now."

We arrived at the picnic table where Gordon, Esther, and Zennia waited on one side. Christian and I sat down on the other.

Gordon made a show of looking at his watch. "About time."

Leave it to Gordon to make a big deal out of three minutes of waiting.

"My apologies, everyone," Christian said. "I was enjoying nature. Centering my thoughts in these terrible times."

Gordon rolled his eyes. "Whatever. Let's get this meeting done with."

Esther patted Gordon's hand. Even if he had lost his own hotel business, Esther was much too tolerant of the guy.

"As you've all heard by now, we're down to two guests," she said.

"Don't forget the reservations for this coming week," Gordon said.

"I expect once Queenie's death hits the major news stations, those people will cancel faster than you can say fiddledeedee."

Gordon slapped the table, and I jumped. "Not if we get moving now. Dana can write a release for the local papers, post some specials on our Web site."

"We could angle it toward a couple's retreat," I said. "Offer a room-service breakfast, champagne and chocolates in the evenings."

Esther slid off the end of the bench and began pacing the patio. "Champagne might make me tipsy, but it wouldn't let me forget I was staying at a spa where two people have died."

"Only one person has died at the spa. Queenie was over on her own property," I said.

"But the guests don't see it that way," Esther said. "And with no guests, I'm afraid I can't employ you all full-time."

My breath caught in my throat and I looked at the others. Two sets of wide eyes and one set of narrowed eyes looked back at me.

"Which one of us is getting the ax?" asked Gordon, owner of the narrowed eyes.

"I'm not firing anyone." Esther settled back down on the edge of the bench. "Instead, everyone can work part time, at least for the next few days until we figure out whether we'll have any guests left." She looked at Zennia. "I can handle breakfast and lunch for two people. You'll be in charge of afternoon snacks and dinners."

"I can prep the veggies in the evening to shorten your work on the lunches," Zennia said.

Esther shifted her gaze. "Christian, I'll cut your classes to two a day, both in the morning."

"One Pilates, one yoga. Got it," Christian said.

Now her look fell on me. "Dana, work half days for your blog and other tasks. You can pick your hours."

"Fine," I said. If my work time was being cut, I might need to arrange my hours around the second job I'd be forced to get.

She had saved Gordon for last. I noticed the hand resting on the tabletop trembled a bit. "Gordon, you'll need to cut your hours as well."

"Don't think you're getting rid of me," Gordon said. He stood up, hands balled on the table.

"Now don't get your knickers in a twist," Esther said.

An image of Gordon in old-fashioned underwear

flashed into my mind, but I blocked it out. Now was not the time to laugh.

"My role," he hissed, "is to keep this farm afloat. You can't possibly run this place alone."

Esther rose from her place on the bench and faced Gordon. I heard Zennia gasp and felt Christian stiffen beside me.

"My husband and I ran this farm long before you showed up. I appreciate your help but I won't tolerate your sass anymore."

I held my breath, sure he'd internally combust, flip the table over, kill a chicken with his bare hands, drown me in the pool.

Instead, he turned and stomped into the house, hands in fists at his side, like a five-year-old whose mom wouldn't buy him a Happy Meal.

I watched his back until he'd passed through the dining room doorway. Gordon always seemed angry and suspicious of the world, lugging around a backpack full of bitterness. Had he killed Maxwell in a rage? Whenever anyone called him on his attitude, he backed down, but maybe he'd exploded with Maxwell. And what about Queenie? I still didn't know how he'd seen the emergency vehicles from the farm.

"I'm sorry about that," Esther said. Her lower lip trembled. "I don't like to argue with my staff. Or in front of them."

Zennia gripped her hand. "Gordon is too combative. I've offered him ashwagandha root, a known soul soother, but he refuses to recognize his problem."

Esther fingered a button on her shirt. "He has such passion for this farm, such vision. And now it's going under, just like his bed and breakfast." She looked around the table. "Meeting adjourned." She remained on the bench, staring at the wood surface.

Christian headed back toward the cabins, and I walked into the house, Zennia right behind.

"Want me to fix you an early dinner?" she asked. "I know you didn't have a chance to eat lunch."

"No thanks. I'll stop for Chicken McNuggets on my way home." Mom probably had a healthy meal planned, but after the day I'd had, I deserved something yummy and heart stopping.

Zennia groaned. "How can you possibly eat those? Did you know McNuggets and Play-Doh share a common ingredient? Dimethylpolysiloxane."

"I haven't eaten Play-Doh since I was three. Maybe I should give it another try."

Zennia gave me a playful shove into the hallway.

I stopped by the office to update my time sheet, then hopped in my car. After a quick stop at the drive-thru, I pulled up to the house.

Ashlee met me at the front door and snatched my take-out bag from my hand. "Dana, you poor thing. How are you? Let me help you with that."

I reached for my sack of processed chicken parts, but she'd whisked it away, along with herself. Plates clacked, the bag rustled. By the time I reached the kitchen, Ashlee had placed the carton and sauce container on a plate and set the meal on the table.

She rearranged the oranges and bananas in the ever-present fruit bowl, wiped a few stray crumbs off the table, and stepped back. "You'd probably rather eat in front of the TV." She lifted the plate from the table and moved toward the living room.

"I can carry my own dinner."

I made a grab for my cooling chicken, but she twisted around and kept walking.

"Nonsense. You've had a hard day." She set the plate on

the coffee table and placed the remote control next to it. "Anything to drink?"

Had aliens invaded Ashlee's body? Where was my real sister? "Mom? You here? Mom?"

Ashlee plucked at my sleeve. "Sit down. I'll get Mom."

"Are you all right?" I asked her.

She gripped my shoulders and practically pushed me into the recliner. "You're the one who isn't all right. Please, eat. I'll take care of everything. And when you're done eating, you can tell me about Queenie's death. You know people will be asking me."

Ah, so the extra attention was Ashlee's way of buttering me up for information.

Mom appeared from down the hall. "Dana, I'm so glad you're home. What a horrible day. How are you?"

"Why does everyone keep asking me that?"

"Martha from my bunco group called a while ago to tell us about Queenie," she said. "You can't keep finding dead bodies like that."

"I'm not doing it on purpose."

Ashlee took my plate. "I'll reheat these in the microwave."

"I can't imagine what you must be feeling," Mom said. "Another death, such a shock."

When Ashlee returned, she carried the chicken, plus my slippers. "Thought you might be more comfortable." She set the plate on the table again and the slippers by my feet.

"Stop that. You're freaking me out."

"Dana, your sister knows you must be upset about these deaths. She's trying to be supportive."

I slipped off my sandals and stuck my feet in the slippers. "Happy?"

"It's not me I'm worried about," Ashlee said.

The doorbell rang and I practically knocked Mom

down on my way to the door. Probably the UPS guy, but I'd welcome any disruption in this *Twilight Zone* scene.

Jason stood on the doorstep, the evening sun highlighting the red in his hair. I smoothed down an eyebrow with an index finger, not that one smooth eyebrow would do any good with the rest of me in a jumble.

"I wanted to stop by and see how you're doing."

I grabbed his arm. "I'm glad you're here. Would you like to come in?" I pictured Ashlee giggling and drooling all over him and regretted my offer.

"I don't have time, thanks. The paper's putting out an extra edition because of the murder."

"Do the police have any more information?"

Jason glanced past me into the house. "Not sure how much I should say. Don't want you scooping my scoop, so to speak."

I took him by the elbow and guided him down the walk toward his car, out of earshot of Mom and Ashlee.

"Please, I need to know if the police are close to an arrest. The spa is in serious trouble. I could be out of a job, and Esther might lose her dream."

Jason rubbed his goatee. "They've narrowed the time of death to between ten and midnight. And she was strangled with the netting on her beekeeper veil."

"But no idea why? Or who?"

"Not yet. But don't give up hope." He wrapped an arm around my back and I momentarily laid my head on his shoulder, enjoying the warmth. He pulled out his car keys. "I've got a story to write. But promise me you'll be careful."

I felt a chill, and I was pretty sure it wasn't because Jason had removed his arm from my shoulder. "What do you mean?"

"Those two deaths have to be connected. And you've

found both bodies. The killer might wonder if he left behind any clues. If you found anything you weren't supposed to."

"But I didn't. I don't know anything." My voice squeaked as I spoke.

Jason opened his car door. "Doesn't matter. He might come after you next."

26

After a night of staring at the ceiling and listening for any unusual floorboard creaks, thanks to Jason's warning, I awoke to a minor headache and a major bad mood. The smell of fake eggs simmering in a coating of non-stick fake cooking spray didn't help.

"Want some eggs, Dana?" Mom asked, more chipper than Barney the Dinosaur.

"Just toast." I wrenched two slices out of the bag. Were those sprouts in my bread? "I really need some white bread."

"Nonsense. This brand is full of fiber. Good for digestion."

"You sound like Zennia."

Mom slid her eggs onto a plate. "I should meet this Zennia. She could give me some healthy cooking tips."

"No." Having Zennia teach Mom about wheatgrass and fish granules was not an option.

"My goodness, but you're surly this morning."

I pulled the toast from the toaster, singeing my fingertips, and smeared I Can't Believe It's Not Butter across the surface, crumbs falling in a heap as I attacked the bread with the knife.

"Got a lot on my mind." I slapped the bread on a plate and stalked off to the living room.

Since Esther had given me the option of setting my own half-day schedule, I spent the morning sorting through the rest of the boxes I'd brought home from San Jose. Call me superstitious, but I'd left a stack in the corner of my bedroom, untouched, somehow believing that if I opened the final boxes, it meant I was never leaving home again. Now, I unwrapped the picture frames and glass figurines and set them on my dresser top, telling myself the situation was only temporary.

With the boxes emptied and broken down for recycling, I threw together a turkey sandwich, eating at the counter, and then drove to the farm. Only three cars sat in the lot. For a moment, I felt like I'd flashed back in time to last week, with Esther and the rest of us waiting for opening weekend. But no, opening weekend had come and gone and so had most of the guests.

Gordon sat at the computer in the office, his suit jacket draped over the back of the chair. His greased hair gleamed in the lights as he studied the screen with a frown.

"How are the reservations today?" I asked.

"Cancelled. We've still got three couples lined up, but they probably haven't heard about the second murder yet."

Lord, the farm was truly going out of business.

"I thought about marketing angles last night," I said. "We could have two approaches. First, make the place a family day-trip destination. Offer classes on pig tying or conduct chicken races. Let kids pick their own vegetables. On the other side, we could ratchet up the spa services for the yuppie crowd, advertise in the health and wellness magazines."

Gordon grunted. "Not bad. But that doesn't help us today. I'm working with the meat and toiletry suppliers, trying to get a discount. Shouldn't be more than a few minutes and then you can have the computer."

"I'll come back." I wandered out the back door and through the herb garden, inhaling the scent of dill. The midday temperature was already too warm, and on its way to getting hotter. I should have worn shorts again today, instead of my jeans.

At the pigsty, I leaned over the rail and patted Wilbur's head. He oinked in return.

"Don't be mad if I tie up your feet," I told him. "I'm only doing it for Esther. And to keep you and your buddies well-fed."

Behind me, the click-clack of heels sounded on the pavement. Tiffany tottered toward me in a minidress, her blond hair piled on her head, a large satchel in one hand.

"Didn't realize you were still here," I said when she stopped at the sty.

She dropped the bag on the ground. "I'll be leaving as soon as my ride gets here." Another suspect taking off, and nothing I could do to stop her. Would I find incriminating information about her after she left, like I had with Logan?

Wilbur nuzzled my fingers with his slimy snout and I moved my hand away, wiping the snot on my jeans. I'd better say something if I wanted to gather any last information. "You didn't drive yourself up?"

"No, tagged along with a buddy heading up to Oregon. He's coming back tomorrow, but I want to get the hell out of here, so I called one of my friends."

"I'm surprised you didn't catch a ride with Logan."

"Believe me, I would have if I'd known he was leaving."

"Think you'll get in touch with him once you get back home? I noticed you two were getting awful close."

Tiffany tilted her head. "Logan's gay, you know."

I blinked. News to me. Guess my gaydar was broken, not that I had one. "Then why were you two looking so cozy the last couple of days?"

Tiffany tugged at her hem. Maybe if she bought longer skirts, she wouldn't tug at them all the time.

"Sometimes it's nice to talk to a guy who you know doesn't want to sleep with you."

Was this the same girl who'd planned to boink Maxwell for a movie role?

Then she winked at me. "But don't worry, I had a whole lot of fun while I was here."

Fun at a spa where a man suffered a violent death? Tiffany was whacked.

Clucking from the nearby coop brought to mind the mysterious note I'd found on Maxwell's nightstand the day of his death. "Did you leave a note in Maxwell's room, asking him to meet you behind the chicken yard?"

Tiffany tittered. "Yep, sure did."

"Not to land that movie role?"

Tiffany twirled a tendril of hair hanging down from her topknot. "He brushed me off when I approached him before about playing Isabella, so my next plan was to seduce him. Once I got him in bed, he'd change his mind. Others have."

I took a step closer into her personal space, trying to catch her off guard. "When he brushed you off, was that when he pushed you?"

She fought to keep her face calm but she couldn't stop her eyes from widening for an instant. "I don't know what you're talking about."

I crossed my arms over my chest. "Someone saw Maxwell laugh at you, then push you to the ground."

"I don't know who you heard that from, but they're crazy. Maxwell would never laugh at me."

Funny how she denied the laughing part, rather than being pushed down.

"Guess I heard wrong. When did you leave the note in his room?"

"After yoga. I saw him leave his cabin, found the door unlocked, and left it. 'Course, he got killed right after that, so I figured the police kept the note. And here I only came to the spa to win that role."

"You weren't celebrating your new movie?"

Tiffany dabbed at the corners of her lips with her ring finger, but her gloss was already perfect. "That was the excuse I gave. But I've got a mole at Maxwell's studio, and she told me when he decided to stay here. Figured it was my one chance to catch him alone."

This girl was shameless. Of course, Maxwell had created almost the same plan to win back Sheila. But Logan seemed to think he'd done it for love, while Tiffany had used her sneaky devices for fame.

A car horn beeped near the front of the house. Tiffany picked up her bag. "Bet that's my ride. See ya."

She toddled off, all eye candy and sex appeal. If the police arrested her for Maxwell's murder, she'd look fantastic on the stand. But I didn't think Tiffany had killed Maxwell. My money was on Sheila or Logan.

I left the pigsty and walked down the path. If I had my timeline correct, Maxwell had confronted Heather about the necklace immediately after breakfast. Logan spoke with him before yoga class, and Maxwell was angry.

The chickens clucked at me as I went by.

Was Maxwell upset about Heather or about Logan applying to another studio? He'd left yoga early, then later taken the necklace to Sheila in an attempt to reconcile. Tiffany saw Maxwell leave his cabin and slipped in to drop off the note.

I cut through the camellia bushes and onto the patio. The pool water shimmered in the sun, the surface smooth.

Maxwell had then returned to his room after being rebuffed by Sheila, and someone had killed him. Had Sheila followed Maxwell back to his cabin, furious at his offer of reconciliation? Perhaps the glitzy necklace had set her off, yet another example of how Maxwell only thought of himself.

Or maybe Maxwell had confronted Logan about his job application and reminded Logan that the screenplay really belonged to the studio. Logan could have stewed while Maxwell was in yoga, then attacked him upon his return.

But what about the murder weapon? Either one could have easily hidden the knife before and after the attack, Logan in one khaki pant leg or Sheila in the long sleeves of those loose blouses she loved to wear. But where did they hide it afterward?

I followed the path past the far side of the pool and around to the cabins.

Esther stood before Maxwell's cabin, fingering the number seven on the door.

"Need help?" I asked.

Esther jerked her head at me. "Goodness, I didn't hear you come up." She plucked at a button, her favorite habit. "I can't believe how everything went so wrong. People are cancelling their reservations."

"Gordon mentioned that."

"I have a meeting at the bank to ask for a business loan to bridge the gap here until people come back."

Would this next paycheck be my last? "If the police could solve the murders, I know business would rebound."

Esther nodded without enthusiasm. "That's what I keep telling myself."

"Things will get better." I winced at how clichéd that sounded. "What can I do?"

"Would you be a dear and make a list of what needs to be done to make the hot springs ready? I told Gordon about the area and he thinks it's critical that we offer something like that to the guests. Most spas don't have a hot springs, so we'd be special."

"Oh, Esther, I'm glad you're opening up the springs."
I knew she wouldn't have agreed to my idea without
Gordon's say-so, and I felt a tiny spark of warmth for the
guy. "I'll walk out there again and take a closer look
around. You'll have the list by the end of the day."

"Perfect. And would you mind terribly cleaning up the
place a bit? You can use the pool net in the tool shed. I'll
mention our plan at my bank meeting. Might help me get
the loan if they see we're planning ways to attract new
business." Esther looked down at her faded frock. "Guess
I'd better change." She gave my hand a squeeze and walked
away.

Once the sound of her footsteps faded, silence surrounded me, broken only by the drone of a far-off plane.
With Tiffany packed up and gone, Sheila was the only remaining guest. I hadn't seen her yet today, but she and
Christian might be enjoying an afternoon together.

Pausing briefly, I grabbed the doorknob to Maxwell's
room and entered. Probably stupid of me not to lock the
door yesterday, but I'd been distracted by Logan's e-mail.
The box sat exactly where I'd left it, but my mind was on
Esther and whether she'd really get the bank loan.

The police had to solve the case for the farm to survive,
but the way Jason talked they weren't making any progress.
And I wasn't doing much better. But I had a feeling if I
could find just one more clue to the puzzle, the solution
would appear, so obvious I'd slap myself for not having figured it out sooner. But I needed that last piece. And I didn't
know where to find it.

I picked up the box, groaning at the weight, and eased
out the door. As I came around the side of the cabins, I
could see Gordon at a picnic table, the pergola providing
shade as he scribbled in a ledger.

"Might as well enjoy the fresh air since we have no
guests to disturb," he said as I approached.

Always a positive thinker, that guy. I heaved the box onto the table and sat on the bench across from him. "Where's Sheila?"

"Shopping with a girlfriend." He studied the pages before him. "I'm crunching the numbers. Even with the staff working half time, we're still in the red."

"Let's hope Esther gets that loan today."

Gordon grunted and jotted in the book. He glanced at the tabletop. "What's with the stuff?"

"Maxwell's belongings. The studio is worried his laptop contains industry secrets."

He gestured to the book sticking out the top. "I'll never understand everyone's fascination with yoga. You can't call it exercise when all you do is twist your body in ridiculous positions."

I bent my elbow and flexed my bicep. "Take a look at Christian's muscles. I'd say yoga gives you a workout."

Gordon capped his pen. "Christian and his muscles won't be here much longer if I have anything to say about it."

"You can't cut the yoga and Pilates classes. People expect those offerings at a spa." And if we stopped giving customers what they wanted, they'd have no reason to come back or tell their friends. Surely, Gordon, the great spa ruler, realized that.

"We'd keep the classes, but get a new instructor. Esther doesn't allow fraternizing with the guests and I won't tolerate the impact a failed relationship could have on this spa."

Uh-oh. Sheila and Christian hadn't been exactly subtle, but I didn't think Gordon had caught on to their relationship yet. Sheila had enough trouble with a dead ex-husband. No need to pile on the guilt by getting her boyfriend fired.

"Christian and Sheila are only friends," I said.

Gordon frowned. "Who said anything about Sheila? I'm talking about Tiffany."

I jerked my head back. "You're mistaken."

"I've seen the way Tiffany bats her little fake eyelashes at Christian. And he's practically drooling on his yoga mat. Don't tell me there's nothing going on."

I started to protest more, but stopped. If Gordon wanted to believe Christian had hooked up with Tiffany, just as I had for a while, that'd keep him from discovering Christian's real relationship with Sheila.

"Too bad Tiffany left," I said. "Now you'll never catch them in any hanky-panky."

"He'll have an affair with a new guest. He's got that reputation. And I'll catch him. I know they meet at that elm tree."

So Gordon knew about the tree. Had he found the underwear under the bench, too?

The proverbial light bulb lit up in my head, at 100-watt power.

"I know what you've been doing, you big pervert," I said. The look of panic that flitted across Gordon's face was all the confirmation I needed.

I'd discovered Gordon's dirty little secret.

27

"What the hell are you talking about?" Gordon demanded. "Just what do you think you know?"

"That you've been spying on that lover's bench. It's how you saw the ambulance at Queenie's trailer." I said.

"Why do you keep harping on that?"

I pointed a finger at Gordon and prayed he didn't bite it off. "When you barged onto Queenie's property after her death, you said you'd seen the emergency crews from the hot springs. But you couldn't have. You were lurking around the bench, trying to catch Tiffany and Christian doing the deed."

Gordon adjusted the knot on his tie. "You make it sound so seedy."

Was that a confession? "Why lie?"

Gordon balled his hands into fists and I thought about ducking under the table. "I don't think you appreciate all that I do for this spa. See how you immediately called me a pervert?" He pulled at his tie so hard this time, I worried about his ability to breathe. "I'm running a business here, and I won't tolerate rule-breakers. You shouldn't either," Gordon said. "I want this farm to succeed. The minute you lower your guard, employees slack off, don't dedicate themselves to the work."

"Most people are more reliable than you give them credit for," I said.

"Not in my experience. If I let Christian sleep with one guest, pretty soon, he'll sleep with them all. And his affairs will harm the spa's reputation." He flipped his notebook closed. "I've got to meet some suppliers about the linens, then see about a quote for the hot springs. When Zennia gets here, let her know we're down to one guest for dinner."

He went into the house. A few minutes later, I saw his car drive away as I brushed crumbs off the picnic table. With Gordon gone, I was alone at the farm. At least until Zennia arrived. The mention of the hot springs reminded me that Esther had asked me to clean it, but first I'd use the brief alone time to hash out some marketing plans.

I walked into the house, noting the silence, and stopped at the kitchen sink for a glass of water. I'd never been in the house when it was empty, and the quiet made my skin prickle.

"Dana!"

With the glass to my lips, I jerked at the sound, water sloshing out the sides and wetting my face.

In the doorway, Heather held a pile of folded towels, her thin legs poking out the bottom of her cut-off jeans. Her long brown hair hung loose, framing her wan face. She handed me a towel and I blotted my face.

"Sorry," she said. "I didn't think anyone else was here. This place is so spooky with all the guests gone."

"Have you had a chance to talk to Esther? We had a staff meeting yesterday about how she's going to run the farm until things improve." The new hours and cut wages would no doubt affect Heather, raising those kids on her own.

Heather leaned against the door frame. "Saw her this

morning. She explained about the half days. I'd have been at that meeting except I had a custody hearing."

"How's that going?" With Heather's ex trying to label her an unfit mother, even a hint that Maxwell thought she'd tried to steal the necklace could have caused big trouble for Heather during the hearing. She'd ended up telling the detective about the misunderstanding, but she must have been worried when Maxwell first threatened to report her. Worried enough to kill him?

I studied her twig-like arms, much like Tiffany's. She looked too weak to plunge a knife into a grown man, but sometimes killers got lucky and hit the right spot on the first try. But why kill Queenie? Heather was no golden-haired temptress. But she could be the person Queenie saw spill blood.

"Over for now," Heather said, snapping me out of my ghoulish musings. "I wasn't sure which way the judge was leaning, with my stupid ex lying about me, but the court ruled in my favor. Even got me good child support. That'll come in handy now that our hours have been cut."

"I'm glad everything worked out for you," I said. "Guess that whole incident with Maxwell and the necklace didn't matter after all."

Heather scowled. "Maxwell was a jerk. We don't need people like that around here."

She might want to keep those statements to herself. People might think she was glad to see Maxwell dead.

Heather's hand shot out from under the towels and she touched my arm. "Esther told me you were the one who found Queenie," she said. "How're you doing?"

"I'm coping." What was the appropriate response? If I said I was fine, I'd seem cold and heartless. If I admitted to a constant state of uneasiness, I'd look weak.

Heather used her free hand to tuck her long hair behind her ear. "I just hope this doesn't mean the end for Esther and the spa. Even with my ex paying support, I need the money."

She wasn't the only one. Half days wouldn't provide enough for me in the long term.

"I'm keeping my fingers crossed," I said. "But speaking of income, guess I'd better earn mine."

Heather went into the laundry room while I turned into the office. For half a second, I considered locking the door. I hadn't ruled out Heather as the killer yet, even if her motive was weak. But if I started locking office doors, where would the paranoia end? Would I be afraid to eat Zennia's food in case it was poisoned? Well, Zennia's food already gave me the willies.

I was halfway through a brochure that even Gordon would be impressed with when I heard a car engine followed by two doors slamming. Had Zennia brought a friend to work?

I saved the file and cut through the lobby to the parking lot. Sheila and Kimmie were stepping onto the sidewalk. Oh, joy.

"Dana, hi," Kimmie said, a bulging bag hanging off her arm.

"You two out shopping?" I asked.

"I told Sheila she needed a girls' day to take her mind off these murders."

Sheila held up her own shopping bag. "We drove to Santa Rosa this morning and hit the downtown mall. So many wonderful shops."

"I'd have bought more, but my trunk's full as it is." Kimmie placed a hand on Sheila's arm. "We really shouldn't talk about shopping in front of Dana, here. Not everyone has as much money as we do."

This woman was too much. I crossed my fingers behind my back in preparation of my lie. "Working at the spa provides me with plenty of shopping money, thank you. No need to worry about me."

"Just trying to be thoughtful. My dear husband always says I'm much too nice."

He probably said that after five shots of whiskey and with a hint of sarcasm, but that was only a guess on my part.

"Come on, Kimmie, you can help me cut the tags off my new clothes," Sheila said.

"And after that, we can find that boyfriend of yours. Last time I was here, I asked him about the various branches of yoga, but he never got around to answering me. I'd love to find out more."

"And then you can stay for dinner," Sheila said. "Bye, Dana. Have a good night."

Zennia pulled into the parking lot as the two women walked away. I waited for her to park and join me on the sidewalk. She carried a reusable grocery sack.

"How's the farm today?" she asked.

"Tiffany left this morning, so Sheila's our last guest. But she's bringing a friend to dinner tonight, so you'll be cooking for two."

"Better than cooking for none." She held up the bag. "Did you want to stay as well? It's tofu taco night."

I froze my face before I could wrinkle my nose. "Thanks, but I'm going to clean the hot springs and take off. How about next time?"

Actually, I was pretty sure I'd never eat tofu tacos.

"Suit yourself," Zennia said as she disappeared inside the house.

I walked around the side to the tool shed and grabbed the pool net, accidentally pulling down a weed whacker and broom that were hanging on the wall. With a curse, I repositioned the tools and dug around until I found a trash bag.

The walk to the springs left me hot and sticky. The trees

blocked out the sun, but the branches trapped the humidity. By the time I reached the turnoff and fought my way through the bushes, I was covered by a thin layer of sweat and dust. I brushed an oak leaf that clung to my arm onto the ground and stared at the overheated water, which only increased my glum state. If I was in the mood for a cup of lukewarm tea, the water would be perfect, but in this heat, all I wanted right now was a nice glass of an ice-cold beverage.

I dropped the pool net on the ground, then bent down to open the trash bag top. My cell phone fell from my shirt pocket and landed with a thunk. Grumbling, I opened the bag, stuck my phone back in my pocket, and leaned over to retrieve the net. Plunk. What was this? An old Carol Burnett skit? I slid the phone partway in my pocket, then looked at the hot springs. Warm water was probably not as beneficial for a cell phone as for clogged pores. I set the phone by a tree and swept the net over the water's surface.

Leaves, twigs, and dead insects gathered in the net and I dumped them into the trash bag. Two more passes, and I was finished. With the net still in one hand, I picked up the trash bag with the other and made my way to the trail. I had to stop once to remove the trash bag from a branch that had punched straight through the plastic. Esther had a lot of work before the hot springs would be ready for guests. Who knew what my role in clearing and building would be.

After wrestling with the plastic bag, I emerged on Chicken Run Trail and walked back to the house. My shirt stuck to my back, leaves clung to my arms, and a mosquito buzzed in my ear. First thing I was going to do when I got home was take a shower.

At the back of the house, I dumped the leaves and twigs on the compost pile, put the net and empty trash bag in the shed, and stopped in the kitchen for a drink of water. As I walked toward the office, I could hear Kimmie and Sheila chatting in the dining room with Zennia, who was explaining how tofu was made. I updated my time card and walked out of the house without stopping to say hi. No need for Kimmie to see me all sweaty and dirty. She might not recognize real work when she saw it.

At home, I waved to Mom in the kitchen and headed straight to the bathroom, where I washed the day's grit from my body. That done, I towel-dried my hair, donned fresh clothes, and returned to the kitchen.

"Need help with dinner?"

"No, almost done with the barley. We'll eat as soon as your sister gets home."

I sat down at the counter and sorted through the day's mail. Nothing for me, but no bills for Mom with flaming red letters on the envelope either. "How was bunco?"

"Not bad. Of course, as soon as Judith offered me condolences, Betty took up half the time talking about how much she missed her Harold."

"Did he pass away recently?"

Mom stirred the barley. "At least twenty years ago, but give her any opening, and she'll bring up his death. The next gathering should be better."

Guess she was going back. One small step in the healing process.

Ashlee burst into the house in her work smock, never one to make a subdued entrance. "Dana, guess what."

"You met another ex-con today. You're eloping."

"Ha, ha, you're so funny. Maybe I won't tell you how I ran into Jason down at Get the Scoop."

My heart sped up, but I tried for casual. "So you talked to Jason."

"He mentioned the film festival over in Mendocino tomorrow and said he'd be calling to ask if you're available."

I tried to stifle my grin. No need for Ashlee to know how goopy Jason made me feel. But a movie or two, a long walk on the beach, a romantic candlelit dinner. All the elements of a cheesy personal ad. Or an intimate evening with Jason.

I must not have hid my excitement because Ashlee clapped her hands.

"You like him, you like him."

I half-expected a crack to appear in the sliding glass door from her high-pitched squealing.

"Stop. Now." But inside, I was jumping up and down.

Ashlee glanced at her smock, where a fine layer of cat hair covered the front. "Let me change, then we'll figure out what you should wear."

"Who says I'm even going?"

"Oh, please. You're so going."

She was right. If Jason asked, I'd say yes.

Ashlee returned a moment later in shorts and a tank top. She studied the surface of the counter near my elbow. "Where's your cell phone? He might call any minute."

"Relax. I have voice mail. We're about to eat."

"Actually," Mom said, holding up a wooden spoon. "The barley is taking longer to cook than I expected. You have time."

Ashlee punched me lightly on the arm. "Go get your phone."

I hopped off the barstool. "Fine, I left it in my shirt pocket."

In the bathroom, I lifted the hamper lid, found my shirt still on top of the dirty clothes stack, and felt around the pocket. No familiar lump. I reached into the pocket in denial, but the space was empty. I dropped the shirt on the floor and felt around the other clothes in the hamper. No phone.

Which meant no call from Jason.

With a sinking feeling, I dumped the hamper upside down and rooted around on the floor, eventually realizing my efforts were futile.

How could the phone be in the hamper when I'd left it by the hot springs, at the base of that tree?

28

I set the hamper upright and crammed the clothes back in, all the while telling myself that Jason would leave a nice voice mail, which I would return first thing in the morning. Provided he even called at all.

Ashlee was waiting for me in the kitchen, her dating antenna at full alert. She saw my empty hand. "Where's your phone?"

"Back at work."

"Go get it."

I spread my hands. "I'm not rushing out to the farm to pick up a phone. Besides, it's out by the hot springs and that's a hike I like to limit to once a day."

"But Dana, if you don't call Jason back tonight, you won't have time to make plans. The film festival starts early."

"The movies run all day. Besides, Jason might have remembered he has plans tomorrow. Or changed his mind."

Ashlee grabbed my hand. "Take it from a dating expert. When you like a guy, you make the effort to let him know. Not returning his phone call right away is a sure sign you're not that interested."

I let out a laugh. "You read that trick in *Cosmo*?"

"I've used that trick myself to let a guy know what to expect if and when we go out. One date, unless he impresses me."

Was she right? Would Jason be offended if I didn't return his call tonight? Would he decide I didn't care?

"I'll think about it."

"Don't think, act. Britney was with me when I was talking to Jason. She told him that if you weren't interested, he should give her a call instead. You know what a poacher she is."

Hussy. Trying to steal my guy. But Jason wasn't my guy. And he certainly wouldn't be if I ignored his calls.

And I already felt somewhat anxious now that I knew my phone wasn't at my fingertips. Odds were small that Logan would ever return my call when I had my phone with me, but I could almost guarantee he'd call now that my phone was missing. "Fine. I'll run out there now."

Mom placed a casserole dish on the table. "You'll have to wait. Dinner's ready."

I slumped into a chair and placed a small helping on my plate. Dinner was the longest meal of my life, longer than Thanksgiving dinners at Uncle Fred's, when he'd show us slides from his summers in Idaho and then do tricks with his dentures. Ashlee nattered on about some new guy she'd met at the vet's office. Mom asked about his parents, job, and education, while I ate my barley in silence. Apparently Bobby Joe wasn't such a catch that Ashlee was ready to move into exclusive territory with him. My sister did like to hedge her bets where men were involved.

After I'd cleared the dishes and Mom had placed them in the dishwasher, I grabbed my car keys.

"Dana, it'll be dark soon," Mom said. "I'm not sure I want you wandering around that farm at night. Not with the police still searching for the killer."

I twirled the key ring on my finger, listening to the keys

clack together. "Both Maxwell and Queenie must have been targeted for some reason. It's not like Michael Myers from *Halloween* is roaming the woods in search of a random victim."

"Isn't Jason Voorhees always the one lurking in the woods in those *Friday the 13th* movies?" Ashlee asked.

Mom frowned. "Seriously, Dana. We don't know why Maxwell and Queenie were killed. I don't like it."

"If I'm the next intended victim, then the killer will be looking for me here at home this time of night, not the farm."

Mom turned to Ashlee. "Could you go with her? I would but I have my first pottery class tonight."

Another new activity for Mom. Another sign of progress.

Ashlee shook her head. "Can't. I've got that date. Remember?"

"Guys, I'll be fine. The farm is only five miles out of town, not fifty. I'll bring a flashlight in case, but I'll be back well before dark."

Mom bit her bottom lip, not convinced.

Ashlee sighed and reached into her purse, pulling out her car keys. "I'm making the ultimate sacrifice here, Dana, but I'll go with you. It'll cut into my prep time but we should be back before my date gets here." She jangled the keys. "As long as I drive."

A memory of my last ride with Ashlee came to mind with the roar of the engine, the centrifugal force pushing me against the seat, the overwhelming urge to pee my pants.

"Forget it. I'll drive."

She tossed her keys on the counter. "Fine, but don't drive like an old lady, the way you always do."

We'd be back long before dark but just in case, I dug two penlights out of the utility drawer in the kitchen, verifying the batteries worked before handing one to Ashlee and sticking the other one in my purse. Mom hugged Ashlee and me with a fervor that implied we were going on a cross-country three-month trip instead of driving across town to retrieve my cell phone.

Outside, the sun was low in the sky as Ashlee and I got into the car. She immediately flipped down the passenger side visor to check her reflection in the mirror. Then she whipped out a tube of mascara from her purse and extracted the wand. I shook my head and pulled onto the street.

The roads this time of day were practically devoid of traffic. The setting sun bathed the pear trees along the highway in a golden light, the last rays bouncing off the silver foil strips meant to deter the crows. At the farm, I parked and Ashlee and I went into the house. I hit the wall switch for the lobby light on my way through the darkening room.

Zennia was in the kitchen, hanging a pot on the rack. She turned at our footsteps. "Dana, what are you doing here?"

"Forgot my cell out by the hot springs." I nodded toward Ashlee. "This is my sister, Ashlee."

"Nice to meet you," Zennia said. Ashlee smiled in return.

"Sure you want to go out there now?" Zennia asked. "You might get lost in the dark."

I almost launched into my woeful tale about possibly missing Jason's invitation to Mendocino, but didn't want to sound pathetic. "I'll manage," I said.

"Before you go, take a couple of my hazelnut and pepper cookies for sustenance."

I eyed the flat circles sitting on the kitchen table. Cookies were always good, even with pepper, right?

Zennia handed me the biggest one, black flecks clearly visible. "I was going to set out the plate for Sheila and Kimmie when they return from the movies, but I'm worried about their taste. I'd try one myself, but I'm allergic to molasses."

She offered a cookie to Ashlee, who shook her head. "Thanks, but I'm on a diet."

I eyed the pepper once more, then took a bite. Visions of sawdust piled high in the Gobi Desert filled my head. I kept chewing, willing my mouth to generate saliva. With Zennia watching me, I managed to swallow the grainy crumbs, feeling them scratch my throat as they worked their way down.

Spare Zennia's feelings and lie? Or spare Sheila from a bad cookie experience? Customers came first.

"A bit dry, I'm afraid."

"Oh, poo."

Actually, poo was a lot moister than these circular sand cakes.

"Guess I'll make parfaits instead," Zennia said. She glanced at the wall clock. "Then I've got to get going. My accountability group meets tonight."

"We'd better get my phone. See you tomorrow." I stuck the penlight in my jeans pocket and walked out the back door, Ashlee trailing behind. The sun was behind the mountain now, the evening light fading. I quickened my steps through the herb garden and past the pigsty. The chicken coop yard was empty, the chickens no doubt tucked in for the night.

We passed the corner of the cabins and I led the way onto the trail.

"Hang on a minute, just how far away are these hot springs you mentioned?" Ashlee asked.

"Not too far. And I promise we'll hurry." Now that I was actually in the woods, the trees looked taller, the twilight calls from the birds and animals louder. I was suddenly glad Ashlee had invited herself along.

"Dana?"

I froze for a moment, confused that the sound hadn't come from Ashlee. But it was a man's voice.

I turned back toward the cabins and saw Christian down by Sheila's door, holding a bouquet of flowers, dressed in an ironed white dress shirt and slacks, the first time I'd seen him not wearing exercise clothes. If it weren't for his ever-present ponytail, I might not have recognized him.

"Hold up a minute," he said.

Was the world conspiring to keep me from my phone? Did Jason not bother to call and God was trying to spare me the disappointment?

"I thought you left at lunch," I said.

"Sheila let me know that you're aware of our relationship, so I guess I can tell you." Christian held up the roses. "I came back to see if she wanted to sneak off to dinner over in Mendocino, but she doesn't seem to be in her cabin."

I looked at the roses in his hand, a classic romantic gesture, and thought about how I'd run right out to retrieve my phone in the off chance that Jason wanted to go out. Was he the type to buy a girl roses, too?

"Zennia mentioned Sheila was at the movies with her friend Kimmie," I said.

"Guess that's my lesson to call next time. Never assume a gorgeous woman is alone, even on a Thursday night." He looked at Ashlee. "Speaking of gorgeous women, I don't believe we've met."

He offered the hand not holding the roses and Ashlee shook it, fluttering her eyelashes all the while. Christian then gave a little bow and held up the bouquet.

"Lovely roses for a lovely miss."

Ashlee giggled and pretended to curtsey.

Seriously? Was there no end to the number of men Ashlee could attract? And what about Sheila? Had Christian forgotten about her? Of course, if she killed

Maxwell, Christian might be in the market for a new girlfriend after the police arrested her.

"Look, I need to get out to the springs for my phone before it gets much darker." Even as I spoke, the shadows were blending together, darkness approaching.

Christian looked at the trees over my shoulder. "You shouldn't be wandering around at night, not with the wild animals and everything that's been happening."

"It'll only take a few minutes."

He smiled at Ashlee. "Allow me to escort you, for your own safety. Since Sheila isn't here, my evening is wide open."

At least he remembered Sheila's name. Ashlee's charm hadn't wiped out his memory bank.

Ashlee held a hand to her chest. "We would love a big strong man like yourself to walk us out there. You can protect us from the bears."

"Wonderful," Christian said.

"Great, let's go," I said, disappointed in Christian for flirting with Ashlee when he was dating Sheila. My faith in men slipped a notch.

We walked down the path, chatting about the miserable state of the farm after the deaths. As we stepped farther into the trees, the last of the light from dusk was blotted out, making my steps less sure as I strained to see any gopher holes or loose rocks.

I dug the penlight from my pocket and switched it on, the beam creating a comforting circle of illumination against the ever darker woods. Ashlee followed my lead and turned on her own light. An owl screeched in a nearby tree, making me shiver.

"By the way, Dana," Christian said, "Sheila and I appreciate you keeping that little secret."

In the shadows, I could barely make out the outline of his face.

"You mean the secret about your relationship?" I asked, adding emphasis to the last word in case Ashlee had missed it a while ago. "Sheila goes home tomorrow, and then you two can stop worrying," I said.

"Thank goodness. We've gotten a bit sloppy the last couple of days. It's hard to hide our feelings for each other."

Oh, geez, please tell me he wasn't going to get all mushy. And if he started sharing info about their sex life, I might throw up Zennia's cookie.

"You guys had to hide your relationship?" Ashlee asked. "How romantic. Just like Romeo and Juliet."

"Well, I don't like keeping secrets from Esther," Christian said. "She's too nice."

I thought about my earlier conversation with Gordon at the picnic table. "Gordon's the one you have to worry about."

"True. He'd fire me in a nanosecond. Well, he'd browbeat Esther into doing it."

"Don't worry, Gordon was way off on his suspicions."

"What do you mean?"

I heard a rustle in the bushes as a small animal ran by. At least I hoped it was small. Ashlee gripped my arm for a moment.

"He somehow got the idea that you and Tiffany are an item," I said.

Christian tripped over something on the dark path and stumbled. I swung the light around to help him see, though I didn't spot what he had tripped over.

"Why would he think that?" he asked, straightening up and running a hand along his ponytail.

"Not sure. But he was spying on that bench off the Hen House Trail where I found a pair of underwear, so perhaps he saw the underwear, too." Should I have mentioned our conversation? If Christian confronted Gordon, Gordon would know I was the one who told him and he'd be even more unbearable to work with. "Hey, don't tell Gordon I mentioned his spying on you, please."

"You've kept my secret, so I'll keep yours." He clapped a hand on my back and chuckled, though his laugh sounded tight. No doubt he was mad to discover Gordon was a sneaky little spy.

"I decided to let Gordon think what he wanted, even though Tiffany and Maxwell were the ones at the bench. I figure if he focuses on Tiffany, he won't suspect Sheila."

"Who's Tiffany?" Ashlee asked. I'd almost forgotten she was there.

"Tiffany Starling, another guest at the spa," I said.

"Wait, is she an actress? The one from *Machete Mayhem*? She had the best death scene ever, running around with only one arm and leg. Well, hopping really."

"Um, yeah, that sounds like her type of role." I shone the light to the right. "Here's the turnoff for the hot springs. Little harder to spot at night."

"You've got to be kidding me," Ashlee said. I moved the light over to her, and she pointed toward the bushes. "I'm not going through there. I'll get all scratched up before my date."

"But I don't know of any other way to get to the hot springs. It's not much farther." And no way was I going into those bushes alone.

"I don't care how far it is. I'll wait here."

Christian doffed an imaginary hat. "And I shall wait with you, milady."

In the beam of the light, I could see Ashlee smirk. "Forget it. You have a girlfriend."

I felt like clapping. I wasn't the only one disgusted by Christian's maneuverings after all.

"Besides," Ashlee added, "wild animals are a lot more likely to be in those bushes than out here on this trail. You should go with Dana."

Gee, thanks for mentioning the wild animals.

Christian shrugged. "As you wish."

I led the way through the brambles and shrubs, Christian silently following behind. When we broke through, I searched the ground with the penlight until I spotted my phone by a tree, exactly where I'd placed it for safe keeping.

"I'll get it, my dear," Christian said. He scooped down in the beam of the light and grabbed the phone. As he turned toward me, he seemed to hook his foot in the tree root and fell forward. The phone flew from his hand. I listened as it skidded across the dirt in the dark, the scraping sound followed by a small splash.

Well, crap.

I kept the light on Christian. "You all right?"

He stood up and dusted off his hands and knees. "Dana, I'm sorry about your phone. Sounds like it went in the springs."

"That's okay." What else could I say? That he'd blown my big chance to attend a film festival with the first guy in this town who'd sparked my interest? That I'd given up my Friday evening to traipse through the woods for absolutely no reason now, even if my evening only involved watching the latest horror film and eating unbuttered popcorn?

"I'll pay for a new one," Christian said.

Might have to take him up on that, considering the current state of my finances and the shaky future of my employment. I shone the light along the edge of the water, though I knew it was useless. "Guess we can head back now."

"I feel terrible." He did sound sorry.

"Seriously, don't worry." I could worry for the both of us about whether or not Jason would actually call and only get my voice mail. No need to trouble Christian with my dating woes, even if he was the one who dropped my phone in a giant pit of hot water.

He brushed his hands off again. "Say, you never told me why you think Tiffany and Maxwell had something going."

"Because she wanted a role in his latest movie," I said absentmindedly as I walked over to the edge of the pool for another look, more because I was annoyed my phone was gone than anything. "'Course, when Maxwell was killed, Tiffany mentioned how she hadn't slept with him, but maybe they got real cozy on that bench without doing the deed. Or maybe it was another guy."

"Like that Logan fellow, Maxwell's assistant."

"Nah, he's gay." A thought struck me and I swung the penlight around to shine in Christian's eyes. "Don't tell me Gordon's right for once and you're two-timing Sheila."

Christian laughed, a hollow, forced laugh that chilled me to my bones.

"Don't be absurd. I love Sheila."

I studied him in the beam from the flashlight, but all I saw were sharp lines and shadows. "But I've seen you eyeing Tiffany at the pool more than once."

"Tiffany's a good-looking girl, that's all."

Something else was tickling my brain. I scratched my poison oak just as Christian scratched his chest.

I stared at his shirt. He had poison oak! And I'd seen Tiffany scratching a rash on her butt back at the spa. My mind flew to that little green plant growing by the bench. "Leaves of three, beware of me," was something I'd learned as a child. I couldn't believe I hadn't made the connection until now.

Ashlee had mentioned rumors about what a ladies' man Christian was, but would he be so blatant as to sleep with two guests staying at the spa at the same time? What a cad.

Then I thought of the book in Maxwell's room, the one talking about the history of yoga. The book mentioned universal consciousness, but Christian claimed the purpose of yoga was to report to a deity. And whenever someone asked Christian yoga questions, he dodged them faster than a fourth-grader dodged the big red ball in gym class.

"You know, I heard a rumor that you went to India to study with a swami and that's why Esther hired you. Is that right?" I asked. Should I be asking him such a question out here in the dark? I reached up and felt the smooth front of my St. Christopher medal like I was stroking a security blanket.

"Of course not. But you wouldn't believe what you can learn from the Internet," Christian said.

He was two-timing Sheila, plus he barely knew a thing about yoga? "Everything about you is a lie." Whoops, probably shouldn't have said that out loud.

Christian took a step toward me. "Guess you've discovered my secret. Just like Maxwell. And we all know what happened to him." The menace in his voice left no doubt to what he was really saying.

Ashlee and I were alone in the woods with a killer.

29

My hands went numb, and I almost dropped the flashlight. I might be in some serious trouble here. I willed myself to shut up, but my mouth ignored my brain.

"Maxwell realized you were a fake, out to woo his ex-wife. But why?"

"What does a spa have? Rich, lonely women who pamper themselves because no one in their life is doing that pampering. Which is where I come in. But stupid Maxwell had to defend his ex-wife's honor and ruin everything. I could have made a fortune." In the beam of the flashlight, I could see Christian clench his fists as he stepped closer. "Instead, Maxwell found out my real name. Tried to blackmail me into helping him write a screenplay about my con jobs, swore he was destined for an Oscar and this was his big ticket. Well, I punched his ticket, all right."

"Oh, God, you killed him." My hands began to shake, and the flashlight beam jittered back and forth as I took a step back. "That means you must have killed Queenie, too. You were the one she saw with Tiffany."

Christian didn't respond. He stared at me in the soft light, the calculating look on his face making it clear he was deciding my fate.

My teeth started chattering as a deathly chill snaked its way into my stomach. I needed to get the hell out of here. "What did she mean about the spilled blood? Did she somehow see you kill Maxwell?" I glanced toward the dark ground, hoping to spot a rock. Or a tree branch. Anything I could use as a weapon.

"Close enough. And while that beekeeper was crazy, she was just sane enough to be a problem." He sneered at me. "Just like you."

Christian charged at me, knocking me off balance and propelling me back, his muscular frame giving me no room to maneuver.

We fell into the springs, and I opened my mouth to scream. Warm water ran down my throat. I felt like I was taking a bath from the inside out. I struggled to the surface, coughing and sputtering. Christian immediately pushed me back down, then maneuvered on top of me.

My lungs burned. My throat ached. I fought the instinct to breathe as the world grew dim around the edges. Through my panicked haze, I realized I was still clutching the penlight. I kicked at Christian and connected with his shin. His grip on my shoulders loosened.

Using the precious seconds of freedom, I reached up and grabbed Christian's ponytail with one hand. I held the penlight with my other and swung with my last bit of energy. The light connected with flesh. Christian's hands released my shoulders. He no longer held me down.

I kicked toward the surface until my head popped out of the water. I gasped for breath and swam away from where I thought Christian might be. I could barely see, the sky dark now, the moon casting a paltry glow. My hand scraped rock and I held on. Behind me, Christian splashed in the water.

"My eye! My eye!" he bellowed.

I dragged myself out of the springs. The weight of my

clothes threatened to pull me back in and I belly-crawled across the dirt until my feet were clear. As I grabbed for another handful of earth, I wondered if Ashlee was still standing on the trail, waiting for us, with no idea what was happening.

I lay still for a moment, my arms aching, my lungs heaving. A sliver of fear shot through my gut as I realized I could no longer hear Christian moving in the water. Quiet ripples sounded from the springs. I shivered in my wet clothes.

Pine needles crunched directly behind me. I rolled to the side. A thump sounded where I'd been. My eyes had partially adjusted to the darkness and I could discern Christian's form lying on the ground.

He rose up with a roar. "You stabbed me!" His voice held a mixture of rage and disbelief.

I scrambled to my feet and ran toward where I thought the path was, fighting my way through the brush, branches slapping me in the face, catching on my clothes. I'd dropped the light when I'd struck Christian in the water and I stumbled onto the path, falling to my knees as my eyes focused on a circle of light. Ashlee!

She rushed up to me, helping me to my feet. "Jesus, Dana, are you all right? What's going on?"

Behind me, I could hear Christian breaking through the trees, like Godzilla on a rampage. "We have to get out of here, Ashlee. Christian killed Maxwell. And he knows I know. He wants to kill me, too."

Ashlee stood there. "Is this a joke? 'Cause it's not funny."

I grabbed her shoulders and shook her. "It's not a joke. He'll come after you next."

I pushed Ashlee down the path, in the direction of the farmhouse. She finally snapped into action and we ran. Behind us, I could hear a final rustle of bushes and then steady footsteps.

Christian was coming. And he was faster and stronger.

I could hear him closing the gap. If we stayed on the path, he'd overtake us before we could reach the house, and help.

"To the right," I gasped to Ashlee. I veered off into the trees, running smack into a pine tree in my haste. The bark scratched my hands and forehead, burning my skin. I swung around the tree, plowing ahead, my hands out front, Ashlee right beside me. In her panic, she emitted a high-pitched keening sound, intermingled with gasping, as she ran.

Christian cursed at our change in course and followed. The distance between us grew as he tried to find us among the trees. But we couldn't stop now. I'd seen enough horror films where the girl cowered in the forest, only to have the killer catch up and bludgeon her. And no way was Ashlee or I getting killed because I'd just had to retrieve my stupid phone.

We weaved between the trees, my arms scraping against the branches, Christian somewhere behind us. Were we going in the right direction? Instead of reaching the farm, would we end up at the base of the hills, lost in the endless wilderness?

Emerging from the trees, I fell and sprawled in the dirt. I noticed that the ground around me was empty of brush as Ashlee dragged me to my feet. We were back on the path. But what part?

I could hear Christian fumbling around, sounding far away. Now might be our one chance to call for help.

"Ashlee, get your phone out. Call 911."

She handed me the penlight and fumbled in her pocket. When she hit the ON button, the display lit up, brilliant against the dark night. I winced at the glare as she pressed the numbers. I leaned my head next to hers and heard a ringing sound across the line, intermingled with static.

Please let the call go through, please let the call go through.

"911, what is your emergency?"

Relief flooded through me and tears sprang to my eyes as
Ashlee spoke. "We're in the woods, behind the O'Connell
Farm and Spa, and . . ."

"Hello, is anyone there?"

Static filled my ear. I pulled away as Ashlee lowered the
phone and looked at the display. A single reception bar appeared on the screen.

"Hello?" the operator asked again, her voice faint.

The line went dead. The sudden silence emphasized the
fact that I once more couldn't hear Christian. He could be
anywhere. And if he'd seen the light from the phone, he
knew exactly where we were.

I turned off the penlight and gripped Ashlee's hand as
we crept down the path, my Keds creating mere whispers
in the dirt. My shin collided with a hard surface. "Shit!" I
clapped a hand over my mouth. Couple more outbursts like
that and Christian would hone in on our location.

I turned the light back on and shone it on the object I'd
hit. The bench! At least I knew where we were. But we
were nowhere near the house.

"Check your phone again," I whispered.

Ashlee flipped it open but not a single reception bar appeared.

A loud crash sounded in front of us. Christian burst
onto the trail, his shape barely visible in the faint moonlight that filtered through the trees. With him squarely in
the center of the path, the only option was behind us.

Then I remembered Queenie's trailer. It might have a
landline phone. Or the shotgun.

"Ashlee, follow me," I shouted. With Christian right in
front of us, whispering was pointless. I turned and ran,
fighting through more brush, the point of a branch ripping
down my arm like a knife.

"Dana, I'm going to catch you," Christian called to me.
"If you slow down, I promise to make the end nice and

quick. For you and your sister. So stop and make it easy on yourself."

Easy on me? Ha! More like easy on Christian. Just give up like the sacrificial lamb Queenie would have spouted on about.

I ran into the field and stopped, Ashlee bumping into me. Queenie's trailer sat in the middle, bathed in the soft moonlight. Oh, how I wished she'd barge out, shotgun in hand. Had Christian killed her because she'd seen him with Tiffany at the bench? Was he the one she was talking about when she mentioned the blood?

But now was not the time to worry about Queenie. I needed to focus on saving Ashlee and me.

Maybe her cell phone would work now that we were away from the trees. Before I could tell Ashlee, I heard Christian step into the field.

I sprinted forward, staggering in the pitted dirt. Then, a thump sounded behind me and I heard Ashlee scream.

"Dana, help! He's got me!" she shouted.

I stopped so fast that I fell over, then immediately regained my footing. In the moonlight, I could see Ashlee lying on the ground, Christian crouched over top her. I ran straight at him, charging like a defensive lineman for the Oakland Raiders, throwing my entire weight against him.

He fell back onto the dirt and I pummeled him with my fists while he tried to block the blows. But I couldn't possibly overpower him like this. And I didn't want to waste the time trying.

I jumped to my feet and ran for the trailer. Ashlee had risen from the ground and I dragged her along behind me, only letting go of her hand when I reached the steps.

I hit the metal stairs at a run and jerked the doorknob. The door flew open, slapping me in the face. I staggered back and almost lost my footing, but Ashlee pushed me from behind. I gripped the door's edge and pulled my way inside, tearing through the crime scene tape, Ashlee on my heels. I slammed the door shut behind her and pushed the lock in the knob, knowing it wouldn't hold for long.

"What are we going to do, Dana?" Ashlee's voice came out in a shriek, distorting her words.

I tried to look around, but the trailer's interior was as dark as a crow's feathers.

"Where's your flashlight?" I asked.

"I dropped it back in the field."

I felt along the walls for a light switch. My hand connected with the plastic toggle and I flicked it up. Nothing. No power. Damn.

"Let's try to find a weapon, anything."

I could hear Ashlee rummaging nearby as I felt around in the darkness, running my hands over the fridge, the countertop, the tiny table. I brushed past a drawer handle and tugged it open. Rubber bands, wrapped straws, and sauce packets lay at my fingertips. My hand closed around a handle and I inched my fingers upward. A round smooth surface, tiny sharp points on the end. A spork? Our best weapon was a spork?

I dropped the plastic utensil. "Find anything?" I asked.

"No." Ashlee choked the word out like she was being strangled.

Footsteps sounded on the metal steps. I flailed around in the dark, fumbling for anything, connecting with nothing. The sound of the knob twisting, first one way, then the other, reached my ears. My heartbeat picked up speed, the thumping competing with the sound of Christian banging on the door.

All my senses converged and an image of Queenie's trailer appeared in my mind from the morning I'd found her body: The smell of death, the sound of the bees, the touch of the metal doorknob, the taste of fear. And the sight of a skillet hanging on the side of the cabinet. I felt for the wood, ran my hand along the side, and grabbed the cast iron skillet at the same moment the trailer door burst open.

Gripping the skillet handle with both hands, I swung at Christian's head, clearly outlined in the open doorway. I could hear Ashlee scream from behind me as the skillet bounced off his face with a sickening gong.

Christian flew off the steps. He landed at the bottom and lay quiet. I stood for a moment, looking for any stray movement, any indication he was faking. He'd killed two people. He wasn't above laying a trap. But he remained motionless.

I watched Christian while Ashlee tried her cell phone again. This time, the reception held, the call went through. Help was on the way.

Still clutching the skillet, I sat down on the top step of the trailer. And wept.

30

The next morning, I heard my bedroom door open and felt the mattress sink as someone sat down on the bed. I opened my eyes, winced at the brightness of the room, and lowered my lids again.

"Dana, how are you feeling?" Mom asked.

I tried to sit up, fighting the sheet wrapped around me. "Like I got chased through the woods by a crazy guy."

"Promise me you'll never do something so dangerous again, especially not when your sister tags along."

"Trust me, if I'd known Christian murdered Maxwell and Queenie, we never would have walked into the woods with him." I shuddered at the memory. "At least, we've caught the killer. People should feel safe enough to stay at the spa."

Mom patted my knee through the sheet. "When I encouraged you to help Esther, I never for a moment believed it might put you at risk. To think I almost lost you both makes me sick."

"I'm glad I could help." I took a deep breath, feeling the tears gathering at my eyes, and tugged on the sheet. "I know I failed you when Dad died. You needed me, and I only thought about myself."

Mom kissed my forehead. "You didn't fail me. You had your own grief to deal with." She stood. "But I'm glad you're here. And I hope you stay a long while." She walked out.

I lay back down and pulled the sheet up to my chin, warm from my head to my feet. My moving back home had actually helped. Mom was rejoining her clubs, enjoying life again. Maybe that dream job in San Jose would have turned out to be a nightmare. Perhaps my place was here at home, with family.

Ashlee barged in without knocking.

Then again, I might need to rethink this whole staying in Blossom Valley thing.

"Jason's here," she sang.

I rolled over and pulled the pillow over my head. In my bruised and battered condition, even talking to Jason sounded like too much work. "How can you possibly be so perky after what happened last night? Go away."

"Dana, you have to talk to him. I already gave him my side of the story, but I still don't know what happened at the hot springs." She tried to lift the pillow, but I held on with both hands. "You have to get up. We're famous now. When I went to pick up donuts this morning, all these people practically attacked me, asking questions, wanting to know what had happened."

I lifted a corner of the pillow. "Did you say donuts?"

"Yep. Mom wasn't too thrilled, but she figures we almost died, so we deserve a donut."

"Yum, old-fashioned glazed."

"I ate that one. Sorry. But there's a maple bar and a bear claw." She slapped my foot under the covers. "Never mind the donuts, go talk to Jason."

I sat up and glanced in the mirror over my dresser. My hair looked like squirrels had tried to build a nest and given up. "You're nuts. I can't talk to him looking like this."

Ashlee studied my face. "So run a brush through your hair, slap on some makeup. I'll keep him entertained with stories about your prom while he's waiting." She ran out as I threw my pillow at her. It landed in the hall.

Oh, no, Ashlee wouldn't really tell Jason about my attending prom with a guy all the kids called Dancer Dave, would she? I'd better get out there.

With a groan, I tossed off the covers and stood, wincing as pain coursed through my arms. The scratches and bruises stood out against my pale skin, the bandage I'd slapped on the deeper scratch itching as I moved. Why wasn't Ashlee stiff and sore? I donned the first long-sleeved ironed T-shirt and pair of clean jeans I could find, then headed to the bathroom for a quick face washing and hair brushing.

When I walked into the living room, Ashlee had hit the part of the story where Dancer Dave had tried to flip me over his back and instead dropped me on the floor. In front of the entire senior class.

Jason laughed. I told myself he was just being polite.

The moment he saw me, he jumped up from the couch and rushed over. "Dana, you okay?"

"I'll live." And so would Christian, according to the paramedics who'd treated him at the scene last night. News I was happy to hear. I didn't want to be responsible for taking a life, even if he had killed two people.

Ashlee cleared her throat. "Well, guess I'll go tidy the kitchen."

My sister had never volunteered to clean in her life, but I appreciated the gesture. I smiled as she walked past, and she winked in return.

"You're sure you're all right?" Jason asked. "Christian didn't hurt you, did he?"

I touched my sleeve, where the bandage still itched under the fabric. "Nothing serious."

"I'm really glad to hear that." He paused for a moment, clearly torn. "As long as you're okay, you know I have to ask you about what happened. Feel up to it?"

Thinking about last night got my heart rate up and I paced a bit. "Sure, but there's not much to tell. Christian offered to walk Ashlee and me out to the hot springs to retrieve my cell phone." At the mention of the phone, I remembered Jason was the reason I'd gone out there, and I felt myself blush.

"And?" Jason prompted.

"When we got to the springs, I realized that Christian was dating both Tiffany and Sheila. That must have been what Tiffany meant when she'd said she'd enjoyed her stay, even with two murders and a failed attempt at a movie role. Not only that, but Christian lied about studying with a swami in India. Maxwell must have figured it out from his yoga book and confronted Christian."

Jason pulled out his notebook. He probably slept with that pad under his pillow. "Exactly what he told the cops."

I stopped pacing. "What else did he say?"

"Everything. Confessed to killing both Maxwell and Queenie. He's wanted in four states back east for swindling rich women out of their fortunes. One of those women also died in a mysterious accident, and the police are checking to see if Christian helped her death along. Things were getting too hot for him so he moved out here."

Four swindles and a possible murder? Yikes. "So he came to Blossom Valley under the guise of being a yoga expert to pick his next con victim," I said. "You know, Ashlee mentioned hearing some gossip about Christian liking rich, older ladies, but I totally blew her off." I should really pay more attention when my sister spoke.

"Maxwell apparently realized that Christian was a fraud, even figured out his real name and did some Googling. Once he found the newspaper articles and knew Christian's story, Maxwell called him to his cabin after yoga class and threatened to tell the cops if Christian didn't agree to help Maxwell write a screenplay about the cons. Christian killed him instead."

"Shame on Maxwell for not going straight to the police. Christian mentioned that Maxwell wanted an Oscar. I guess his quest for fame overrode common sense." I shook my head at such an idiotic move. If Maxwell had told the police about Christian at the start, he and Queenie would still be alive. "Did you say Christian isn't even his real name?"

Jason tapped his pen on his notebook. "Right. His name's Bruce Collins. That's why he attacked you when you found his money clip."

The big shove at the chicken coop. "What does his money clip have to do with the murders?"

"He claims it was a gift from his most recent victim. Engraved with his real name. He knew he'd dropped it somewhere by the animals and got there just as you picked it up."

"But I never saw the engraving. And I wouldn't have realized that Christian was really Bruce Collins." I shivered. "Guess I should be thankful he didn't decide to kill me right there with only the chickens for witnesses."

"Apparently he never saw you as much of a threat. Until last night, that is."

I pictured my plunge into the hot springs and shivered again. "What exactly did Queenie see that made him kill her?"

"She caught him in the woods, burying the bloody knife he used to kill Maxwell. She ran off before he could do anything about her, but then he heard you talking to Esther about the crazy honey lady. That's when he found out she'd also been spying on him and Tiffany at the bench. He had to kill her before she exposed him."

"So I helped get a woman killed."

Jason placed a hand on my arm. "You can't blame yourself. Christian did all the killing. He felt Queenie was too much of a threat, once she saw him hide the knife like that. And you know, he couldn't steal Sheila's fortune if she found out he was two-timing her with a young hottie."

"Young actresses do it for you?" I asked, raising an eyebrow.

Jason looked me in the eye. "I prefer marketing girls."

I broke eye contact and wondered why my face felt so enflamed. Little young for a hot flash.

"Which reminds me," Jason said. "I don't know if Ashlee mentioned the film festival to you."

I stepped forward. "Yes?"

"That's out now."

"Oh." Well, he'd probably decided he didn't want to date me anyway.

"With your mad dash through the woods and catching a killer, I've got to prepare another extra edition. It needs to be done tonight." At least he'd come up with a plausible excuse. "But when my work's done, I'd love to take you out. We could make a day of it, wine tasting, hot air ballooning."

I felt like my feet were already off the ground. "Why, sir, are you trying to get me alone in a balloon basket?" I asked, complete with Southern drawl. Good grief, I was channeling Scarlett O'Hara.

He ignored my accent and took my hand. "When I heard you'd been in danger, I was almost out of my mind. I'm glad you're okay."

I leaned toward him, my eyelids starting to close.

The doorbell rang.

Oh, for crying out loud. I pulled my head back and Jason dropped my hand.

"Guess I'd better get that," I said. I walked to the front door and yanked it open a little harder than necessary.

Esther and Gordon stood on the porch, Esther beaming in a floral dress and clutching a white purse. Gordon was dressed in his usual suit, making me wonder if he even owned a pair of jeans.

"Dana, thank goodness you're all right. I was so worried," Esther said.

"Yeah," Gordon said. "Glad you weren't killed or anything." He stepped inside without waiting for an invitation, and I pushed the door a bit wider so Esther could walk in, too.

She caught sight of Jason, and the beam widened. "Oops, didn't know you had company. I just wanted to stop by real quick and let you know the good news."

"What good news?" I asked.

"The bank okayed the loan," Esther said, clasping her hands together and raising them up in a victory gesture, purse swinging. "With Christian in jail, the loan officer felt the spa might be a success after all."

"Even though Christian was an employee at the spa? That doesn't worry them?" Surely that would have some negative impact to business.

"Apparently not," Gordon said. "The police have their man. The guests can feel safe again. Once we line more up, of course."

"Fantastic," I said.

"And I should point out that having an employee of the farm catch the killer is great for advertising. What could be safer than staying at a place with its very own Nancy Drew?"

Guess he was talking about me. I'd have to buy a magnifying glass and find some friends named Bess and George.

Esther patted Gordon's arm and he brushed at the fabric of his sleeve.

"We wouldn't have gotten the loan without Gordon's help," she said. "I wasn't feeling too good about how the meeting went yesterday, so once I heard what happened last night, I dragged Gordon down to the bank first thing this morning and had him go over the numbers with the officer. That made all the difference."

Gordon gave a dismissive wave, but he couldn't quite keep the corners of his mouth from twitching upward. My God, was he about to smile?

"Enough about that," he said, regaining his usual serious expression. "Dana, just make sure you're at work tomorrow by nine. We have lots to do."

Esther whipped her head around to look at Gordon. "Mercy me, aren't you the slave driver." She turned to me. "Monday morning is fine. You need extra rest after such a frightful experience."

"Really, Esther, we don't have time," Gordon started, but Esther turned on him with a swift glare. He stopped, then shrugged. "You're the boss."

Glad he'd finally realized that. If I didn't watch out, I might start to like Gordon.

Esther reached up and pinched his cheek. His face turned crimson while I choked back a laugh. "And you're my right-hand man." She walked toward the door, calling over her shoulder, "See you Monday."

I watched as Gordon pulled the door closed behind them. The killer was in jail. And with the loan, my job was secure for a while. Not bad for a night's work.

I felt a hand on my shoulder and turned around to look into Jason's green, green eyes.

"I thought they'd never leave." He leaned in and laid his lips on mine in a firm yet tender kiss.

An added bonus to staying. Blossom Valley suddenly had a lot more to offer.

Besides, I had to make sure Wilbur didn't become someone's Christmas ham.

Tips from the O'Connell Organic Farm and Spa

Esther and I wish you could join us for a visit here in Blossom Valley. Until then, I've selected a few tips to share from the spa's daily blogs.

Growing Arugula Arugula typically grows best in cooler environments. The soil must be fertile, have proper drainage, and be loose enough to allow air circulation. Arugula prefers full sun, but the taste of the leaves turns bitter when hot weather arrives. The outer leaves can be harvested from each plant on a continual basis until the season is over. The trick is to keep Wilbur and all his pig friends out!

Making Your Own Lemonade Making homemade lemonade is easy peasy. Use five or six lemons to squeeze out one cup of lemon juice into a pitcher. Stir in one cup of sugar and five to six cups of water, depending on how strong you want the flavor. Chill the mixture. When serving, garnish the drink with a mint sprig or lemon slice. Pucker up!

Eating Well for Hair Health A poor diet can affect the quality of your hair. Dry hair may indicate too little vitamin A or healthy fats, while limp hair marks a deficiency in vitamin B6. If your hair looks sad, stock up on salmon, nuts, eggs, and oatmeal—all popular foods here at the spa—to see if your hair can regain its bounce and shine. You might become a star in your own shampoo commercial.

All about Wheatgrass Juice Zennia Patrakio, our very own spa chef, swears by the benefits of wheatgrass juice. A mere two ounces has the same amount of vitamins and minerals as three pounds of vegetables! The juice also improves digestion and boosts your immune system. If the taste of straight wheatgrass is too strong, add a twist of citrus or mix it with other juices or smoothies for the same benefits.

Getting More Fiber and Vitamins The much-maligned Brussels sprout is a powerhouse of fiber, vitamin C, and disease-fighting compounds. To make the sprouts taste better, sauté with a generous pat of butter and sprinkle with salt and Parmesan cheese. Then, pinch your nose shut and eat away. Bon appétit!

Eating More Bananas Available year round and completely portable in their own peel, bananas are an excellent source of potassium, fiber, and vitamins B6 and C. We always have bananas available for the guests here at the spa. For a nutritious breakfast, Zennia likes to top whole-wheat toast with natural peanut butter and banana slices, make a yogurt parfait with layers of vanilla yogurt, sliced bananas, and granola, or whip up a banana and strawberry smoothie. Don't be surprised if you see her swinging from the trees!

Making a Daisy Chain To make a daisy chain, gather twenty-five daisies from a nearby field or your own planter, if you happen to grow your own. With your fingernail, create a slit in the middle of each stem. Pry apart one slit and insert the stem of another daisy until the head is resting on the slit opening. Repeat this step for the rest of the daisies. For the last slit, pull the head of the first daisy through to complete the circle. You can wear the chain as a crown or necklace.

Gathering Chicken Eggs The O'Connell Farm and Spa offers fresh eggs from chickens on-site, and we encourage anyone with a yard to start their own coops. Collect chicken eggs at least once a day, twice if possible. Gather the eggs from any empty nests first. Be sure to wear gloves in case eggs are broken or the chicken has messed its nest, though this is unusual. If a chicken is still sitting in the box, encourage the chicken to leave the nest by producing loud noises, then grab the egg.

Treating Poison Oak Any time you're walking along trails or out in the woods, beware of poison oak. Oil from the plant actually causes the rash. If you've been exposed, clean the area with rubbing alcohol and rinse with cold, not hot, water. While scratching the rash does not spread the poison oak, it can leave you susceptible to infection. Apply calamine lotion when the itching is unbearable, but keep the area dry and open to air often to speed healing—and to show off your impressive rash to your friends.

Please turn the page for an exciting sneak peek of
Staci McLaughlin's
next Blossom Valley Mystery
coming soon from Kensington Publishing!

1

A gust of dry, warm air swept onto the porch step and swirled around my sandals, tickling my toes and sending a shiver up my calves as I tilted my head for a good-night kiss.

A shriek sounded from inside the house, followed by a bang. I jerked my head toward the front door, recognizing the sound as coming from my sister, Ashlee. I turned back to Jason, noticing how his reddish gold goatee glinted in the porch light.

"Everything okay in there?" he asked me.

No way was I letting Ashlee's latest emotional melt-down interrupt my big kiss with Jason. Who knew when our next date might be?

"Nothing we need to worry about."

Jason reached over and tucked an errant chunk of blond hair behind my ear, sending a ripple of excitement down my back. "Sorry your bowling score wasn't any higher tonight, Dana," he said.

I felt my face heat up and hoped it didn't show in the dim light. "The strobe light blinded me. I couldn't see the pins."

"Must have had your eyes closed to score a seventy-four."

"Hardee har har." I just hoped he didn't print my score

in the local paper. As the lead reporter for Blossom Valley's only paper, he sometimes had to get creative to fill the space. "I'll wear sunglasses next time. Be prepared to quiver in your bowling shoes when I approach the lane with my mighty ball."

Jason moved closer, his ironed Ralph Lauren dress shirt almost brushing the front of my lacy sweetheart top. "You've got me quivering right now."

A smile played across my lips as my hand found Jason's, his long slender fingers intertwining with mine. "Where were we again?" I closed my eyes and leaned in.

Another bang, this one followed by an undecipherable shout from my sister. The moment evaporated faster than a slushie on a hot summer sidewalk. Whatever Ashlee was mad about tonight, it sounded like a doozy.

I dropped Jason's hand and dug my keys out of the pocket of my jeans. "Guess I'd better go in."

"Sounds like someone needs help." Jason half turned toward the door, obviously torn between going in with me and escaping while he could.

"Only a licensed therapist can provide the help that Ashlee needs." I stuck the key in the lock. "Thanks for a great night."

"I'll call you, arrange that bowling rematch." He offered me a wink and a smile with that promise, then stepped off the porch.

I shot a quick glance at his butt before I entered the house. The front hall was silent, save for the ever-present ticking of the grandfather clock. I checked my teeth in the hall mirror and noticed I had spinach lodged over a canine. Great. Maybe Jason had missed that.

A ripping sound off to my left reached my ears, followed by muttering. I walked toward the living room and stopped at the entrance.

Glossy photos were strewn across the tan carpet, most

torn in half. Ashlee sat cross-legged in the middle of the wreckage, her normally brushed and styled blond hair, three shades lighter than mine, hanging down from an untidy bun, tear tracks evident on her flushed cheeks.

"Ashlee, what's wrong?" I asked, pretty sure her crisis involved a man. Ashlee went through boyfriends faster than world champion competitive eater Joey Chestnut went through a plate of Nathan's hot dogs.

She lifted her head at my voice, her clenched fist squeezing two halves of a photo. "Oh, Dana. Bobby Joe is such a pig. He's been cheating on me!"

I raised my eyebrows. Ashlee and Bobby Joe had been dating since they'd met at the cricket-chirping contest back in May. Though I knew their relationship wasn't long-term, I'd assumed it would at least survive through the upcoming Fourth of July weekend. Nobody likes to watch fireworks alone.

"Are you sure? Did Bobby Joe tell you he cheated?"

Ashlee sniffed, her face a portrait of wounded pride. "He told me. Right after I found the evidence, the big coward."

My mind flashed to lace underwear stuffed in the glove box of his truck. Or maybe a bra tangled around a wrench in the oversized toolbox he carried in the truck bed. "What evidence?"

"Text messages." Spittle flew from her mouth along with the words.

I screwed up one side of my mouth, not hiding my doubt. "That's your big evidence? Text messages?"

Ashlee grabbed another picture, this one showing Bobby Joe holding a large striped bass, and ripped it in half with a vicious yank. "I don't need more proof than that, especially when I read about what a great time the tramp had last night and how she can't wait to see him again."

Okay, a text message like that might be enough proof

after all. And Bobby Joe had admitted he cheated. I bent down and gave Ashlee an awkward one-armed hug. "I'm sorry he turned out to be such a jerk. I know you really cared about him."

"Yeah, I guess. 'Course, he was starting to be a drag. You can only go four-wheeling so many times." Ashlee shrugged my arm off her shoulder and attempted to smooth down her hair. "But I've never been cheated on before. These things don't happen to me."

I resisted the urge to mention that she dated most men for two weeks or less, not giving them much time to stray, but now didn't seem like the time. "Anything I can do to help?" I asked instead.

Ashlee stood, photos falling from her lap like tiles from a roof during an earthquake. "No. I gotta update my Facebook page. Change my status to 'Single'." She stomped from the room, leaving a trail of torn photos in her wake.

I used my hands to sweep the pieces into a pile and dumped them in the wicker garbage can that sat next to the beige and brown floral couch. With my limited number of ex-boyfriends, I had little advice to offer Ashlee. Luckily, her prognosis was most likely a battered ego rather than any actual heartbreak. She'd line up a new boyfriend by tomorrow and forget Bobby Joe's betrayal in a week.

I headed to my own bedroom, pushing Ashlee's troubles from my mind. A smile formed on my lips as I remembered my evening with Jason and stayed there as I drifted off to sleep.

The alarm screeched at six the next morning. I shot an arm out from under the sheet and slapped at the cheap plastic box until I was rewarded with silence. With a groan, I tossed back the covers and stumbled out of bed. I took a quick shower and donned my summer uniform of khaki walking shorts and a navy blue polo shirt with STAFF stitched on the back that everyone at the O'Connell Organic Farm and Spa wore, a long way from the blouses and skirts of my marketing days at a computer software company.

I'd moved back home four months ago after a lengthy stint of unemployment down in San Jose, thanks to a layoff where I worked. With my mother still grieving my father's unexpected death, I'd convinced myself she needed someone around to keep an eye on her health. But since my father had died of a heart attack, Mom now insisted that we abolish all processed and sugary foods and stop frying our dinners, which meant no more kids cereal in the mornings, no more fried chicken for Sunday dinners, and no more giant bowls of ice cream during *Scream* movie marathons. Now it was whole wheat pasta and poached fish with fresh fruit for dessert. As if adjusting to life back home wasn't hard enough, I didn't even have any Chocolate Fudge Brownie ice cream to ease the transition. At least not without a disapproving glare from my mother.

Casting aside my musings, I headed for the kitchen to face breakfast. Box and gallon jug in hand, I sat at the oak table under the watchful eyes of the family portraits that lined the wall and swallowed my bran cereal without really tasting it, not that there was anything to taste. Pushing the empty bowl away, I gulped my orange juice and glanced at the clock. Only 6:30. Mom and Ashlee were still asleep. Who knew how long Ashlee had stayed up last night, changing her Facebook status and tweeting about her suffering? She might be in bed for another hour or two, but I preferred to start my day early.

Besides, Esther might need help with the chickens.

I grabbed my purse, locked the front door behind me, and slipped behind the wheel of my Honda Civic. Already, the sun beat down on the roof, warming the car like a hothouse, a precursor to another scorching day. The weatherman called for this heat wave to continue through the July Fourth weekend, but I was keeping my fingers crossed that his satellite was broken and a cold snap was imminent. A girl could dream.

Easing out of the driveway, I waved to Mr. McGowen, who had been tinkering in his yard every day for the last thirty years, and drove the few blocks through the downtown. The owner of the Get the Scoop ice cream parlor was already setting out the patio tables and chairs in front of his plate glass window, business so busy with the current stretch of hot weather that he'd started opening for breakfast. Only a handful of cars were parked in the Breaking Bread Diner lot, though I knew from experience the place would crowd up as the morning wore on. Having the best omelets in town always guaranteed a hungry crowd. With no commuter traffic, I was through Main Street in less than a minute and on the highway, headed for the farm.

When I'd moved home, the *Blossom Valley Herald* want ads had listed few jobs, exactly zero of which was for marketing. But then Mom had met Esther, owner of the new O'Connell Farm and Spa, at a grieving spouses support group, and Esther had hired me to market the place. With less promotional needs than expected, the job quickly evolved into a Jill-of-all-trades position. When I wasn't marketing the farm, I helped the maid clean the cabins, the cook serve the meals, and Esther tend to the animals. I was just happy to be employed, something that had been in jeopardy after a guest was murdered on opening weekend back in May and almost closed down the farm.

Two months later, with the killer behind bars, the farm and spa was finding its footing again. In fact, all ten cabins were booked for the long weekend, ensuring me plenty of work around the property.

I took the freeway off-ramp for the farm and bounced down the lane. Time for repaving. I slowed as I approached the small lot and parked near the side path that led to the kitchen. A pickup truck with oversized tires and a compact already filled two spaces.

Sparrows chirped in the nearby pine trees, a melody to accompany the staccato crunch of my sandals on the gravel. I stepped onto the dirt path next to the vegetable garden, admiring the plump Brandywine tomatoes, a deep red against the lush green vines. A cucumber peeked out from beneath a broad leaf. Zennia, the spa's forty-two-year-old cook, would no doubt snag that cuke for a lunchtime salad. Little did that vegetable know that his fate was already decided and the end was near.

I wound around the camellia bush, passed the pool and patios, and entered the kitchen by way of the herb garden.

Zennia stood at the counter, layering homemade granola and Greek yogurt into a parfait glass. She straightened as I entered, her long black braid sliding over her shoulder and hitting the counter, almost dipping into the yogurt container.

"Dana, morning." She added a handful of granola to the top of the parfait, then grabbed her honey pot and held the drizzle stick aloft.

I nodded at her dish. "Looks delicious. Wish I hadn't wasted all my stomach room on boring old bran cereal." I grabbed a blackberry from the bowl on the counter and popped the fruit into my mouth.

"Hope you didn't fill up too much. We're having curried lentil burgers for lunch."

My stomach seized. Where did Zennia find these recipes? Torture Cuisines R Us? I forced a smile. "Great." Before my expression faltered, I snatched one last blackberry from the bowl and headed down the hall.

In the office, I plopped down in the desk chair, punched the power button on the computer, and swiveled idly, studying the room as I waited for Windows to load. The wall closest to the door held an overstuffed bookcase, extra books stacked on the faded green carpet. A metal guest chair sat between the bookcase and the door. The opposite wall held a wood filing cabinet under the window and a floor lamp in the corner. Pictures of the farm in earlier years, along with a handful of family photos, filled the walls.

When all the icons had appeared on the desktop, I checked my e-mail, then wrote the day's blog. Today's topic covered the benefits of watermelon, celery, and other foods that could rehydrate your body during a heat wave.

After posting the blog to the spa Web site, I logged onto Facebook and read the latest news. Ashlee had changed her status from In a Relationship to Single, and posted, "Cheaters suck! You stink more than your bad breath, Bobby Joe!!" Sheesh. At least she was being mature about the whole thing.

I closed the Web browser and returned to the kitchen. Four more parfaits had joined the original at the counter. Zennia stood nearby, drying the now-clean blackberry bowl.

"Need help serving breakfast this morning?"

Before she could answer, Esther huffed and puffed her way into the kitchen from the hall, her denim shirt with the embroidered kittens misbuttoned. Her gray curls drooped in the morning heat, and her plump cheeks were flushed.

"Goodness gracious, those ducklings have escaped," she gasped.

"Again?" I said, trying to remember if this was the second or third time this week. The newest additions to the farm, the ducklings weren't the first animals to escape their pen, but they were definitely the most frequent offenders. "Esther, I know you want the guests to see the ducklings the minute they park so they'll be in the right mood for their farm stay, but don't you think those ducks are more trouble than they're worth?"

Esther finished catching her breath. "I know they run away a lot, but they're so darn cute. And the kids love them so."

I didn't point out that we'd had no more than three kids stay with us. Besides, she was right: the ducks were pretty cute.

Esther patted my arm. "You're always such a dear, Dana. Would you round them up with me?"

I looked at Zennia to see if she needed my assistance with breakfast, but she waved her hand in a shooing motion.

"Call me quackers, but I'll help," I said.

Zennia chuckled as I walked out the kitchen door, Esther shadowing me through the herb garden. No little ducks hiding under the mint leaves. I stopped at the tool shed for an empty cardboard box, then wandered by the pool area.

The surface of the water was as smooth as the patio tables. I craned my neck to peek under the chaise longues in case the ducks had decided to seek refuge from the summer heat, but the space was empty.

I suspected the ducklings were entertaining the pigs again, but I held out hope they'd still be waddling down the sidewalk and we could intercept them. No such luck. One glance at the pigsty showed little yellow feathers coated in mud and only God knew what else, although I had a pretty good idea.

I placed my hand on the top railing. The fence around the sty was the same style as the slat fence around the pond out front. Three rails with large gaps in between. "Ever think of enclosing the ducklings in a more escape-proof fence? Maybe add a bottom board to keep them in?"

"Oh, I couldn't do that to the precious little things," Esther said. "Then they'd feel like prisoners."

"We could give them an hour of yard exercise every day. Isn't that what they do in real prisons?"

Esther tittered. "Oh, Dana, you're a hoot."

I hadn't actually been kidding, but apparently Esther wasn't keen on fencing in her pets. I scanned the area near the gate for the rubber boots that usually sat there, but the boots were missing. Someone had probably left them at the chicken coop or off in the vegetable garden. Not the first time the boots had walked away.

With a resigned sigh, I slipped off my sandals, opened the gate to the sty, and placed one bare foot into the muck. Mud and mystery objects, cool and slimy, squeezed between my toes. I shuddered as I added my other foot to the mixture, ready to catch these fuzzy felons and get out of the pen.

Wilbur, an occasional escapee himself, snorted at me. The four other pigs started a backup chorus of squeals and snuffles. Joy.

I grabbed the least muddy duckling, careful not to squeeze too hard, and handed it off to Esther, who dipped the duck in a nearby bucket of water and placed it in the cardboard box. I grabbed another duck, and we repeated the process.

By the fifth bird, my hands and wrists were covered in mud, the brown goo inching toward my elbows. The sixth pooped in my hand, but really, what difference did it make at this point?

I looked around the pen for the final escapee, not seeing any yellow peeking through the brown. The pigs had quieted down and now huddled in a group at the far side of the pen, watching the day's entertainment. If I didn't know any better, I'd swear Wilbur was smirking as he watched me play the farm's version of hide-and-seek.

Movement caught my attention across the pen. A brown blob crept toward the fence and the freedom beyond the rail. I caught Esther's eye and jerked my head toward the duckling just as I heard the first strains of my cell's ringtone coming from my pocket.

I raised my gunk-covered hands and continued to listen

as Coldplay got louder, wondering who was calling at this exact moment. Oh well, if it was important, they'd call back.

I took two steps toward the moving blob, the pigs shuffling and snorting in nervous anticipation. These pigs really needed more excitement in their lives.

Chris Martin started singing again. I abandoned the errant duckling and slopped over to the gate, ignoring the sucking sounds from my feet. I snatched a nearby rag from a fence post, rubbed my hands mostly clean, and gingerly slid my phone from my pocket. The display showed my home number. Ashlee should be at work by now, leaving only Mom to call me here. But she was old-school when it came to interrupting someone's workday. This might be serious after all.

I pressed the green button and held the phone to my ear, crinkling my nose at a whiff of pig smells.

"Dana," Mom said, her voice clearly strained. "I need you home right now. Your sister's in trouble."

"What's wrong with Ashlee?" I asked, the grip on my phone tightening as I ran down a mental list of possibilities. Had she crashed her car again? Been fired? Gotten in a fistfight down at the Prescription for Joy drugstore over the last tube of Cotton Candy lipstick?

"It's Bobby Joe," Mom said, the words spilling out so fast, I expected them to drip from the receiver.

I sighed, not hiding my exasperation. "Is she still upset about that? She told me last night that they weren't even serious. Tell her to find some new guy at work today, and she'll forget all about Bobby Joe."

The pause on the other end made me wonder if my cell service had cut out, something that happened often at the farm.

Then I heard Mom again, her voice practically a whisper. "He's dead."

GREAT BOOKS, GREAT SAVINGS!

When You Visit Our Website:
www.kensingtonbooks.com

You Can Save Money Off The Retail Price
Of Any Book You Purchase!

- **All Your Favorite Kensington Authors**
- **New Releases & Timeless Classics**
- **Overnight Shipping Available**
- **eBooks Available For Many Titles**
- **All Major Credit Cards Accepted**

Visit Us Today To Start Saving!
www.kensingtonbooks.com

All Orders Are Subject To Availability.
Shipping and Handling Charges Apply.
Offers and Prices Subject To Change Without Notice.

Devour These Mysteries By
Joanne Fluke

Chocolate Chip Cookie Murder
0-7582-1505-3

$6.99US/$9.99CAN

Strawberry Shortcake Murder
0-7582-1972-5

$6.99US/$9.99CAN

Blueberry Muffin Murder
0-7582-1858-3

$6.99US/$9.99CAN

Lemon Meringue Pie Murder
0-7582-1504-5

$6.99US/$9.99CAN

Fudge Cupcake Murder
0-7582-0153-2

$6.99US/$9.99CAN

Sugar Cookie Murder
0-7582-0682-8

$6.99US/$9.99CAN

Cherry Cheesecake Murder
0-7582-0295-4

$6.99US/$9.99CAN

Available Wherever Books Are Sold!

Visit our website at www.kensingtonbooks.com